SIXPENCE AND SELKIES

MANNER AND MONSTERS BOOK 5

TILLY WALLACE

Version 15.03.21

ISBN 978-0-473-56983-9

Published by Ribbonwood Press

www.ribbonwoodpress.com

To be the first to hear about Tilly's new releases, sign up at:

www.tillywallace.com/newsletter

1

AFTER THE BIGGEST society wedding of the London season, the mood of Hannah, Lady Wycliff, was a leaf on the wind—swirling in different directions depending on the whims of a breeze. Joy would sweep through her at being witness to a day so marvellous that it filled the newspapers with tales of the beautiful bride, the handsome groom, and the magical enchantments. Then a wave of sadness would break over her. Never again would she and Lizzie be two giggling girls, as close as any sisters could be.

When she returned from her honeymoon, Lizzie would step into the role of Duchess of Harden and society had laid weighty expectations upon her. Not to mention the soirées the duchess would host, the charity work for the underprivileged she would undertake. Hannah wondered if her dear friend would manage to find any spare time for her once she threw herself into the full whirlwind of the Season. A quiet voice in the back of Hannah's head pointed out that if she had remained unmarried, she might by now have slipped into the role of companion and been a constant support to Lizzie in her new life.

If Hannah were brutally honest with herself, her wallow in self-pity was fuelled by the tiniest sliver of jealousy. Lizzie had married the man she loved and experienced the full pleasures of married life. Hannah felt trapped in the first few pages of a romance novel, as though the reader had lost interest and the characters could not advance to the next chapter. She longed for more heated kisses from Wycliff, but the thought of boldly asking for them made her blush. Nor could she read his behaviour.

When she had sought her friend's counsel, Lizzie thought he might be taking a slower approach in order to woo Hannah and allow her time to become accustomed to his affections. While she appreciated that her husband cared enough to progress slowly, sometimes slow was, well, *too* slow.

Tick tock. The clock on the mantel marked the progression of time for those in the room. Though it must be said that, due to her mother's freezing her in time, for Hannah the clock struck the same two-second beat over and over again. What if, in order to advance matters, she had to remove the spell from her body and let the curse steal her life? Oh, the irony if she couldn't truly live until she died!

Hannah stabbed her boiled egg a little too vigorously and it shot out of its porcelain cup. The *plop* as it hit the tablecloth made Wycliff stare at her over the top of the newspaper, his intense black eyes as unfathomable as ever. Hannah had no inkling whether she had committed some terrible wrong, or if he were about to confess his undying love.

The very thought of that made her snort, which turned into a cough.

"Are you all right, dear?" her mother asked from her side.

"Yes, something caught in my throat, is all," Hannah replied.

She couldn't imagine Wycliff doing anything so... fanciful as giving a heartfelt pledge of love and devotion. Nor did she know where such silly ideas were coming from. More and more, she stewed in her growing feelings for her husband. How did one know if one was in love? A distinct physiological change would make a diagnosis easier. Or Timmy could peer into her heart to see if Wycliff's name was written upon it.

Pursuing that line of thought made more questions burst into her mind. Did love always evolve at an equal pace in each person? What happened if it didn't? Or, horrors, what if one person fell deeply in love, only to discover the other party simply thought of them as a good chum?

"Your egg is escaping," Wycliff murmured.

Rather like wrangling bolting horses to a halt, Hannah managed to pull her wayward thoughts back to the scene at the table. The egg spun in a slow circle, its escape impeded by its oval shape and an inability to roll in a straight line.

She scooped the egg up on a spoon and dropped it back into the chicken-shaped porcelain cup. Hannah swallowed a sigh. If only all her problems were so easy to deal with. Before it shot off again, she placed a finger on the top to exert downward pressure and then sliced horizontally through the shell with her knife. The decapitated piece fell to the plate and Hannah peered within at the bright orange yolk. Their chickens laid eggs with the most vibrant centres, as though each held a little burst of sunshine.

"I have a request, Hannah." Wycliff spoke with cautious, measured tones.

Hannah picked up a small spoon in one hand and a slice of toast in the other. She managed a weak smile. "Oh?"

Wycliff fidgeted with the edges of the newspaper, then scrunched it up and discarded it beside his plate. "As you know, I instructed my farm manager to buy a ram and a number of ewes of the new breed of merino sheep. I intend to return to my estate to see the flock and attend to some long overdue business matters. Would you care to join me?"

He kept a steady gaze upon her as he made his request, but his Adam's apple bobbed up and down.

This time, a genuine smile touched her lips. He was trying, and perhaps another jaunt in the country-side was just the tonic their marriage needed. "Why, of course I would. How wonderful to see your ancestral home."

Seraphina reached out and took Hannah's hand. "We need to consider timing, Hannah, depending on how long you wish to be gone."

She stared at her mother's gloved hand. With the passage of each day she wondered if her heartbeat's failing was such a curse anymore. She had a husband who would protect her beyond death. Did a pulse make any difference in whether one was happy or not?

Hannah patted her mother's hand and glanced up at the veiled face. "I know. But I have never been to Dorset and it has been so long since we used to go to the seaside as a family. How I miss building sandcastles."

"It seems journeys are on everybody's mind this morning." Her father spoke up from the head of the table. "I thought I would take Timmy back to see Doctor Colchester. There is much the lad could learn from a fellow aftermage, and I think assisting on country rounds will be less intimidating for him than our regular London clientele."

"An excellent idea, Hugh," Seraphina said.

At that moment, Barnes rode into the breakfast room on Sheba and leapt to the table as they neared. Barnes ran up and down the centre of the table and bounced on his fingertips. The puppy made for her usual spot in the sun at Wycliff's feet.

"Perhaps we should take Barnes and see what

Doctor Colchester can discern about him?" Hugh pointed to the hand with his knife.

Barnes flopped to the tablecloth and twitched rather like a landed fish.

Hannah laughed at his antics. Given he had no eyes, ears, or mouth, he still managed to convey rather a lot through gestures, like a tiny mime. "I don't think he wants to go to the country, Papa. Would you like to go to Dorset, Barnes?"

The hand turned over and onto his fingertips. He jumped up and down like the large spider Mary imagined him to be. Then he did some form of contortion. It took Hannah a moment to realise he seemed to be pointing to the severed tattoo on his wrist.

"Of course! Barnes was a sailor. He wants to go to the seaside," she said.

Barnes stopped in front of Seraphina, sat back on his stump, and crossed two fingers. It appeared to be a plea to be allowed to go.

"Do you think a disembodied hand loose in the countryside is a good idea?" Seraphina cocked her head. "We only recently extended his range to include the garden."

"Can you even swim, Barnes?" Wycliff asked.

"Not overarm, he can't." Hugh chuckled at his own joke.

"Many sailors cannot swim. To learn indicates a lack of faith in their ship being watertight, or in their captain's ability to keep them from trouble," Seraphina said.

Hugh peered at his wife and concern pulled the creases deeper at his eyes. "If we are all away, Sera, what will you do? Fancy joining me in the countryside?"

Seraphina reached out and took Hugh's hand. "I miss our walks in the countryside, but I have a task to complete. I shall return the fusil dryads to the Fae realm and advise Queen Deryn of the fate of her grandson."

"The puppets will not be incinerated, then?" Hannah asked between mouthfuls of toast. Much discussion had taken place about the fate of the fusil dryads, the small wooden bloodsuckers responsible for the deaths of two men. While technically they had committed the crime, it had been at the command of Baron Medwin, the faery queen's grandson. In that regard, the puppets were somewhat like a rifle or sword, being the weapon wielded by another, who used it to monstrous ends.

"No. While they are dangerous creatures, it seems unfair for them to spend an eternity locked away in the Repository because of what the baron ordered them to do. I am certain Queen Deryn will find a secure place for them and ensure they do not return to our realm." Seraphina clutched an empty teacup in her hands.

"How I wish I could see the Fae court." Hannah half closed her eyes and conjured a fantastical scene in her mind. What a wondrous sight it would be—full of the most beautiful beings and other magical creatures. The book Wycliff had found for her said that the Fae possessed unicorns, who shone like glittering silver by moonlight. What woman didn't want to gaze upon a unicorn?

Wycliff narrowed his eyes at her. "You mean accompanying your mother to the Fae court sounds better than my offer of a farm visit to see sheep?"

Hannah stared at her husband, her mouth opening and closing while she tried to respond. Although really, there was no choice to be made. A trip to the Fae realm was virtually impossible for an ordinary person like her without serious repercussions. Many mortals lost track of time and returned to their lives decades later, or fell so in love with the Fae that they pined and died without them. Hannah could not take such risks, but she did expect her mother to conjure images of what she saw upon her return.

Seraphina laughed and waved a hand at Wycliff. "Don't tease the poor girl, Wycliff. Sheep have their own magical properties—particularly when it comes to falling asleep. Since we are all venturing away for some time, perhaps you might consider taking Frank and Mary with you to Dorset? I could construct a spell that binds Barnes to within a certain distance of Frank. He is large enough to work as an anchor point to stop our diminutive friend from running off."

"A disembodied hand, a stitched-together monster, and a maid prone to fainting in the country? Well, at least we won't lack for entertainment." Wycliff's dark eyes sparkled with humour as his gaze returned to Hannah.

Barnes leapt up and down with excitement and ran round the tabletop in circles.

"We shall take Sheba with us, too. I am sure she will love the open spaces and walks through the forest." Hannah would need to tell Mary of the forthcoming trip. There would be much packing to do.

"If Hannah wants to stay in Dorset for longer than a month, Sera, I could collect you from the Fae doorway down that way and we could visit Mireworth for a few days. Assuming her ladyship does not mind our intrusion?" Hugh winked at his wife and daughter.

Hannah's mind spun. While she knew there were ways to the Fae realm, she didn't understand exactly how one moved between them. That led her to wonder if it were similar to the way Wycliff could travel to the underworld. His form had disappeared as he stepped on that shadowy path. "Do the Fae use doorways, and not paths such as Wycliff saw leading to the underworld?"

"Yes, dear. Fae doorways are fixed in certain places, whereas I suspect the path Wycliff can see is more fluid, and appears as needed. Fairy rings and standing stones mark Fae doorways. Although some are purely for show, of course, they guard the real doorways so people don't inadvertently stumble through," Seraphina explained. Then she turned to her husband. "That would be most convenient, Hugh. You could signal me when you are at the Dorset doorway. That will ensure I don't lose track of time—you know I do not like to be away from you overlong."

"You would be most welcome at my—our—estate," Wycliff said. "Although I must apologise in advance for its sad state of neglect and disrepair. Most of the house is shut up and not lived in. The housekeeper has a few rooms maintained on the ground floor, but it will be basic accommodation. Not unlike being back on the campaign trail," Wycliff added.

Seraphina laughed. "Your home would be a palace compared to the hovel Hugh used to live in when I first met him. I do believe he shared it with rats and a family of owls, and there was so much dirt on the floor that potatoes and mushrooms grew in the corners."

Hugh squeezed his wife's hand and a look of pure love and devotion shone in his eyes. "I had nothing, and yet when you gave me your heart, I became the richest man in the world."

Hannah dropped her attention to the empty eggshell on her plate. If Wycliff ever gazed at her with a fraction of the love her father bestowed on her mother, she would consider herself a most fortunate woman.

2

THAT AFTERNOON, Hannah sat on the window seat in her mother's turret as the powerful mage prepared the monthly renewal spell. With a piece of yellow chalk, Seraphina drew a coffin shape on the wooden floor. Then she added another boundary around the first line. The three-inch space between the two lines was filled with runes and symbols that Hannah didn't understand, but a chill washed over her skin and raised goose bumps as each image was drawn.

One satisfied with her work, Seraphina threw the chalk onto the bench and waved to Hannah. "I am ready for you now, my dear."

Hannah walked to the chalk outline and swallowed the lump in her throat. Though they had performed the same ritual every month for over two years now, it never became any easier to place herself in the drawn coffin. She gathered her skirts in one hand to stop them from brushing the patterns as she stepped in and lay down. With her hands crossed over her chest, Hannah closed her eyes and waited.

Her mother shuffled closer to the edge of the drawing and placed one gloved hand on Hannah's head, the other over her heart. Then Seraphina began to chant in a low tone. An invisible hand squeezed Hannah's heart, and just as she thought she could endure it no longer and might cry out, her mother fell silent and the interior grip loosened.

"All done, Hannah." Seraphina patted her daughter's head.

She opened her eyes, sat up, and curled her feet under her. "And?"

After every instance of performing the spell, her mother issued the same reassurance—the curse lay dormant in Hannah's body, she remained in a frozen point in time, and they had another month to work on a cure.

Today, her mother remained silent.

In a rare move, Seraphina raised her veil and revealed her ruined face. The greyish skin and blue blotches spoiled her once pale complexion, but nothing dimmed the love in her blue eyes. "I do not wish to alarm you, Hannah. My spell holds and the curse will not have you this month. But it has...moved."

"Moved?" Whatever did that mean? Had it pooled in her toes?

"That is the easiest way to explain the change I sense within you. It is like an army laying siege to a castle encircles their target. I fear that after all this time, the dark magic is testing my spell, perhaps seeking a way to break through. But it will not succeed, Hannah. Death will not have you." Seraphina took her daughter's hands and the two women sat side by side on the floor.

Hannah had delayed death for two years. Her heart should have stilled a few weeks after she had first dabbed the poisoned powder on her face, and she should have joined the gentle ranks of the Afflicted. The many months that had passed since had given her ample opportunity to face her fear of death. When viewed objectively, her situation was not so terrible. After she died, at least she would arise in her bedroom, surrounded by her family. They would never know how many of those who had used the tainted powder had roused to find themselves buried deep in the ground with no hope of escape from their graves. When her parents had tried to exhume those they suspected of being Afflicted, the families had denied them permission.

"We cannot hold it back forever, Mother. But do not worry, for I am not afraid. Not anymore." Wycliff would protect her and her mother both. Legislation might declare them to be dead, and as such unable to hold property or fulfil other legal obligations, but they would still continue with their lives. "Besides, when that day arrives, you and Father will finally have one of the Afflicted willing to sit in a bathtub of potion while you call down a lightning strike."

Seraphina burst out in laughter and wrapped her

arms around Hannah. "I do so admire your spirit. When I return from the Fae realm, we will discuss what we do next. The time has come for us to take a bold step to defeat our invisible enemy."

"You will journey to the underworld," Hannah murmured.

It was the logical progression of their search for a cure. Seraphina would journey to the next life and seek out the creator of the dark magic spell, with the assistance of a hellhound to shake the truth from the mage responsible.

"Yes, but don't tell your father just yet. You know how he will worry." Seraphina pulled the veil back over her face and shuffled to her bathchair. She muttered a spell and her body levitated the short distance necessary for her to resettle in the chair.

Sir Hugh would not be the only one to worry. Concerns gnawed at Hannah, too. To walk beside the hellhound, Seraphina would need to sever the strand that bound her soul to her physical form. They had no idea what effect that would have. What if the strand connecting soul to dead form was the very thing that kept her mother animated? Hannah's concerns extended beyond her mother to include Wycliff, too. If only there was a way for her to make the journey with her husband. But only the dead could cross into the shadow realm.

"What if you don't return?"

"There is no point worrying about things that have not yet happened. Do you really think Wycliff would leave his mother-in-law in Hell?" Seraphina tilted her head and the muslin swayed.

Hannah bit her lip to keep from laughing. "I suspect there is many a husband who would happily deposit his mother-in-law in Hell, but I don't believe Wycliff is one."

Her mother's shoulders shook in silent laughter. "You may be right. But as I said, don't go gathering worries before their time. Now, off you go. You have much to organise and I need to finalise the spell to bind Barnes to Frank."

THE NEXT FEW days passed in a whirl of activity. Trunks were packed and Mary agonised far longer over what belongings to take than Hannah did. The maid bubbled with both excitement and dread about a trip to the seaside. It transpired that she shared Hannah's reservations about the ocean. Though neither of them could swim, at least Hannah had happy memories of playing in the sand as a child. Mary had never seen the ocean.

"I'm not going into the sea, milady, but I would like to wriggle my toes in the sand," Mary said as she closed the lid of the trunk.

"I'd quite like to sit on the sand myself." Another thought occurred to Hannah. Wycliff had mentioned teaching her to swim. What would that be like—to have his arms hold her as the waves tugged at her body?

Would he hold her tight or would she slip from his grasp?

"We're all done, milady. I'll have Frank carry the trunks down." Mary placed her hands on her hips and surveyed her work.

A regular tapping made Hannah look around. It sounded like a breeze knocking a branch against glass. Except no trees reached Hannah's first floor windows. "Mary, where is Barnes?"

The hand had been assisting them by selecting pieces of jewellery, which they rolled up in a blue velvet case.

"Oops." The maid lifted the lid of the trunk and then jumped back.

Barnes climbed over the side and dropped to the floor as though he had been deprived of oxygen. Sheba rushed over and administered a reviving lick.

"That could have been an uncomfortable trip, Barnes," Hannah murmured as she closed the trunk once more and ushered the group from the room.

That night, the family had a quiet dinner before they were to part ways in the morning. Hugh would transport Seraphina to the doorway to the Fae realm, where she would be met by Helga, a woman in Lady Loburn's employ. The robust and sensible servant was often used to assist the dead mage on her trips. Helga was painfully short-sighted without her spectacles, and would remain unaffected by the beauty of the Fae. The Miles home would remain silent except for Cook, who looked forward to her own sort of holiday.

The old woman would sit by the fire, she said, and knit.

Seraphina had crafted a mage silver ring for Wycliff, which she presented at the end of the meal. "I made it in the shape of a bone, like Hugh's ring. I thought that an appropriate shape for both a physician and a hellhound."

Wycliff slipped the ring onto the smallest finger on his right hand, and the magical metal adjusted to the perfect size. "Thank you."

THE YARD BUSTLED the next morning with two carriages hitched up and all the horses pawing the ground, impatient to move off. Frank and Old Jim loaded the trunks onto the correct vehicles. Sir Hugh had hired a large travelling coach and four horses to take Hannah and Wycliff to Dorset, and the vehicle would provide ample space for them and their luggage.

Frank fussed over the equines, checking the harnesses and scratching withers as final arrangements were made. Then the trunks were secured to the rear by ropes. Cook pushed a basket into Hannah's hands containing a meal to tide them over until their stop that evening.

Seraphina sat in her bathchair to one side, the chickens surrounding her like ladies-in-waiting. "Barnes," she called out, "it is time."

The hand scampered over, ducked around a

chicken, and climbed up the side of the bathchair. Seraphina picked up Barnes in her gloved hands and held him before her face.

Hannah had a flash of an illustration in a picture book that accompanied the fairy tale of the Princess and the Frog. If her mother kissed Barnes, would he be transformed into a frog leg?

The mage whispered and the words became a blue-tinged gust that swirled around the hand until he stood in the middle of a head-sized vortex. Then a piece broke off and raced toward Frank. The blue wind grew in size as it spun around the giant's middle. When the swirling covered all of Frank's torso for a split second, the wind became solid, like water that flash froze, with an accompanying loud crack. Then blue chunks fell away but never touched the ground, having dispersed into the air.

"Done," Seraphina said.

She placed Barnes on the ground and the hand turned around and around, as though looking to see if he had grown a tail.

The mage pointed a finger at the disembodied hand. "You are tethered to Frank, Barnes, and I have given you a two-hundred-foot range. I think that will cover most scenarios. Should you try to venture farther than that, you will encounter a solid wall that will not let you take another step in the wrong direction. If Frank moves beyond the allowed distance, you will be dragged to within the necessary distance. Try not to be on the other side of something solid if that happens."

Frank stared at his middle, a deep frown on his face.

Mary clung to his arm. "It won't hurt my Frank, will it?"

Hannah swallowed a laugh. Mary worried about Frank, who was the anchor, but it was poor Barnes who would suffer if the tether tried to pull him through a tree or a wall. Or imagine if a gust of wind caught the hand—he might become a kite gliding high above Frank as he strode across the countryside.

Seraphina waved away the maid's concerns. "Of course not, Mary. Frank won't feel a thing. But do remember Barnes is connected to you before you take off in any kind of conveyance, and ensure he is nearby. Otherwise the poor fellow will be bounced along in the road behind you."

A low chuffing noise, somewhat like the new and experimental steam engines, came from the constructed man. He rarely laughed and the odd sound suited him, as though warmth and humour rolled off him like puffs of steam coming from a kettle.

Wycliff and Hugh checked everything over again and the time had come to say goodbye.

"Before you depart, I have one more enchantment to weave. Hannah, Wycliff, would you take my hands, please?" Seraphina held out her gloved hands.

Hannah glanced to her husband, then took her mother's hand. Wycliff approached more cautiously, but he took hold of Seraphina's other hand.

"Good. Now if you two would join hands," Seraphina instructed.

They did as asked, the three of them now hand in hand and forming a loose circle. Seraphina's head dropped forward and she murmured in a strange tongue. Whispers raced over Hannah's skin and tickled, as her mother's magic washed over her body. On the last syllable from her mother's throat, the gold ring on Hannah's left hand wriggled of its own accord. Wycliff stared at his own hand and she assumed the same thing was happening on his finger.

Seraphina let them go. "It is done. I have added an enchantment to your wedding bands to let you signal one another if necessary. It won't be as elegant as contacting me, nor will it enable direct communication, but should the need arise, you have only to rub the gold ring and think of the other person. That will make their ring wriggle as you just experienced. I am still pondering how to enable you to talk to one another across distances—and whether a miniature you carried might be ensorcelled to work as a conduit."

Hannah stared at her hands. One gold ring, one silver, and each touched by a different type of magic. She leaned down and kissed her mother's cheek. "Thank you. I will see you in a month's time, Mother."

"Have a glorious adventure, Hannah, and we can swap stories when I see you next." Seraphina reached up and stroked her daughter's cheek before letting her go.

Next, Hannah hugged her father, and she even

managed a quick cuddle with Timmy, which made the lad blush as he scampered away to the family's carriage.

Mary stood next to the large travelling carriage and fidgeted with her hands.

"Whatever is it, Mary?" Hannah asked as she looked around the yard one last time.

The maid leaned close and whispered, "Do I have to ride inside? His lordship is ever so fearsome. I'd rather sit up with Frank, if it's all the same to you, milady."

Mary remained oblivious to Frank's gruesome, stitched-together appearance and saw only the gentle soul that dwelt within. Yet Wycliff's stern good looks struck fear in her heart. Hannah decided it was best not to tell her about the souls attached to Frank. Men were forever bound to his form by the stitches Lord Dunkeith had used to attach the limbs taken from others...but Mary did not need to know that.

Hannah nodded. "Of course you may, Mary. But if bad weather threatens, I will insist you sit inside. Wycliff is bringing his mare, so he won't always be in the carriage. He will ride at times."

"Oh." Mary's face brightened. "I'll sit with you then, milady, when his lordship is on his horse."

Wycliff tied his mare to the ring at the back of the carriage and scratched the horse's withers. The saddle and bridle were stored in a rear trunk, for when he wished to ride.

"Where will you sit, Barnes?" Wycliff picked up the hand.

Barnes gestured up and Wycliff placed him on the high driver's seat.

"He wouldn't have much of a view from inside, unless he swung from the curtains," Hannah murmured as Wycliff helped her up into the carriage. Then he handed up the spaniel, who sat on the seat and peered out the window.

Hannah waved to her parents as they set off. An odd disturbance churned in her stomach, as though things would never be the same again. Silly, she chided herself. This was her second trip away in as many months and it was only the disruption to her normally quiet routine that made her unsettled.

They skirted the fringes of London and headed southwest. As twilight fell, they broke their journey at a quaint tavern in Winchester. Light and laughter rolled from within. Frank eyed the activity and growled, preferring to stay in the stables with the horses. Not everybody was like the Miles family. Strangers often stared and he preferred to stay in the shadows, lest he distress others with his appearance. Mary split her time between fussing over Hannah inside and worrying about Frank outside.

Wycliff procured two rooms next to each other, and Hannah discovered she was to share one with Mary.

Who snored.

3

THEY SET off from the tavern early the next day, as Wycliff was keen to reach Mireworth before dark. They halted only for short rest breaks and ate luncheon by a stream as Frank watered the horses. After lunch Wycliff rode his mare, but after two hours, they paused to remove the horse's saddle and tie her to the back of the carriage.

Afternoon was lengthening toward sunset when Wycliff sat forward and peered out the window. He pointed to the left. "We will be able to see Mireworth soon if you look this way."

Then worry pulled at the corners of his eyes and he frowned.

Curious as to what caused him concern, Hannah leaned toward the window and fixed on the view. Trees clustered in a woodland area that looked ideal for explorations with Sheba. The road followed the dips and bends of the land and excitement built in her stomach at what she would spy as the foliage drew back from the sweeping driveway. The grand curve hugged the side of the house and formed a complete circle with a patch of tall grass in the middle.

"Oh," Hannah managed to say as she schooled her disappointment. "She must have been grand in her day."

Once golden stone was smoke-stained and smeared with grime, with only a few muted pale patches still visible. Staring at the house was not unlike gazing on the rot-ravaged face of an Afflicted. The windows were dirty and cracked, and some were boarded over. Dead vines clung to the stone in places like skeletal hands with a death grip on the structure. Weeds had made a valiant effort to take over the gravel of the drive and made better progress in the cracks around the house. At the exact moment of their arrival, a dark cloud took up residence over the roof and Hannah wondered if her mother, in a mischievous mood, had sent the thunder-cloud on purpose.

In her mind, Hannah ignored the exterior and contemplated the bones. The skeleton showed Georgian origins in the clean lines of the facade and the symmetry of windows on either side of the central portico. Now, the once grand house appeared tired and forgotten, like a broken toy shoved in an attic. Time had eaten away her beauty and Hannah wondered if only ghosts and bats were left to wander the halls.

"Once, Mireworth was marvellous," Wycliff murmured. "Then some ten years ago, a big storm damaged the roof and Father had no money to repair it. She slid into ruin after that, but I hope to wrest her back from neglect and restore her." He flung open the carriage door and jumped down before offering a hand to Hannah.

The spaniel leapt free with a bark. Frank lowered himself to the ground, and lifted down Mary and then Barnes. Sheba and the hand made straight for the circle of grass and disappeared in the overgrown lawn.

"Oh, milady, surely we're not staying in there? It looks right haunted." Mary hugged her arms to her body and she glanced from Frank to the house.

Wycliff ground his teeth and a stony look dropped over his features as he stared at his inheritance.

Hannah dug deep to find any good in the situation. "I'm sure no ghosts will bother us, Mary." The ones following Frank everywhere caused no concern, and she hoped those that clung to Mireworth would be equally polite and unobtrusive.

A man hurried around the side of the manor house. "Lord Wycliff! How marvellous. We were not expecting you today."

Wycliff hailed the man and they shook hands. "Hannah, this is Swift, the estate manager. Swift, this is Lady Wycliff."

The man appeared to be in his thirties, with a face darkened by the sun and worn into creases by inclement weather. Of average height, he had broad shoulders and warm brown eyes. He halted on seeing Hannah and adopted a wide-eyed, startled look.

"How do you do, Mr Swift? I am looking forward to seeing these merino sheep with their superior wool. Wycliff has told me much about them." Hannah smiled at him encouragingly and wondered whether, while Wycliff had told her of the sheep, he had neglected to tell his manager that the estate had acquired a mistress as well.

The man swept off his cloth cap and nodded. Tufts of brown hair stuck together and he appeared to be in need of shearing. The manager tortured the hat in his hands and glanced from Hannah to Wycliff. "They are mighty fine sheep, milady. Best-looking ones in the county, if I do say so myself. But your lordship, we did not know you would be bringing her ladyship with you. We have no proper accommodation."

"My wife does not require her own suite. We can make do together." Wycliff took her hand and squeezed it. Although whether to reassure himself or her of his words, she did not know.

"Yes, my lord. But if you recollect, we have only the cot in the study." Mr Swift whispered in such a loud voice that Hannah easily overheard. She looked away and pretended an intense interest in whatever weed was trying to prise its way under a window frame. With tiny yellow flowers, it appeared to be creeping clover.

Wycliff ran a hand through his hair and stared up at the sulking house. "Blast. I had forgotten, it has been so long since I last visited."

"Come now, Wycliff, I know the house is uninhab-ited, and I did not expect to find grandeur and a surplus of servants. You may as well tell me the worst of it." Hannah slipped her hand into his elbow and they walked toward the cracked portico.

"Well, she's not entirely uninhabited. Mrs Rossett, the housekeeper, has her room by the kitchen." Leaves made deep piles at the front door and Wycliff kicked them aside. "I don't normally go in this way."

"I am quite capable of using the kitchen entrance like everyone else." Hannah glanced around the house, prepared to find the servants' entrance.

"You should at least use the front door on your very first visit," he muttered, and rattled the door handle, which didn't want to budge. In the end, he put his shoulder to the thick slab of wood. It burst open and Wycliff nearly tumbled inside.

Hannah was about to step in behind him when he called, "Wait!"

She froze and stared into the gloom. Perhaps he had spotted some wild creature and wanted to chase it out? The next thing she knew, he had swept her up into his arms.

A bashful smile crossed his face. "It is customary, I believe, to carry one's bride over the threshold the first time she enters her new home."

Warmth bloomed through Hannah at the romantic gesture. No wonder he had practically knocked the door down rather than let her slip in through the kitchen.

Once inside, he set her back on her feet. The stained glass doors of the square entrance way opened to an enormous, rounded space. Light struggled to filter through a glass dome high overhead and cast the room in permanent twilight. Two staircases swept up either side of the space in a gentle curve, meeting at the top to create a balcony that overlooked the tiled floor.

"Oh, Wycliff! It's beautiful." The newel posts drew Hannah to them—each a four-foot-tall griffin.

Their heads formed the starting point of the balustrade, their wings stretched back protectively over the first few posts. She placed a hand on a feathered head. Carved in a rich golden wood, the workmanship was so exquisite she expected the creatures to step forward and demand to know her business in the house.

In her mind, she stripped away the years of neglect and dust and imagined the dome cleaned to allow sunlight to stream in. She mentally scrubbed the tiled floor, polished the wooden balustrades, and laid stair runners in fiery tones. The house possessed magnificent features on an imposing scale, and once restored would rival any grand home in Mayfair.

"Most of the house is shut up and unused. I've not lived here since before the war. The study on the ground floor is kept habitable for when I visit, and I need only a cot to sleep on. I foolishly did not think to tell them we would need more beds for everyone." Wycliff gestured to one side. A twin set of doors stood directly opposite on the other side of the foyer.

Hannah was no wilting flower; she could roll up her sleeves and do a hard day's labour when required.

"We will make do. Let us assess the situation first and then decide on a course of action. Mr Swift, are there beds in the rooms upstairs?"

"Yes, Lady Wycliff. Some are broken down. Others might not be in good shape after all these years," Mr Swift answered, having followed them inside.

The solution to the problem seemed obvious to her: Fetch a bed from upstairs and bring it down. The study was habitable and she preferred its closeness to the kitchen. There was no need to ramble up and down stairs and along dark halls every day. Besides, that would be akin to stalking through a cemetery at night. The house should be left to its peaceful slumber. For now.

"First things first. Wycliff, why don't you see to the horses? Then you can go upstairs with Frank, find a dissembled bed in good repair, and carry it down to the study. Mary and I will introduce ourselves to the housekeeper and find linens, if you will point me in the right direction?" Hannah reached out and took Mary's hand. Mostly to ensure the maid didn't run back to the carriage. She had gone as pale as a wraith and her bottom lip trembled.

Wycliff gave her quick instructions to find the kitchen at the rear of the house, and then gestured for Frank and Swift to follow him back outside. Frank picked up Barnes, who sat on the tall man's shoulder.

Sheba hesitated for a moment, conflicted as to which direction to take. The spaniel had a soft spot for both Barnes and Wycliff. Then she decided on solidarity with her gender and trotted along at Hannah's heels. Hannah and Mary took a few turns in the corridor and soon pushed through heavy double doors that signalled they had stepped from the family areas into a servants' hall. Along one wall, placed high above the door frames, was a row of brass bells, each mounted in a square of dull metal. Under every bell was affixed a name plate to denote the room, such as dining room or library. Hannah spotted one in a faded script that read *Lady Wycliff*.

Ignoring the tug of curiosity to follow the bell's wire to its point of origin, Hannah pushed through the next door to the kitchen and found a stark contrast to the rest of the house. Light streamed in from a row of windows on one side and a skylight set directly above the worn oak table. The floors were swept, the bench tops and table clean. A row of gleaming copper pots hung from hooks, and a wonderful sweet aroma filled the room. A set of glassed doors allowed a glimpse to some sort of conservatory, accessible from the kitchen.

A woman sat at one end of the table, closest to the ovens. A regular clacking came from the knitting needles in her hand and a ball of yellow wool spun at her feet as the yarn pulled free. She glanced up and narrowed her eyes. "And who might you be?"

Hannah stopped by the table and smiled pleasantly. "I am Lady Wycliff and this is Mary, my maid. The spaniel is Sheba. I assume you are Mrs Rossett?"

Mrs Rossett resembled a barrel—short, rotund, and sturdy. She appeared to be somewhere in her late fifties, with greying hair pulled back in a tidy bun. Piercing grey eyes stared at Hannah for a long moment and then turned upon Mary. The maid's head dropped and she shuffled sideways to escape the withering scrutiny. The housekeeper never stopped knitting, although she growled at Sheba, who had stalked too close to the ball of yarn. Once chastised, the spaniel sat and cocked her head as though waiting for further instructions.

Having made some internal decision, the woman heaved a sigh and set aside her knitting. She pushed her chair back and stood, which increased the resemblance to a barrel; the woman couldn't even have reached five feet in height. "There are no rooms ready for you, your ladyship. We were given no notice."

"I'm aware of that, Mrs Rossett, and will be perfectly content in the study with Wycliff. The men are putting the horses away and then they will forage upstairs for a larger bed. I need your assistance with linen and blankets, please. Mary and I will make up the bed once the gentlemen find one. Then it remains for a bed to be found for Mary."

Hannah wanted to let out a sigh and drop into a chair. The kitchen had a comfortable atmosphere and her tired body longed to linger, while her stomach wanted to investigate the delicious aromas coming from the range.

Mrs Rossett narrowed her gaze at Hannah. "You would make the bed yourself?"

What an odd question. "Of course. My mother might be a mage, but she never believed in using magic to do something your own hands are capable of. If you would be so good as to provide me with a broom, a bucket of water, and a cloth, we can give the study a once-over while we wait for the men. Once we finish, supper would be lovely."

Mrs Rossett tilted her head back and let out a hearty roar of laughter that seemed more suited to a seven-foot-tall pirate. Mary jumped and Hannah shot out a hand to settle the girl. The puppy yapped and leapt to her feet. "You do not know how relieved I am that the rapscallion has finally found a capable woman to marry."

"Rapscallion?" Hannah assumed the housekeeper meant Wycliff, but she couldn't fit the description to her serious husband, even though she caught rare glimpses of humour under his steely facade.

"Oh, yes. That one was right trouble when he was a lad. Always getting into things he shouldn't. Why, once we had to grease his head with lard after he got it stuck between the stair railings." She headed toward a dim corridor and gestured for them to follow. "I keep a supply of bedding aired and clean, just in case he might appear. He seldom gives me sufficient notice."

Hannah's feet refused to move while her brain conjured an image of the young Wycliff having his ears greased to fit back between the railings. There a story she would tuck away for later use. "Is there a room close by that Mary could use? Frank—that's our man—prefers the stables and being close to the horses."

"We can air out the room next to mine for her. That

way we'll be company for one another." Mrs Rossett kept up a steady stream of conversation, detailing the exploits of a young Wycliff. It transpired that the housekeeper had begun her life in service at the tender age of eight, sweeping out the fire grates. Over the years, she had risen through the ranks to housekeeper. Wycliff kept her on, even though the house sat silent and mostly empty.

Hannah returned to the study with a pile of bedding, while Mary carried a broom and cleaning supplies. By chance, there was already a pie in the oven and they left Mrs Rossett to begin on sufficient vegetables for dinner since with much to do, everyone would be hungry by the time night fell.

While Hannah and Mary cleaned, thuds and bangs preceded the men carrying in the pieces of the bed through the double doors. Next they made the return journey to bring down a mattress. Barnes leapt onto the study light fixture and watched from above.

The cot was taken to a room by the kitchen for Mary's use. The room picked for her possessed a window overlooking a slice of overgrown walled garden, where once vegetables for the household would have grown. In the study, a narrow desk and a cabinet needed only a wipe with a damp cloth to revive them and the open window would soon drive out the lingering dust.

By the time they had everything in order, night had fallen and Mr Swift took his leave to return to his home and family. Hannah and Wycliff, followed by the others, made their way to the kitchen, to be greeted by a delicious aroma and the table set with a plain, but ample, meal.

"Viscount or not, milord, you had better wash those filthy hands before you sit at my table." Mrs Rossett waved a knife at Wycliff and then pointed to the sink.

"Yes, Mrs Rossett," Wycliff murmured like a meek schoolboy. Then he ruined it by winking at Hannah and leading her to the soap and hot water.

4

Despite Mrs Rossett's formidable appearance, the housekeeper harboured a soft side. Not only had she found a pretty bowl with purple pansies painted on it for Sheba, the housekeeper filled the dish with offcuts from dinner, then folded an old blanket and placed it by the range, where the spaniel could stretch out in the warmth. The dog attacked her dinner with gusto and her tail wagged as she ate. So far, Sheba's country adventure was going splendidly.

Hannah took a seat at the table to the right of Wycliff. Frank sat to Wycliff's left and stared at his plate. Mary, sheltering next to him, dished up an enormous helping for her man and cast nervous glances around his bulk at Wycliff. Mrs Rossett sat to the other side of Hannah and closest to the range.

Hannah pondered whether or not to say anything about this unprecedented state of affairs. In the end, she decided to act as though it were perfectly normal for the lord and lady of the house to dine in the kitchen with the staff. To be fair, Hannah didn't even know where the formal dining room was, nor did she want to contemplate what sort of condition it might be in. Mice and rats probably dined and then danced upon its table while bats clung to the corners underneath.

Barnes hopped up on the table and plonked himself down close to Frank. Mrs Rossett, to her credit, did not scream or fetch a broom. She merely pointed. "*What* is that?"

"That is Barnes. There once was more of him, but he met an unfortunate end and this is all that remains," Wycliff said as he passed a bowl of potatoes to Hannah.

"He can be mischievous, so please don't let him startle you." Hannah worried the hand might misbehave so far from her mother's control.

"Oh, I don't think he'll cause me any problems. If he does..." Mrs Rossett slammed a short vegetable knife deep into the wood of the table. "I'll skewer him to the table. Do we understand each other, Barnes?"

The hand froze to the spot as the knife hilt quivered. Then he gave a thumbs-up signal and dropped back to the bench, out of range of small knives.

Relieved she had one less problem to worry about, Hannah cast about her for a topic of conversation. "Thank you, Mrs Rossett, for providing such a wonderful meal at short notice."

"Think nothing of it. I prefer to have busy hands

and it is nice to have his lordship under his own roof again." The housekeeper beamed at Wycliff like a besotted grandmother.

"His lordship? I think you mean the *rapscallion*. I do hope you have some lard on hand in case of misadventures." Hannah, somehow, managed to keep a wide-eyed innocent look on her face as she asked her question and then turned to Wycliff.

Wycliff set down his cutlery and heaved an exaggerated sigh. "What exactly have you been telling my wife, Mrs Rossett?"

"Why, hardly anything, sir. I've only known her ladyship a mere handful of hours. I haven't told her nearly as much as I'm going to over the next few days." The housekeeper winked at Hannah and then let out her booming laughter.

Hannah found herself laughing at the horrified look on Wycliff's face.

"I'm not so sure bringing you here was such a good idea after all," he muttered as he returned his attention to his dinner.

"Really? I believe it will turn into quite an educational trip." Hannah grinned at him. He might be the most notoriously grim and rude viscount in London, but in Dorset he was the mischievous boy and she looked forward to hearing more of his antics.

A lively discussion erupted around the table, while Frank remained silent. Mary managed to speak up at one point and didn't quiver in fear when Wycliff asked her if her accommodation was sufficient. After dinner, Hannah and Mary helped clear up and wash the dishes. Wycliff took Sheba for a walk outside and Frank disappeared to the stables, where he had a room in the loft.

The night lengthened and soon Mary said her good-nights. Mrs Rossett brewed a cup of tea for Wycliff and he kept one hand curled around the cup while he scanned the local newspaper he held in the other.

A weariness crept over Hannah's limbs and warred with a case of nerves. Her husband seemed settled for the time being and that provided her with ample time to complete her evening routine. "If you'll excuse me, Mrs Rossett, I will also seek my bed."

They had managed to turn the study into more of a functional bedroom and less of an officer's campaign tent. The men had pushed the plain wooden bed frame up against one wall, which contained bookshelves to the height of the chair rail. Above that was an enormous map of the world. Hannah and Mary had made up the bed with clean sheets and found a cheerful patchwork quilt in a mix of floral patterns to spread on top. They moved the desk closer to the window, to give them a few more inches of space and to serve as her dresser. Her small travelling case sat to one side, holding her brushes, a bottle of perfume, and her velvet roll of jewellery.

Hannah managed to coax a fire into life in the

hearth, to throw its cheery light over the room and to dispel the gloom. The rugs were threadbare, but functional. Only one pane in the window was cracked and it did a valiant job at keeping the drafts at bay, as long as the dusty drapes were pulled. Tomorrow she would find a piece of wood to cover the gap.

The drapes would need to be taken down and given a good beating—another job to add to her list. Wooden boxes of various sizes were stacked in one corner as though a boy had built a fort. Wycliff had muttered about the boxes containing small items such as silverware or porcelain that had once resided in the upstairs rooms.

A small settee with holes chewed in its golden brocade was set at the foot of the bed and before the fire. Hannah threw a forest green blanket over the piece to make it more homely and to cover the holes. There was no screen for her to hide behind while she changed. Her trunk stood open beside the desk. Hannah removed her dress, shift, and stays and placed them on top. Then she slipped on her nightgown and dressing gown.

She sat on the settee with a book in her hands, but the words swam on the page. Her mind churned as though she made butter in her head. She had not shared a bedroom with Wycliff since their stay with the Pennicotts. But much had changed since then. She recalled the day in the glade, when he had confided how the hellhounds had attacked his platoon. Then he had kissed her in a way that made her think the same molten heat was being poured into her veins.

There was no doubt they would share a bed while at Mireworth. Only one question remained: Would he sleep under or on top of the blankets?

She didn't have to wait long to find out. In a few minutes, Wycliff entered and closed the door behind him. Hannah dared glances from under her lowered lashes as he undressed. Silently he stripped off his jacket and hung it over a chair. His waistcoat and cravat were tossed over the top. Next, he pulled off his boots and stockings and set them next to the chair. His shirt came off over his head and was balled up and tossed to the top of the crates.

Heat flared over her cheeks at the sight of his well-formed and naked torso. She felt a small moment of pride at the barely perceptible silver scar on his shoulder, where she had dug out a ball shot from a badly aimed pistol. She had not been given any opportunity to examine the wound since.

Clad only in his breeches, he crossed the rug to stand in front of her, and reached out to take the book from her limp fingers. Closing the pages, he set it beside her. Taking her hands, he raised her to her feet. One hand slid to her waist, and with the other, he caressed her cheek.

Hannah closed her eyes and focused on his touch. She leaned into his palm as he cupped her face.

"There is much unsaid between us, Hannah," Wycliff murmured as he traced the line of her jaw and down the side of her neck. "I offered you a marriage in name only, but I believe our feelings on that subject have altered. Yet I find myself on uncertain ground as I contemplate whether to advance or retreat. The next step is not my decision to make—it is yours. I need only a single word to indicate whether this is what you want to do. If your answer is no, I shall sleep on the settee. If yes, well...I promise you will not regret your decision."

The idea of physical intimacy no longer frightened Hannah. Rather the opposite. Due to her evolving relationship with Wycliff, she found herself curious and wanting more. Which meant they should advance, wherever that path took them. It was an easy decision for her to make.

With one word fixed in her mind, she opened her eyes to his intense gaze and whispered, "Yes."

His arm tightened around her and Wycliff kissed her. Hannah let go of any last reservations and placed herself utterly in her husband's warm and very capable hands.

HANNAH AWOKE the next morning a married woman in every sense of the word. But as she stretched out her arms, instead of finding hellhound warmth, she discovered cold sheets. Given the chill on his side, Wycliff must have slipped from the bed some time ago. A frown pulled on her brow as she dragged the blankets up over her naked body. She might be a married woman, but she was still alone.

She had imagined that taking the final step toward physical intimacy would be the missing piece needed to craft a happy ending for their marriage. Instead of a marvellous contentment coursing through her mind and limbs, Hannah confronted a cold hollow in her chest.

Hannah suffered no misgivings or regrets about the previous night. True to his word, Wycliff had treated her tenderly and cradled her in his arms afterward until she drifted asleep. She had foolishly thought that being physically close to him would mean that she now stood close in his heart. But as she replayed the night in her mind, there had been no words of love spoken between them.

Had she sought his devotion when she offered her body? *Yes.*

In that moment, she realised that love for her husband had taken root inside her, but she suspected it was not reciprocated. While she did not doubt Wycliff admired and desired her, the cold sheet beside her shouted that lust was not the same thing as love. Hannah knew enough of the world to understand that a man did not need to love a woman to take her to his bed. In her naiveté, she had believed their situation to be different.

Why hadn't he said that he loved her? She could conjure only one reason why he had never said the words—because he didn't feel them.

Hannah sat up with her back against the bed frame while a tear formed in the corner of her eye. With the heel of her palm, she wiped it away. "There is nothing to be achieved by staying in bed all day and moping," she muttered to the empty room.

Or almost empty. One spider stubbornly refused to be evicted and had re-spun its web overnight.

A cup of hot chocolate would go a long way toward heating the chill inside her, as would cuddles with Sheba. Since she had much to do, Hannah chose a plain gown of sturdy cotton and laced up practical boots for roaming the gardens and fields around the house. She walked on the balls of her feet to the kitchen, not wanting to disturb any slumbering ghosts. The house creaked and groaned around her and at times, she felt as though she violated a crypt.

In the kitchen, the oven was stoked but there was no sign of Mrs Rossett. Sheba wagged her tail from the blanket by the range, but the spaniel was content to stay put in the warmth. Wycliff had most likely let her out on his way through earlier. Hannah patted the dog, then filled the kettle with water and set it to boil. The glass doors to one side of the kitchen drew her, as curiosity itched to be satisfied about what lay beyond. Last night it had been too dark to explore.

Hannah pushed the doors open and gasped. Within was a conservatory that once would have provided the house with delicate produce and flowers for the tables. It would have grown fragile plants that could not survive outside, where they would be buffeted by the winds whipped off the ocean.

The floor was laid with red bricks in a herringbone pattern. In the very centre stood a raised pool, in the centre of which stood a brass statue of a woman wearing a linen gown laced around her torso with braid. Her arms were outstretched and she appeared to have a shawl draped over her shoulders. When Hannah peered closer, she realised it wasn't a shawl at all, but feathery wings. The image scratched at her memory and women from myths and legends throughout time raced across her mind. The statue represented someone, but she couldn't call the name to the tip of her tongue. She would ask her mother when next they spoke.

Her attention drifted to the knee-high pool around the statue. The water, fish, and any lilies were long gone and a layer of dirt clung to the once brightly coloured tiles laid around the sides and bottom. Overhead and all around her, the panes of the conservatory were coated in years of dirt and grime, but the soaring metal structure revealed its beautiful shape. The conservatory formed a rectangle with a vaulted ceiling, with garden beds running around the outside edge in a scalloped pattern that left a circular path free around the pool.

"Her ladyship loved to tend the plants in here." Mrs Rossett came in on silent feet and joined Hannah. "We had tomatoes all year round under her touch and the most beautiful orchids."

"Perhaps you will again, one day." Hannah reached out and touched a pane. It would take weeks, if not months, of hard labour to breathe life back into the house. Not to mention the finances they would need to repair the obvious damage caused by the storm long ago, and years of subsequent neglect. The list of chores in her mind grew exponentially until their imaginary pages swirled around her like a paper blizzard. No wonder Wycliff had left early, no doubt driven by a similar tally of tasks calling for his attention.

"You have a job ahead of you, milady." Mrs Rossett stared up at the roof where, on either side of the metal frame, bird droppings added an additional thick layer of material to remove.

Hannah couldn't do everything, so chose one thing as a place to start. "There is an old Chinese proverb—a journey of a thousand miles begins with a single step. As my first step, I will concentrate on restoring the conservatory. Along with providing us food, it will be a marvellous place to sit in winter, since it faces south and will capture the sun."

"There used to be rattan furniture in here. It's stored somewhere, assuming the rats haven't found it," Mrs Rossett said.

Rats? A quiet shudder ran down Hannah's spine. Why was it she could handle mice with no concerns, but one mention of their larger cousins and she considered the benefits of fainting like Mary?

"Have you seen his lordship this morning?"

Hannah managed to form a smile by the time she turned to face the housekeeper.

"He was up early and set off to meet Mr Swift. Some problems with the boundary walls to keep those fancy sheep from roaming too far. They took that big ugly fellow of yours with them to help carry rocks, and that extra hand. Can't see what he can do, although he might be useful for scratching the spots you can't reach on your back." The housekeeper chuckled to herself as she walked back to the kitchen.

"I imagine there is much to be done while Wycliff is here, and there will be many demands on his time." Hannah knew how to run a household, but only a little of how to manage an estate this large. She could guess that there would be livestock and tenant farmers to consider. She should examine the books in the study more closely; there might be one on estate management that would educate her further on what to expect and on her new role as the viscountess.

"The kettle has boiled, milady, if you'd like a cup of tea or hot chocolate? And that maid of yours is rousing," Mrs Rossett called as she walked back to the kitchen.

Hannah cast one last look at the barren conservatory and then closed the doors behind her. She pulled out a chair at the kitchen table and sat. "Hot chocolate would be marvellous, please. After breakfast I would like to walk to the village to collect a few things I might need, if you would point me in the right direction?"

Mrs Rossett toasted bread and winked at Hannah.

"Of course. The villagers will love to have a good gawk and gander at you."

"Oh." The cold lump inside Hannah grew a little larger. She didn't want to be an object of curiosity, but there was probably no avoiding it. "Better make it two cups of hot chocolate. For fortification."

5

WYCLIFF HAD AWAKENED EARLY that morning with an odd mix of contentment and anxiety churning through his gut. Rather like oil and water, the two didn't combine, and the constant battle wouldn't allow him to sleep any later than the first hint of dawn.

The contentment came from Hannah. At long last, he had her in his arms, to discover an inquisitive and responsive lover. The closeness he shared with her soothed the hellhound, even as fire burned through his veins to repeat the night's events again. He considered locking the study door and spending the next few days and nights getting to know every inch of his wife's body intimately.

Oddly, his anxiety also arose because of her. What must she think of the derelict house? He had forgotten, or perhaps suppressed, the sad state of the once grand Mireworth. She had degraded into a horror fit for a gothic novel. When they'd been searching upstairs for a bed frame he had altered his vision, wondering how many of his ancestors still roamed the halls. He spied only two lost souls, but couldn't identify them without searching the many portraits stored in the former billiards room.

He had brought his wife to the estate and couldn't even provide her with a bedchamber. Instead, they were camped out in his study, where she used his desk as a dressing table. The spectre of failure loomed over him. What sort of husband couldn't even provide a watertight roof over his wife's head? Admittedly, the roof above them was rather expansive, but the storm-damaged slates from years ago had allowed water to seep into the timbers. The constant drip of moisture over a number of years spread rot and decay like a creeping plague.

One of his many tasks would be talking to the tradesmen about the scale of the work needed on the roof. He cherished a dim hope that he might be able to raise the finances to start critical repairs. They had only a few short weeks in Dorset until his mother-in-law would descend upon them to renew the spell that kept Hannah frozen in time, and allowed her heart to continue to beat. He found himself uncomfortable at the thought of viewing the estate through her parents' eyes. Did Hannah regret her decision to marry him, now that she saw the amount of work and money the estate would consume?

He remembered his conversation with Sir Ewan Shaw the night of the duke's wedding, when he had sought counsel about his relationship. *If you cannot find the words to tell her how you feel, Wycliff, show her instead. Words alone are empty unless accompanied by action. Wrap her in your devotion and your feelings will filter through to her.*

To win his wife's heart, Wycliff needed to become rather similar to the creeping rot or the droplets of water that the timbers and plaster absorbed. Drip by drip, he would show Hannah the depths of his devotion to her. Decision made, and considering he had kept Hannah awake a good part of the night, he let his wife sleep on undisturbed. He kissed her exposed shoulder and drew the blankets around her before he slipped from the bed. On silent feet he gathered his clothes and pulled on his breeches and shirt, but took the rest out into the hall.

There was an overwhelming amount to do and he needed to show Hannah some improvement in the month available to them. Part of him hoped that she would see this as their family home. If her parents found the cure for the Affliction, it could even one day see their children running along the cliffs and swimming in the ocean.

He finished dressing seated on the bottom stair next to a griffin. As he pulled on his boots in the gloom, he made a note of immediate chores. The stone walls needed repair first, to ensure the valuable sheep stayed where they wanted them. Then he would count the few pounds left over to see what could be done about the house. He suspected the choice would be between the roof or the broken windows. A piece of timber would fix the draft in the study and the money saved might buy a few roof slates.

Despite the early hour, he found Mrs Rossett in the kitchen, clad in her dressing gown and slippers, stoking the fire.

"Morning, Mrs Rossett. Do you have anything I can eat on my way to see Swift?" He had agreed to meet the farm manager early, to begin the first of many tasks. He also had to find the time to visit the tenant farmers, particularly those who had fallen behind in their rents.

A more immediate problem that clamoured for his attention could be easily remedied. The spaniel bounced at his feet and Wycliff flung open the door to let her out.

"I made some pasties yesterday. You can take one of those with you and it will fill your belly until morning teatime." The housekeeper opened the larder and removed a large tin. She prised off the lid to reveal a row of fat and golden Cornish pasties.

With their filling of meat and vegetables, each savoury would be a meal almost on its own. Wycliff selected two—one for him and one for Frank, who would be useful for the heavy work ahead.

"Is her ladyship awake?" Mrs Rossett asked as she put the lid back on the tin.

"Hannah sleeps on, Mrs Rossett. She seems quite worn out from her first night at Mireworth." Then his good mood burst forth and he winked and waggled his eyebrows.

The old housekeeper giggled like a young girl and swatted at him with a towel. "Get out of here, you rogue. I'll wait until I hear Lady Wycliff stirring before I start on toast, or perhaps she will need something more robust to revive her?"

Wycliff barked in laughter, let the puppy back inside, and wandered across the packed earth yard to the stables. He found Frank up and mucking out the horse stalls. Barnes sat on a beam above, next to the barn cat. Hand and cat eyed each other as though a fight was about to break out.

"The horses can go out in the field, Frank." Wycliff left the pasties on a ledge, while he clipped a lead to a halter and the monstrous man did the same. Leading two horses each, they soon had their small herd out in a pasture, where the animals cantered away and kicked up their heels.

Barnes slid down the pole and Frank picked up the hand and placed him on his shoulder. Wycliff handed over a pasty, and the two men ate as they followed a beaten dirt track to the cottage where Swift lived with his family. Not far from the main house, the two-storey home was picturesque, with wildflowers growing around it. Unlike the manor house, this one had sparkling clean and unbroken windows and a watertight roof. Smoke curled from the chimney and the laughter of children drifted past his ears.

Wycliff went around back and knocked on the kitchen door.

Mrs Swift opened the door and bobbed a curtsey. "Lord Wycliff, how lovely to see you here! Do come in, sir." Her eyes widened at the sight of Frank, with Barnes sitting like a bird on his shoulder, but the woman said nothing.

Swift rose from the table where he was having his breakfast. The gaggle of children at the table fell silent as Frank entered the cosy room.

One of the boys pointed and let out a long *ahhh* of wonder. "Is he a pirate and that's his parrot?"

Before Wycliff could answer, excited chatter erupted and Frank was surrounded by little ones, most of whom barely came to his knees. One boy stood on a chair, snatched up Barnes, and held him to his face. The hand wriggled and twisted but couldn't break free.

"I see you brought an extra hand." Swift gestured to Barnes with his teacup.

Wycliff chuckled under his breath. Those jokes hadn't grown tired yet. "Yes. That's Barnes and he's good in a pinch. The taller one is Frank."

"You have some odd servants with you, milord," Mrs Swift said as she poured tea and handed the cup to Wycliff.

"Lady Wycliff is the daughter of Lady Seraphina Miles, the mage. They have an eclectic range of staff in their household." Wycliff leaned back in his chair and sipped the tea. The hot brew was just what he needed after their walk.

"Lady Miles? Isn't she dead?" Swift asked.

"Yes, but that hasn't stopped her from continuing her work." Wycliff took a warm scone from the plate offered by Mrs Swift. The Cornish pasty warming his insides would appreciate the buttery company.

A quarter hour later, when the men rose from the table, children dribbled off Frank like water from a stone. The giant plucked Barnes free of the mob and the hand waved farewell from his perch as they headed out the door.

They walked to a nearby field, where the sheep snoozed in the soft morning light. Wycliff surveyed the flock with a growing sense of satisfaction. Even to his untrained eye, their fleece appeared finer and superior to their more common breed counterparts. With the money from Lord Pennicott, he had purchased the ewes, along with a ram, and the resulting spring lambs would augment their stock and establish the new business. In the coming years, he planned to breed enough merino to be able to spread them among his tenant farmers. One day they would build their own mill to produce wool cloth from the fleece.

But first there were practical measures to see to, as a portion of drystone wall had collapsed and needed to be rebuilt. The sheep grazed contentedly, oblivious to the men working alongside them. Frank hauled the larger stones and made a pile while Wycliff and Swift placed them.

"What has been happening in my absence, Swift? Which tenants do we need to call upon?" Wycliff found a rounded stone to wedge between two larger ones.

Swift pulled a handkerchief from his pocket and wiped his brow before replying. "There are three in arrears, my lord. Two are struggling—made some bad choices last winter. They're good folk and a decent harvest this autumn, a bit of leniency, and some sound advice should see them right."

Wycliff nodded. The harvest was susceptible to the weather. He'd rather see his tenants supplement their crops with a more reliable source of income, like sheep or cattle. If the merino breed adapted to the Dorset climate in the way he envisioned, they would one day spin the wool themselves. The increased profit margins would benefit the entire community. Although that was merely a dream; he didn't have sufficient cash to mend his roof, let alone build an expensive mill.

"What of the third tenant in arrears?" Wycliff removed the cork from a water bottle and took a deep drink.

Swift blew out a sigh and stared at the ground, as though searching for an answer in the grass. "Old man Miller. He's a rotten drunk, that one. Never recovered after his granddaughter Amy died before Christmas. He sits out in his yard watching the chickens scratch and the weeds grow. He hasn't paid his rent in over six months and, given the sorry state of his place, has no hope of ever making amends. He needs moving on, if you don't mind my saying so, milord. Put a young fellow on that farm who will roll up his sleeves and get the land productive again."

Wycliff placed the water bottle in the shade. "You know I value your honesty, Swift. Instead of throwing Miller out into the dirt, do we have any small cottages we could offer him?"

Swift paused in his work and swatted a fly by his ear. "There's one or two that are empty and not too derelict. We might need to do a few minor repairs before winter, but we'll find something to suit and he won't have to stagger so far to the tavern and home again."

"There is our solution, then. Miller either moves into the cottage we offer or finds his own alternative. While I'm sympathetic to his grief, I'll not carry dead wood on good land and he has wasted his chance." Wycliff couldn't afford to let prime pasture lay fallow year after year. They all needed to contribute if the district was to flourish. The man had been given ample time to grieve his granddaughter and he'd chosen to wallow in cheap gin instead. "What is happening in the village?"

Swift picked up a stone and assessed where to place it in the wall. "Sarah Rivers has gone missing. Been two days now and no one has seen hide nor hair of her."

Wycliff sorted through his memory to place a face with the name. Youngish woman with blonde hair, if he remembered correctly. "Has she run off with another man?"

Swift shrugged. "Seems unlikely, but you know how the villagers like to gossip. Her man will be out again this morning, walking the shore in case..." His voice trailed off.

"You think she drowned?" The ocean took lives and sometimes gave the bodies back, washing them ashore. Others vanished and were never seen again.

"That makes three in the last year, my lord. Lisbeth Wolfe and Amy Miller were both taken by the sea." The farm manager's gaze darted around the paddock as though he expected a sea monster to emerge from the nearby river and drag away a precious ewe.

Wycliff tightened his grip on the stone in his hands. Lisbeth. Her death a year ago still caused an ache inside him. Sometimes, people trod a dark path and they could not be turned back.

"Drownings are not uncommon, Swift. The tide can turn and pull even an experienced swimmer out farther than they intended." That reminded him of his promise to teach Hannah to swim. Her fear of the ocean would surely fade somewhat if she could stay afloat and swim a short distance. But as much as he wanted to spend time in such a way with his wife, that would be time away from the mountain of tasks to tackle and would do nothing to improve the sorry state of Mireworth.

"As you say, milord, drownings happen when you live by the sea. But folk talk. There are whispers of mermaids returning to the ocean. Of selkie women who shed their skins somewhere along the shore." Swift took a rock from the pile made by Frank and found a spot for it in the wall.

Wycliff snorted. Selkies and mermaids. As if he didn't have enough to do, without tracking down any such creatures to record in the Ministry's registers. Although if Sarah Rivers were a selkie, then her seal-skin would be discarded somewhere near the shore or hidden among the tussocks. "If the women were mermaids, their families would be, too. Why don't we suggest the locals examine each other for gills or scales at bath time?"

Swift barked in laughter and then selected a rectangular stone. "There is another matter, Lord Wycliff. Since you have brought your bride to Mireworth, the village will be expecting some sort of celebration."

Wycliff let out a sigh. He'd rather not. Although planning a ball might give Hannah something to do. He was aware he had abandoned her to her own devices, while he rolled up his sleeves and tried to reverse years of neglect to the estate. A ball would be an opportunity for her to get to know the locals. "I will talk to Lady Wycliff. The manor is not fit for such an event, but we could hold a dance in the village hall."

Swift beamed and slapped his thigh. "That would be grand and it will make Mrs Swift happy. It was her idea and all."

As the men worked, Barnes ran back and forth along the wall. Occasionally he returned with a pebble to slot into a gap. After a few hours of hard labour, the breach was repaired and the sheep secure in the pasture. Wycliff surveyed their handiwork and ticked one job off the myriad on the list in his mind.

"Where to next, Swift?" Wycliff picked up the water jug as they headed back across the paddock.

The farm manager rattled off a number of jobs that all required his attention. It would be a long, hard day. There were two things Wycliff looked forward to at day's end. One was a bath to wash the sweat and grime from his body. The other was shutting the study door on the world and being alone with his wife.

6

THAT MORNING, Mary arose later than Hannah and joined the other women for a companionable breakfast. While the house sat largely derelict and unloved, it warmed Hannah to find quiet solace in the tidy kitchen. It also helped that she had struck up an instant friendship with the older Mrs Rossett. The housekeeper had a never-ending stream of tales about a young Wycliff, or *Master Jonas*, as she remembered him. Hannah wondered if his parents had sent him off to boarding school at an early age because it was customary, or simply for a rest from his constant pursuit of mischief.

The housekeeper gave her directions to the village, saying they wouldn't be able to miss the paths worn into the countryside by generations of feet all heading the same way. Then she handed Mary a carefully printed list of a few supplies she needed. Since Mary could not read, Hannah tucked it into her basket.

"Come along, Mary." Hannah waved to Mrs Rossett, linked arms with Mary, and they set off with the spaniel yapping and bounding around them.

They walked over the fields and around the edge of a coppice, where they reached the path that wound along the top of a cliff. The ocean crashed below them in a centuries-old battle of water against rock.

"It looks ever so fierce," Mary whispered from beside her, her eyes wide as she gazed at the ocean for the first time.

Hannah shared the maid's opinion of the tempestuous sea. "Wycliff said he used to swim here often as a child. No doubt there will be a quiet cove somewhere along the coast." Or at least she assumed he had bathed somewhere with calmer waters. She couldn't imagine leaping into the ocean when the risk of being pounded to death on the rocks were a certainty. That seemed too rash even for a rapscallion.

A breeze whipped up and blew the ribbons on Hannah's bonnet around her face. "The village can't be far now," she said as she batted a green ribbon away.

The village of Selham revealed itself where the sweep of the land created a sheltered cove. Cottages and larger buildings huddled along the shoreline with their backs to the rolling hill. Here, the rocks and harsh ocean gave way to golden sand and calmer waters. A harbour around a point with deeper water served larger vessels, while nearby on the beach smaller boats were hauled up by the locals and dragged back out the next day as they fished.

As they approached, a crowd on the beach caught Hannah's attention. People were gathered on the sand at one end, where upturned boats were stored. They were staring at the water as a fully clothed man emerged from the waves, a limp form draped in his arms. Long dark hair hung low and soaking skirts were tangled about legs turned pale grey.

"Oh, no." Hannah stopped above the beach, unable to look away from the unfolding tragedy.

"Sarah!" A pregnant woman screamed and rushed to the dripping wet man. She wiped hair from the prone woman's face and pressed her cheek to one tinged blue. More people surrounded them, and cries and sobs rose from the assembled crowd.

"Do you think she's dead?" Mary asked.

The man carrying the woman knelt on the sand. Someone shook out a blanket before him and he gently lowered the woman onto it. Then he wrapped the fabric around her form, shooing away helping hands. He draped the blanket over her face last and rested one hand on her hair. He bowed his head and his shoulders heaved.

"It does appear so, Mary." Hannah gripped her hands together at the display of sorrow and grief.

Someone glanced up and shielded their eyes against the sun to stare at them. Another person whipped around and soon numerous eyes glared at their witnessing such a loss.

"We are intruding. Let us leave them to tend her."

Hannah tugged on Mary's arm, and they continued along the path to the village.

The community occupied a pretty spot, with shops and businesses laid out facing the water. Cottages nestled higher up the hill and lanes wound upward between them from the main road. People bustled back and forth. A few men walked next to horses pulling carts. Some passers-by stared at them as they carried out the purchases for Mrs Rossett, but none said a single word. At most, they received a brief curious nod.

The haberdashery window caught Hannah's attention and they stopped to look within at the range of wares displayed. She couldn't help but overhear the conversation taking place behind them.

"Did they find her, then?" a woman said.

"Yes. Poor soul. They are bringing her in now," another answered.

"Did you think it's another one that drowned or...?" The first voice trailed away.

The deeper-voiced woman made a dismissive noise. "Don't start with that old nonsense, Margaret. You're as gullible as any of the children."

Hannah turned, curious as to what old nonsense could be attached to a drowning and intrigued as to what the second woman might have been going to say after *or*. The two women glanced at her, nodded, and fell silent as they hurried along the road. Hannah chided herself for her morbid curiosity. The village lay close to the ocean and many families relied on it for their living. Drownings would be more common by the sea, just as being run over by a carriage was more common on the busy streets of London.

Not that it did anything to allay her fear of the ocean.

Hannah and Mary strolled the rest of the main street and its shops. Hannah made certain they gave their custom in cash, not credit, even if it meant using her pocket money from her parents. Their reception became warmer, and word spread that her ladyship herself had come. Hannah purchased beeswax to polish the furniture, a variety of new brooms to be delivered later, and even a ribbon for herself and one for Mary. At last they turned to walk to the wharf, where they watched seagulls circle, before they set out on the return journey. They arrived at Mireworth well after midday to find Mrs Rossett busy in the kitchen. Mary delivered the basket and told her about the brooms before she set to work rustling up tea and crumpets.

"With so many extra people here and if you are planning to visit more often, I could do with the help of someone, if your ladyship doesn't mind me taking on another maid. One with a green thumb to tackle the kitchen garden would be most useful." The house-keeper looked up from the mixing bowl held in the crook of her arm while she stirred batter with a wooden spoon.

"Of course. Choose someone as you see fit. Mary and I will assist however we can." Hannah preferred to keep her hands occupied. There was no point sending her out to mend stone walls or shear sheep. Nor could she repair a leaky roof. But she could put that morning's decision into action. "I thought I might clean out the conservatory if you had no objection, Mrs Rossett?"

"It would be as good a place as any to start, milady, and I will admit, I did used to like having my afternoon tea in there on a cold, sunny day." She lowered the bowl to the tabletop and added a handful of flour from a large crock. "How did you find the village?"

The sad scene at the beach floated before Hannah and her heart ached for the bereft family. "We saw a woman being retrieved from the ocean. A woman on the beach cried out the name Sarah."

"Oh, no!" Mrs Rossett put a free hand to her chest. "That will be Sarah Rivers. Poor thing went missing two days ago and her family have been searching for her. The rumours I heard were that she and her man had an argument a few nights ago, and she stormed off to have a quiet think."

Hannah stared into her cup of tea and silence fell over the table. Death visited them all, eventually. Only a few would continue to walk the earth after their hearts were stilled. Even if the Affliction took Hannah's life, there was much to be done after her death. She could seclude herself at Mireworth and coax it back into life. That led her to wondering if Unwin and Alder would deliver the *pickled cauliflower* down here that would keep the rot from consuming her limbs. When they returned to London, she would raise the issue of delivery by the post coach.

The items were preserved, so there was no concern they would spoil.

An itch sprang up in Hannah's mind. Cleaning out the conservatory, scrubbing the dirty panes of glass, and refreshing the garden beds would keep her occupied her entire month at the estate. But there was something else she longed to do—explore. The enormous manor house would have many nooks and crannies and she anticipated walking the halls upstairs. What might she find? Lady Wycliff's rooms, perhaps?

"Is the upstairs terribly damaged?" Hannah asked. While she wanted to set off and pry into every cranny, and follow the bell to find the suite belonging to her title, she didn't want to tumble through a rotten floor.

Mrs Rossett took up her mixing again. "I really couldn't say. I stick to downstairs. The roof leaks and his lordship has done what he can to stop it spreading too far. You're most likely to find your way blocked by furniture. Some of the big pieces were moved into dry corridors, and out of the rooms with broken windows or water coming in."

"Oh. I shall ask his lordship, then, before I set off on any exploration. Until then, I shall make a start on the conservatory." Hannah donned an apron provided by the housekeeper and tucked her hair up under a cap to keep it clean.

Mary helped Mrs Rossett, while Hannah found a broom and began the arduous task of sweeping out years of dirt, dust, and dead plants from the conservatory. Fortunately, two large glass doors still opened to the outside, even though the elderly hinges protested. Once she managed to push them open, she chased piles of dirt and debris out the door and off the side of the bricked terrace.

By the time dusk fell, Hannah had swept the bricks in the conservatory, cleaned the dehydrated weeds from the reflecting pool, and made a start on scrubbing the bright tiles around its sides. A thorough cleaning revealed reeds in bright green, flowering lotus in vibrant blues to purple, a crocodile in a muted olive, and patterns in a rich red and a golden yellow. The unfolding scene reminded her of paintings and frescoes from a book she had studied recently.

Hannah sat back on her heels and stared up at the winged statue. "Ma'at," she whispered as the clues fell into place in her mind. What on earth was a bronze statue and pool dedicated to the Egyptian goddess of justice doing in a Dorset manor house?

But that was a question for another day. The light was already fading fast outside and she wiped her hands on her apron. There would be time to wash up and perhaps change her dress before supper.

As darkness dropped over the countryside, Wycliff and Frank appeared from their day in the fields. Both men were damp and Hannah assumed they had washed up in a water trough before entering the house. The group once more gathered around the large table in the kitchen. Hannah's heart stuttered as she sat beside her husband, anticipating what would unfold after they returned to the study.

"What did you do today, Hannah?" Wycliff asked as dishes were passed around.

"Mary and I walked into the village. On the way, we saw Sarah Rivers being brought up from the water." Hannah stared at her plate, the sad sight weighing on her mind.

Wycliff picked up his cutlery and rolled the knife between his fingers. Light caught the metal and flashed like a soul darting upward. "Swift told me her family has been searching for her. At least now they can grieve. The currents around here can be unpredictable, and sometimes the ocean does not surrender what it takes."

"I think I might stick to walking on the beach and building sandcastles. I do not see any need to venture into the sea's cold embrace." Hannah shuddered to imagine how it might be to drown—cold, salty water forcing its way into your lungs as you struggled against the might of nature. Then your body drifting on the tide, subject to the watery mistress's whim as to whether you were returned to your family, or dragged to the dark depths to become food for the fish.

"There are coves with quieter waters suitable for swimming if you still wish to learn," Wycliff said.

Hannah quite enjoyed a warm bath, but the idea of the frigid water tugging her body to bottomless depths struck fear through her. Then she glanced at Mary. The maid had turned ghostly pale at the talk of swimming. Perhaps, as lady of the house, Hannah ought to set a brave example. "If the weather stays fine, I shall venture a paddle at the water's edge."

Wycliff huffed. "That is a first step, I suppose. Which reminds me, before you imparted the sad news of Sarah Rivers, Swift said to me earlier that the locals will expect a ball to celebrate our wedding. Obviously we cannot hold one here given the state of Mireworth, but there is a hall in the village that is often used for dances, weddings, and such. Do you feel up to organising such a thing?"

"A ball, for us? Do you think that is appropriate given that Mrs Rivers' friends and family will be in mourning?" How horrid if the locals thought her crass and unfeeling, putting on a dance while they suffered raw grief.

His dark eyebrows shot up as he considered her concerns. "Life goes on, Hannah, especially in the countryside. But I am not insensible to local opinion and am not suggesting we hold it the night of her funeral or instead of the wake. Perhaps in two weeks' time, to give feelings time to settle?"

"I think a dance is a fine idea, Lord Wycliff. It will give the village something to look forward to, and keep a few idle hands busy." Mrs Rossett smiled from the other end of the table as Barnes dragged the butter dish toward her. The hand seemed to be going out of his way to prove helpful to the housekeeper.

"Well, if Mrs Rossett does not think people would take offence at the timing, I shall do my best. It will also be a fine opportunity to get to know everyone." Making friends never came easily to Hannah. That was Lizzie's forte.

Thinking of her friend caused a wave of sadness to crash through her. Hannah had received only a short missive from Lizzie to say she was enjoying her voyage to Italy, then silence. Her mother had given both women a piece of ensorcelled paper. What was written on one sheet appeared on the other. When ready to craft a reply, they had only to rub a finger over the words to make them disappear. Every night, Hannah checked her sheet, but it remained blank.

Had the ocean claimed Lizzie and Harden? No. It wouldn't dare ruin the honeymoon by dashing their vessel to pieces. She would have to be patient. Her friend would write a full account when she had time. Lizzie was simply preoccupied with her marvellous European adventure, and being doted upon by a husband much in love with his bride.

Hannah swallowed a sigh. What must that be like?

Mrs Rossett passed a pitcher of lemonade to Hannah. "I can come into town with you tomorrow, if you like, and introduce you properly. I'll ask about to find a local girl to help out in the garden for a few hours each day. Will you be here long this time, Lord Wycliff?"

Wycliff glanced at Hannah. "A month at least, I think, Mrs Rossett. Then Hannah's parents will join us for a short while."

She nodded. "We had best prepare another room

for them—my mother will be more comfortable on the ground floor, accessible to her bathchair."

Hannah stared at her hands. She would like to stay for longer, and settle into what she hoped would be their home one day. Her mother would visit to renew the spell that kept her death at bay. But what if she lacked the ingredients needed for the ritual and the curse nibbled a little more at her heart? Before they left for Dorset, her mother had discovered that the dark spell poised to snatch her life had altered.

Thoughts of life and death swirled through her mind and an idea bubbled to the surface. "Wycliff, why is there a statue of Ma'at in the reflecting pool in the conservatory?"

Wycliff frowned. "I have no idea. How did you know who it is? As a lad, I always called her *bird lady*."

Mrs Rossett pushed her plate away and leaned back with a faraway look on her face. "That statue was old when I was a fresh-faced scullery maid. Who knows anymore why it was chosen? That was over a hundred years ago."

"The tiles are distinctly Egyptian and that made me realise the identity of the winged woman. Ma'at is a goddess of truth and justice." Odd that Wycliff's ancestral home had an Egyptian statue, when Hannah and her mother had been pursuing that line to find a cure for the Affliction. Most likely, it was a simple coincidence. Englishmen were fascinated by all things Egyptian. A long-ago Lady Wycliff might have seen the image in a book and requested a duplicate.

After dinner they talked for a while, then Mrs Rossett washed dishes while Mary dried, and Hannah followed directions to put things away. Her palms were damp with nervous excitement as she walked along the hall to their impromptu bedchamber, Wycliff's footsteps an echo behind her own.

He shut the door and Hannah activated the glow lamp by the bed. When she turned, Wycliff had shrugged out of his jacket and stalked toward her with dark fire in his eyes. He caressed her collarbone and his finger slipped under the edge of her gown.

"Jonas," she whispered, and closed her eyes. Hannah leaned into his touch, wondering if this night would be different. Might her husband whisper of his love and fill the odd hollow inside her?

7

Hannah awoke the next morning to find that, yet again, she was alone. A sluggish chill crept through her veins and she tugged the blankets higher to warm her core. Logically she understood that Wycliff had much to do in their limited time at the estate, and he didn't want to waste daylight hours. Nor did she think any fault for her growing loneliness could be attributed to her husband's nocturnal activities. Wycliff was, in her very limited experience, a patient and gentle lover.

So why did waking up alone cause tears to burn behind her eyes? Could it be that the physical act alone did not bring the true intimacy she sought? There was a conundrum—for she could not imagine how to be any closer to her husband. Hannah turned the problem over in her mind as she dressed, wondering if the missing piece was not the closeness of Wycliff's body, but of his heart.

She yanked on the laces of her boots. The only

route she knew to a man's heart was the direct one, assisted by rib crackers and a scalpel.

Once dressed, Hannah headed to the kitchen, but paused in the grand foyer to gaze up at the dome above. Layers of dirt and bird droppings covered the protective outer glass and filtered the light as though she stood at the bottom of a well. The colours in the stained glass were muted to murky reds and browns and one image became indistinguishable from another. Although from what she could see, all the glass appeared intact and in need only of a thorough cleaning. Perhaps she could send Barnes up there with a brush to make a start. At least he wouldn't be injured if he fell from the roof.

An eerie silence enveloped the house. No servants moved about their chores, no one scuttled through hidden passages, no friends or family chattered in rooms above. There wasn't even the tick or chime of a clock to interrupt the quiet. The ghost of a tall and narrow outline hinted at where a grandfather clock might once have stood, marking the passage of time for the household. The timepiece must have been sold to pay the late Lord Wycliff's debts, or was stored in a dry place somewhere.

Hannah found Mrs Rossett and Mary at the kitchen table, chatting over breakfast. The housekeeper rose to prepare a plate as Hannah entered and pulled out a chair.

"His lordship left early again." She congratulated herself on managing to keep a wistful tone from her voice. Despite the fact that she missed his company.

Sheba placed her front paws on Hannah's leg and she patted the spaniel in greeting. At least she possessed this particular dog's affections, even if they weren't large enough to fill the empty space inside her.

"There's always hard labour to be done on a farm. He was muttering about visiting the tenant farmers today. I hear a few are behind on their rents." Mrs Rossett poured a hot chocolate and slid the cup along to Hannah.

After a quiet breakfast, the three women put on their bonnets and walked over to the stables. Frank hitched up the gig for them and then handed each woman up, with a large toothy grin for Mary. Hannah did not miss how the big man's hand lingered on Mary's. It gladdened her heart to see the odd romance blossom and she appreciated the soothing effect Frank exerted on Mary. But she did wonder if there was any future for them. None of them knew how long Frank would remain animated. He might endure for a hundred years...or only as many days.

Hannah realised she could say the same thing about herself. For a moment, melancholy stole her breath. How many beats remained for her heart? The curse was changing within her and fought a silent battle against her mother's magic. Any day might be the one that saw the curse break free and squeeze the life from her.

Seize each day given to you, she reminded herself. The curse could overwhelm her, Frank's stitches could come undone, or a monstrous wave might surge up and wipe out the village. None of them knew their allotted lifespan and dwelling on it allowed fear to steal the enjoyment from each day.

From his perch on the giant's shoulder, Barnes snapped his fingers to attract Hannah's attention.

She pulled her mind back to the friends and family surrounding her. She could guess what the limb wanted when the former sailor was this close to the ocean. "Help Frank with his chores, Barnes, and I promise that this afternoon we will all go to the beach."

The hand gave his version of a salute and then tugged on Frank's ear, no doubt in a hurry to tackle their work for the day.

Hannah picked up the reins and clucked her tongue to ask the placid horse to walk on. Once clear of the estate and on the packed earth road, she urged the horse into a slow trot. It didn't take long before the sweep of the land revealed Selham up ahead. Hannah slowed the horse to a walk as they approached and more people shared the road with them.

Mrs Rossett waved to indicate a large barn. "That's the blacksmith. We can leave the horse and gig there."

Hannah guided the horse into the yard, as a large man emerged from the smoke-covered building. Soot from the forge had caressed nearly every stone and when the sunlight hit the coating, the barn shone a silvery grey.

"Good morning, Mrs Rossett." The blacksmith stood at the horse's head as the women climbed down.

"Good morning. Lady Wycliff, may I present

William Kaye." The housekeeper made the intro-
duction.

The blacksmith nodded to Hannah and pulled off
his cap, but his attention strayed to Mary. "Lady
Wycliff. We were surprised to hear his lordship had
wed. You're a brave woman, if you don't mind me
saying so."

Hannah glanced at Mary when the maid giggled.
What on earth had prompted that unusual reaction?
Ascribing it to the maid's usual unpredictable
behaviour, Hannah turned back to the blacksmith. "I
understand the sentiment, Mr Kaye. My husband does
have a reputation for being somewhat abrupt, and he
does a fine job of concealing his manners."

That comment made Mrs Rossett snort in laughter.
"He does at that! Now, Mr Kaye, we will be a few
hours, by the time we see to all our errands."

The man nodded and yanked his cap back on his
head. "Right-o, Mrs Rossett. I'll unhitch the cob and he
can have the yard until you return."

"If you please, milady. We have much to do." Mrs
Rossett offered Hannah her arm and steered her down
the road while Mary trailed behind. She appeared to be
watching the blacksmith remove the harness from the
horse.

"I think we should find Mrs MacNee and have a
quiet word. She's the publican's wife and they own the
hall," Mrs Rossett said.

As they progressed along the road that separated
the buildings from the shore, Mrs Rossett put names to

the people who stopped to wave or stare. A few wore sad smiles or had eyes that glistened from recently shed tears.

"Was Sarah Rivers well known in the village?" Hannah pitched her voice low as they walked. She didn't want to offend by speaking loudly about the deceased.

Mrs Rossett hummed as she thought. "Everybody knows everybody else's business around here. She was married a few years ago, but the couple weren't blessed with any little ones. Her man is a shepherd for his lordship, and is gone most of the day."

Hannah had her own experience of a husband who rose early to work the land. At least theirs was a temporary measure. How would she cope if endless days alone stretched before her? Then her feet froze to the ground. How silly she had become in a few short months. Before Wycliff had entered their lives, Hannah spent much time in her own company. Quiet solitude had never bothered her as she went about her studies and assisted her parents.

How quickly she had become accustomed to Wycliff's presence and conversation during the day. How quickly she had grown to anticipate his kisses and caresses at night.

"Everything all right?" Mrs Rossett asked, and scattered Hannah's thoughts like a child running toward a flock of seagulls.

"What? Oh, yes, sorry. For a moment I had forgotten something, but it has returned to me now.

Look, I think I can spy the hall." Hannah pointed to a whitewashed building that stood by itself.

"Yes, that's it, and the tavern is right next door. Very handy for providing supper," Mrs Rossett said.

"Would it be all right if I looked at the shops, milady?" Mary asked, fidgeting by the tavern's porch.

"Yes, of course, Mary. We shall catch you up later." Hannah waved to the maid as she gravitated to a brightly decorated window farther along the row. It seemed a pink dress had caught Mary's eye.

Mrs Rossett pushed open the door to the tavern and Hannah followed her inside.

While not a large establishment, the tavern had a warm and friendly air. The floors were swept and the tables clean. A fire crackled in the enormous hearth; the magical orange flames threw no heat, but instead a sweetly scented odour wafted on the air. A ginger cat with luxurious fur sat before the fire and turned its head to regard them with yellow eyes. Hannah thought the creature looked annoyed that the ensorcelled fire made a pleasant smell rather than overheating the room to a cat's liking.

"Morning, Beatrice! It's not often we see you in here," a woman called.

"Morning, Hollie. I have the new Lady Wycliff with me." Mrs Rossett walked closer to the bar.

Hollie's eyes widened and she put down the glass and cloth in her hand to bob a curtsey. "Pleased to meet you, Lady Wycliff. I must say, when Beatrice told us the news that his lordship had married, I thought she was pulling my leg."

"I am aware his lordship doesn't appear to be the marrying type. I confess that on first meeting him, I thought him abominably rude," Hannah murmured.

"Yet there is no man more loyal and he would go to the ends of the earth for those he cares about." Mrs Rossett nodded to herself as she made her pronouncement of Wycliff's character.

Or undertake a journey to the underworld? Hannah wondered.

"Lady Wycliff wishes to discuss using the hall, Hollie." Mrs Rossett gestured out the window in the direction of the other building.

"Indeed. Lord Wycliff and I would like to host a dance for the village. In two weeks' time, if that would be possible?" Hannah asked.

Mrs MacNee beamed in delight at the idea. "Oh, how marvellous, milady. Of course you must use the hall. We can pop over now if you have time, and decide what needs to be done."

From a row of hooks set along the wall, the publican's wife selected a key with a faded gold tassel. Then she led the way through a side door, and across a shared courtyard to the hall. Once unlocked, the door creaked as it swung open. Their footsteps echoed on the floorboards.

Hannah stood in the dusty space and turned a slow circle. It was no grand Mayfair ballroom like the one where Lizzie had her wedding ball. But it had ample space for them to dance, room to set out tables for refreshments, and they could create a few seating areas.

"It hasn't been used for a few months and sand does get into all the corners when the wind howls. It will need a good clean, but there will be plenty of willing hands to help once word gets around. Did you want to decorate at all?" Mrs MacNee asked.

What Hannah wouldn't give her for mother's abilities to set the night alive with magic! Instead, she would have to use more earthly means. Selham was a coastal village. Perhaps a sea theme? Ideas sprang into her mind.

"I think an underwater theme. We could thread shells on strings to make garlands. Lanterns with blue and green glass would cast a lovely light and simulate being underwater. Perhaps strips of fabric to mimic seaweed?" Hannah imagined it in her mind's eye as she conjured the sort of ocean she would dare venture into. No sharks would be allowed to circle the dance floor, but paper fish could dangle from thread.

Mrs MacNee tapped the side of her head as she considered the idea. "We have a young woman in the village who is a right good painter. She has a slight aftermage gift that makes the images move. We could ask if she would paint fish that we could cut out and hang among the seaweed?"

"Oh! That would be brilliant. If we work hard, it will come together in time, I am sure." A tingle of excitement ran through Hannah. What fun to plan her own wedding ball. But what a shame neither her parents nor Lizzie would be present.

They settled on a date two weeks away and Mrs MacNee promised to speak to the painter about providing a variety of sea life. At least collecting shells and stringing them together would give the village children a way to feel included, too.

"I will spread the word and ask for helpers, but I'll leave it for a few days, milady. We have the funeral for Sarah Rivers tomorrow." A frown crossed Mrs MacNee's brow and the light in her eyes dimmed.

Hannah clasped her hands together. "Of course. We must defer any public announcement until after she is laid to rest."

She would talk to Wycliff about attending the funeral. It seemed only right that he be there, and he would have to leave off attending to whatever derelict wall or field called on his time for a few hours to escort her to the cemetery.

That afternoon, as promised, Hannah and the others walked to the shore for an outing. Mrs Rossett told them where to find a sheltered cove. Hannah and Mary both carried a basket containing wrapped sandwiches, fruit, and biscuits. Frank carried a blanket slung over his back like a bedroll. Barnes bounced on the giant's shoulder.

They stopped at the edge of the cliff and Hannah breathed in the salty air. Beneath them, the waves rolled in toward the golden sand. As before, the wind tugged at the ribbons of her bonnet and tested the firmness of the knot holding it in place.

"Oh, milady, we won't get dragged out by the ocean, will we?" Mary clung to Frank's arm and stared at the vast expanse of water with wide eyes.

"No, Mary. We shall gather shells and perhaps build a sandcastle. We will stay clear of the water, unless you wish to have a paddle later?" Hannah had failed to find Wycliff and so could not ask if he would accompany them. Any attempt to teach her to swim would have to wait until another day, assuming her husband could tear himself away from the demands of the estate. Hannah led the way as they followed the worn track down the cliff to the beach.

Barnes jumped to the sand and ran back and forth, then stopped and jumped up and down on the spot before taking off again. Sheba barked at the incoming waves and let out a yelp when cold water lapped at her paws. Hannah laughed to watch their excitement. Mary chose a spot in the shelter of the cliff and out of the fresh wind. Frank undid the strap around the blanket and unfurled it where directed. The women unpacked the food and left Frank to guard it in case the spaniel got any ideas.

Hannah clutched her basket and the two women set off with enthusiasm, picking up shells from the sand or from under seaweed that piled up where the retreating tide had deposited it. Collecting shells for the forthcoming dance had seemed a marvellous idea, until Hannah realised just how very many they would need to thread into garlands to decorate the hall. She hoped there would be lots of little helpers from the village to pitch in and make them, too, once word spread.

When both baskets were brimming with a variety of shells and a few dehydrated starfish, they returned to the blanket and something to eat and drink.

"Shall we build a sandcastle? Or better, construct a sand ship for Barnes?" Hannah asked.

With Mary's help, the two women crafted the hull of a boat from damp sand. Then Hannah gently made a cabin at the stern. Frank found them a large stick to serve as a mast and they tied a handkerchief to it as a sail. Barnes stood at the bow and looked out to the ocean.

"Oh, milady, we could dig a trench around it and fill it with water and he would be afloat on his own little ocean," Mary suggested.

"Brilliant idea, Mary," Hannah said and Barnes rushed to one side of his ship and pointed at the water.

They tackled the next task while Sheba dragged over a stick and settled down to chew one end. The spaniel seemed to think it her life's duty to find and chew as many sticks as possible. Once they had a moat encircling the sand ship, Frank used the now empty flask and filled it with sea water. Trip after trip he made, wading out into the water while Mary gasped and called out for him to beware of each wave.

Relief filled Hannah that the large man was too big and heavy for the buffeting sea to snag and drag out deeper. She would not be able to bear it if the ocean claimed Frank. Soon they had sufficient water around the boat for it to appear to navigate its own small portion of ocean.

Frank hummed a tune and clapped his hands while Barnes danced a strange jig on deck. Mary giggled and for a little while, Hannah held her own enjoyment close to her heart. Then she looked around, and the absence of Wycliff flowed over her with the chill off the water and raised goose bumps along her arms. She pulled her shawl tighter around her shoulders. Never would she have imagined that one day, she would miss the company of the foul-tempered and rude viscount so very much.

8

For a change, Wycliff didn't rise at dawn the next day. Instead, he eased his arm out from under Hannah while full dark still lay over the estate. As usual, he tucked the blankets around her shoulders to ensure no chill touched her skin. Then he gathered up his clothing and crept naked into the cold foyer. For once he was grateful for the hellhound merged with his soul, as hell fire coursing through his veins kept him from freezing as he dressed. A partial shift of his vision allowed him to see his surroundings, since the inside of the house was darker than a crypt.

He helped himself to the tin of Cornish pasties and let Sheba out. Mrs Rossett roused as though some sixth sense told her the rapscallion was raiding her pantry. In mobcap and shawl, she waved the poker before using it to stoke the fire. Outside, dawn spread tendrils of deep orange and red as he walked to Swift's cottage with Frank's silent companionship beside him.

"Red sky in the morning, sailor's warning," Wycliff muttered and then worried that any storm might further loosen the slates on the roof of Mireworth.

Today's task saw Wycliff, Swift, and Frank cleaning out a long neglected waterway. The three men finished the job in under two hours. Dripping wet and smelling of mud and weed, the men walked back to the house to wash and change before Sarah Rivers' funeral.

Once presentable, they used the large travelling carriage to convey the family to the funeral. Mrs Rossett sat inside with Wycliff and Hannah. Mary took a seat up next to Frank. Barnes clung to the edge of the outer rail, but the hand was under strict instructions to stay with the carriage and not wander around the cemetery. Wycliff could imagine the panic among the locals if the hand sat in the dirt upon a grave and wriggled his fingers.

"Here we are," he murmured as the carriage rolled to a stop at the churchyard.

"How picturesque this would be under different circumstances," Hannah said as she peered out the window.

Wycliff jumped down and then held out his hand to Hannah and then Mrs Rossett.

The housekeeper waved to a group of women standing under a large oak, and bustled over. Hannah took his arm and he drew her near. The people of the village gathered on the grass outside the stone church, the murmur of hushed conversation washing over the gravestones.

The day warmed and the service would be held at the graveside, not inside the quaint little chapel. Near a stone angel guarding a grave, a man with a stern expression stood by himself. With tousled, dirty blond hair and a scowl on his face, he appeared to have dressed in a hurry. Stubble clung to his jaw and his cravat had a worse knot than anything Wycliff tied.

There was one thing about the man that made Wycliff approach him—he was an aftermage with a gift for botany. The man might have whatever herbs Lady Miles used to keep the curse inside Hannah from stealing her heartbeat.

Wycliff approached but kept Hannah close to his side. "Good morning, Seager. Lady Wycliff, this is Mr Seager, the local apothecary and a keen botanist. He might be able to provide any herbs or potions you require during our visit."

"Oh! I am pleased to make your acquaintance, Mr Seager," Hannah said.

The man appeared to have forgotten his manners and stared at them for a long while. Then he gave a scant nod in Hannah's direction before glaring at Wycliff. "Your sheep had better not wander into the lower fields. There are many species growing there that I require for my potions and salves, and there will be trouble if the plants are trampled or eaten."

Wycliff ground his jaw at the apothecary's rude manner and snub of Hannah. It wouldn't do to cause a scene at a funeral, but he would remember the slight against his wife. "Swift and I are working to mend what walls require it. Perhaps if the herbs are so important, you should grow them in your garden, rather than foraging over Mireworth pastures? You should take care the gamekeeper does not shoot you, thinking you a poacher."

The man blew out a snort. "You no more own the trees and shrubs than you do the sky or clouds, Lord Wycliff. These plants require very specific growing conditions. My apothecary garden is too sheltered for some that need the salty wind or forest debris."

"My mother, Lady Miles, is a keen horticulturist. She may be able to advise how to alter the conditions in your walled garden." Hannah joined the conversation.

"Lady Miles?" The scowl on Seager's face deepened.

"Yes," Hannah replied.

"The dead mage?" Now the man's nostrils flared.

"Yes." Hannah glanced at Wycliff, but he, too, wondered what the man was getting at.

Seager snorted. "Dead things should fertilise plants, not offer advice about them."

Hannah's fingers curled into Wycliff's sleeve and he wondered which of them would leap at the man first for his insults. For a change, he cut the man dead and steered his wife away before angry words were exchanged. They strolled among the headstones in the sunlight and left the unpleasantness behind them.

Hannah leaned closer to his side. "Today is a rare day. I do believe I have just met someone so rude that, by comparison, he makes my husband appear the epitome of politeness and good manners."

Wycliff huffed a silent laugh. Usually he spoke first, insulted everyone, and left Hannah to apologise after him. Either marriage or his new sense of contentment appeared to have mellowed his temper. "I am sorry, Hannah. I thought he would be a useful person to know and who would most likely have whatever your mother requires. I would have called him out on his behaviour, but did not want to upset the grieving family."

She tightened her grip on him. "You need to stop being so considerate, before you make me swoon."

Good humour rolled through him and he forgot about Seager's abruptness. Wycliff led Hannah along a gravel pathway that wound through the spreading trees.

"Does anyone know how the poor woman came to drown?" Hannah whispered.

Only at a funeral would his wife enquire as to the circumstances surrounding a death. He bent his head closer to hers and inhaled the faint lavender aroma of the soap she used to wash her hair. "She probably slipped while walking along the rocks, or perhaps was pulled under by a wave while searching for shellfish. It happens, Hannah, as tragic as such an occurrence is to the family left behind."

Off to one side and under a large elm tree sat a freshly dug pile of soil. Beside it, a coffin waited on timbers with two ropes coiled in the grass at each end.

The vicar, Mr Hartley, stood in the shade. A pleasant chap of an age similar to Wycliff, he appeared scrubbed and orderly, his light brown hair swept to one side and the Bible clasped in his hands.

"Lord Wycliff, a shame that this sad circumstance mars your return to us," the vicar said on seeing him.

The man had taken the Mireworth living some two years earlier. While enthusiastic, he also seemed realistic about the harshness of life and didn't lecture the parishioners too much about their many vices. In tending his flock, the religious man somehow managed to strike a balance without either boring them or coming across as sanctimonious.

"Indeed, it is always sad when a life ends too soon. Lady Wycliff, this is Mr Hartley, who tends to the villagers' spiritual needs." He turned to his wife and glanced over her head at the gathering people.

"Mr Hartley. I was saddened to hear of Mrs Rivers' losing her life to the ocean." Hannah clung to Wycliff's arm as though he were a piece of wood in a turbulent sea.

The vicar smiled and leaned toward Hannah. "An honour to meet you, Lady Wycliff. Unfortunately, such tragedies are not uncommon when we coexist with the sea, and I do what I can to ease their passing."

Before Hartley got the idea that they were there for a social call, Wycliff pulled Hannah away to stand to one side of the grave. More people joined them so that the crowd flowed between the gravestones. The woman's family stood on the other side.

Hartley gave a sermon about love and forgiveness and then led the congregation in a hymn. The service seemed timed to coincide with the group's ability to stand still on the warm day. As people began to shuffle their feet to relieve cramping muscles, Hartley gave a signal. Two burly men each took an end of the ropes and lowered the coffin into the damp earth.

Mr Rivers approached and scooped up a handful of dirt, which he tossed into the grave. A dull clatter rose up and was followed by another, as the woman's friends and family paid their last respects. Wycliff waited until near the end before performing the same ritual.

Hannah remained silent as they walked back to the carriage, when a figure drew Wycliff's attention. Harvey Cramond stood with his head bowed at the graveside of Amy Miller, a bunch of yellow daisies clutched in his hands. At the time of her demise, Swift had written to Wycliff in London with the mutterings about the woman's death. She had been pulled from the ocean with the obvious sign of a blow to her head. Some blamed her grandfather, saying the old man used to hit her and that he might have flown into a rage when she told him of her plans to marry Cramond and start her life afresh with him. Old man Miller told a different story and blamed Cramond, saying they must have argued when his granddaughter declined his proposal and that he had struck Amy and thrown her into the water.

Wycliff thought the answer simple. The woman had either hit her head and fallen in the water, or walked out into the ocean to end her life, where the action of tide against rocks had caused the injury to her head. He let out a sigh. Now there had been another one, making three deaths in a year, the first of the unfortunate trio being Lisbeth Wolfe.

Lisbeth. The name whispered through his memories like a mournful wind through the trees.

Life became an impossible burden for some women. He curled his fingers around Hannah's hand. He would ensure she never struggled alone. Once Mireworth was restored, he could offer her the sort of life she deserved. Or a comfortable place to see out her death, if the Affliction claimed her.

"I had thought an underwater theme for the ball, but do you think that would be thoughtless given the current circumstances? I would not wish to offend the grieving families," Hannah said, breaking the silence between them.

He turned the idea over in his mind. His initial reaction had been that it was a touch of whimsy and why did they even need a theme for decorations? But as he held her close, it reminded him that he had left her to decide how best to fill her days while he worried about the estate. And she was filling them most ably— not everyone would notice, but every small change was evident to him. "We cannot ignore the ocean. Many men and families rely on fishing to supplement their income. If you are concerned, I will announce the theme. Men are usually considered to be oblivious to such sensitivities. Then you can tell the other women that you tried to dissuade me but were unsuccessful."

She squeezed his arm as he helped her up into the carriage. "Thank you. I thought I might explore Mireworth this afternoon, if you had no objection to my roaming the halls to take inventory?"

"I have no objection, only be careful. You will find some of the corridors...crowded."

"Yes, Mrs Rossett told me about the relocated furniture." Hannah settled on the seat.

Wycliff had sold off what he could in the way of furnishings. Rugs that mouldered easily had been the first to go. Large pieces of furniture like bed frames and old armoires were more difficult to sell, and had been shoved into dark and dry halls like bodies kept in a mausoleum.

"I only wish to learn the layout and contents of the house and I admit, I find old homes fascinating with the history absorbed into their very walls. Do you know when the house was first built?" Hannah made room for him beside her in the carriage.

Wycliff racked his memory for the house's origins. As a young boy, he had found the history of a building boring and had let his mind wander. Now, he wished that long-ago youth had paid a little more attention. "There are parts that are very old, but most of what you see now was built by my great-grandfather a hundred years ago."

THAT AFTERNOON, Swift and Wycliff paid a visit to old man Miller, Amy's grandfather and Wycliff's tenant. Wycliff rode his black mare while Swift tried to keep up on a solid bay. Anger simmered inside Wycliff as they walked the horses up the packed earth lane. Miller's paddocks were full of weeds that set seed and would create a problem for years to come. Pasture sat unused either by stock or crops.

"Damn waste," Wycliff muttered under his breath as he dismounted and tied the reins around a fence rail.

"He's got worse over the years, although Amy did what she could. He's always been deaf to any advice. Calls me an interfering sod." Swift slid off his tall mount to the ground and flicked the reins around the rail.

Wycliff surveyed the house and barn and decided that by comparison, Mireworth didn't appear too bad. At least he was trying to hold his estate together; this man had given up and let his farm slide into disrepair. Dislodged roof slates tumbled to the ground and created sad piles where they landed. Birds nested in the gaps in the roof, straw and nesting material peeking out. It appeared that every window was broken and water had soaked into the frames and damaged the wood. The vegetable patch that should have fed a family grew only thistles and one determined artichoke that refused to cede its territory to its more invasive cousins. Piles of unidentified rubbish and debris lay around the yard, and rats scurried about with no fear of the men.

The scale of the neglect set fire to the anger already bubbling in Wycliff's veins at the wasted fields surrounding them. A scrawny chicken squawked and flapped its wings in its haste to escape his boots.

Old man Miller sat on a rickety chair by his front door, a bottle clutched in his dirty hands. He glanced up as they approached and narrowed his gaze. "What do you want? Come to interfere again, I reckon."

Wycliff paused at the bottom step and crossed his arms. He gripped his upper arms and let the anger surge through him and flow out through his boots. "We are here to discuss the sorry state of this farm. I will no longer tolerate it."

Miller's milky gaze swung to Wycliff and his eyes widened. He staggered to his feet to bow his head and reached out to steady himself against the wall of the house. "Lord Wycliff. I heard you were back among us. I'll pay my rent, on my honour. I only need a little more time."

"Come now, Miller, you have had over six months." Swift spoke with short, clipped words as though he, too, had run out of patience.

"And how, exactly, do you intend to repay the overdue rent when you have no crop in your fields and no stock in your barn? Even the chickens look long past laying and wouldn't even flavour water for soup." Wycliff ground his teeth. Swift was right. What the farm needed was a keen young man with a family to pitch in and wrest the land back under control.

"It's just a little setback, milord. You'll see. A

couple more months and I'll be back on my feet." Miller clutched the bottle in both hands as though he could wring the monies from the glass.

Wycliff had no time to waste on a drunkard. There were too many other tasks pressing on his mind. "Enough excuses, man! Your time here is done. For your granddaughter's sake, Swift has found you a vacant cottage on the outskirts of the estate and closer to the village. You will move there within the week."

Miller dropped the bottle to the ground and it rolled away from him. He wiped a hand across his face. "Everything was fine when Amy ran things, but that Cramond ruined everything. Always sniffing around here. I told Amy to tell him to bugger off. He killed her, you know. Killed her, he did, and no one did a thing about it."

Wycliff arched an eyebrow and glanced at Swift. According to the rumours his estate manager had reported to him, most locals thought Miller had struck her in a drunken haze and when he sobered up, tossed her body in the water to cover up his horrible mistake.

"Amy drowned, Miller, you know that. Was a terrible accident and nothing more." Swift caught the bottle as it rolled to his feet and set it upright in the dirt. A chicken watched with interest as light shone through the glass and highlighted a beetle crawling toward the house.

The old man stood up and swayed, grabbing the chair back to steady himself. "She would never have left me. Took her, he did. Snatched her away and pulled her into the water. That Cramond is a sea monster, preying on our women. I heard he took another, the Rivers woman. How many will he steal before someone listens to me?"

Wycliff pinched the bridge of his nose. This was all he needed—talk of some creature masquerading as a man and dragging women into the ocean. An old memory stirred, but he couldn't bring it to the surface. "Enough. Pack your things, Miller. Swift will bring a cart to move you at the end of the week. This farm is going to a man who isn't too drunk to work the land."

Wycliff turned his back and walked to his horse, ignoring the man's pleas for more time. The hours wouldn't stand still for anyone. Not for a lonely old drunk, nor for the wife of a viscount.

9

AFTER THE FUNERAL, Hannah sat in the kitchen for a moment of quiet reflection. Wycliff had headed off with Mr Swift to visit the tenant farmers. As lady of the manor, she reviewed her own small progress in restoring the estate. The beds in the conservatory were weeded and needed only fresh soil. The reflecting pool was emptied and scrubbed. The windows, however, were a much slower task. The dirt caked on the glass seemed resistant to all but hot water, soap, and large amounts of elbow grease. Not to mention the curved sides of the conservatory frame meant she could only reach so far without needing a ladder and some nimble assistance. She was seriously considering tying a scrubbing brush into Barnes's palm and setting him to work on the more difficult spots.

Then her mind wandered back over recent events, and one in particular that nibbled at her curiosity.

"Have any other people drowned recently?" Hannah asked Mrs Rossett.

"Why do you ask, milady?" The housekeeper peeled potatoes from her seat across the table.

"The other day I heard someone mention *another one*, in reference to Mrs Rivers' death." The conversation occurred the day she had ventured into the village with Mary, and saw the woman's limp body retrieved from the ocean. Two women had spoken of it—one woman had asked if it were *another one*. The other had scolded her not to start *that old nonsense*. The phrasing stuck in the back of Hannah's mind and refused to budge.

Mrs Rossett dropped the peeled potato into a pot of water and set down her knife. "Sarah is the third in the last year. We lost Amy Miller just before Christmas and Lisbeth Wolfe a year ago. All of an age similar to your ladyship, and all in good health."

"All drowned?" Most healthy young women tended to die in childbirth. It seemed unusual for a trio of them to lose their lives to the ocean instead.

"Yes. Although Amy had quite a large bump on her head and there were rumours about how it got there." Mrs Rossett pointed to a spot on her temple.

"The *how* would depend on whether it were pre- or post-mortem." Hannah's mind immediately turned to how bodies acquired wounds and silently told what happened to them. Had the unfortunate Amy been struck on the head and then ended up in the water, or did she drown and the action of the waves and rocks had caused the injury?

Mrs Rossett stared into the basket at her side and selected another potato. "What does that mean, milady —pre- or post-mortem?"

Sometimes Hannah forgot herself in her enthusiasm to examine a death. Not everyone shared her fascination with mortality and its many ways and means.

"Whether the bump occurred before she died, or after. If the blow to Amy's head had caused her death, there would not have been any water in her lungs. Was an autopsy conducted?" Three women dead in a year seemed an awful lot to Hannah. Not that she knew any statistics about the causes of death in rural and seaside communities, but still.

"Oh, no. We don't do that sort of city thing with dead bodies here. They were pulled from the water so it's obvious they drowned, isn't it?" Mrs Rossett wielded her knife with precise skill upon the next potato's skin.

Hannah swallowed her commentary about the benefits of an autopsy and how it advanced medical knowledge. Instead, she stuck to the available facts. "Did anyone question how Amy received the blow to her head?"

Mrs Rossett stared up at the ceiling while she fetched the memory. "Lots of talk at the time. Her grandfather—one of his lordship's tenants—is a mean old drunk and many thought he might have hit her, to stop her running off with Harvey Cramond."

"Did he not approve of the match?" How sad when a woman did not have her family's support to follow her heart's calling.

"Didn't want to lose the free labour, if you ask me. Amy was the only one doing any work there and the place fell apart after she died." The housekeeper tossed the peeled potato into the pot.

There was a common problem for rural families—many hands were needed to tend sheep or nurture a crop. What a shame the woman's grandfather couldn't see that he would have acquired an able-bodied grandson-in-law, rather than losing a granddaughter.

"What of Lisbeth Wolfe? Were there any rumours about her demise?" Hannah's spirits perked up at the ghoulish thought of three deaths to investigate. She would question Wycliff later—he might know more about the circumstances of each.

"Hmm...let me think. I know we were right shocked at the time. Beautiful thing, she was. Hair as black as night, skin as white as snow, and lips as red as rose petals. Many thought she was part Fae."

"Really? Was she?" Hannah had recently learned that her dear friend Lizzie possessed a Fae grandmother, which gifted her features with ethereal beauty. Perhaps another conspiracy against Fae offspring had claimed Lisbeth.

Mrs Rossett snorted. "Not likely, if you'd ever met her parents. Lisbeth was a shy and lonely thing. Girls can be so cruel and it turned my stomach, the way they tormented her."

There was a lesson many women learned. Some chose to lift up their sisters, while others viewed them as the enemy. "Why were they cruel to her?"

"Too pretty, I suspect. That didn't change as they all grew older and her beauty matured. Lisbeth kept to herself, and having a touch of magic made the locals even more suspicious of her. She lived in a cottage in a wild spot, right by the water." Mrs Rossett rose from her seat and took the pot of potatoes to the range.

Hannah sipped her tea and contemplated the life of the unknown woman. "How sad. She must have been terribly lonely."

"Well, his lordship more than made up for that. They were close as two halves of a clam as youngsters. Always running about and getting into mischief. We all assumed he would marry her one day and make her Lady Wycliff." Mrs Rossett turned with wide eyes, as though she had just realised what she had said.

An ache stabbed through Hannah. It had never occurred to her that Wycliff might have intended another woman to be his bride. She searched the dregs of her tea for something to say. "Was his lordship at Mireworth when she died?"

"No. But he did return for her funeral." Mrs Rossett pulled out the sack of flour, the butter container, and a clean bowl. "Now, what sort of pie shall I make for after dinner? I can send Mary out to pick some blackberries, if you like?"

Apparently the subject of the young Wycliff and the ethereal Lisbeth was now closed. "Blackberries would be lovely. I'm going to explore the house this afternoon, and have promised Wycliff I will be careful. I think Sheba should stay here with you, in case she gets trapped." Wycliff had warned her that there might be storm-damaged areas, and Hannah didn't want to risk the spaniel falling through a rotten floor or becoming lodged in stacks of furniture.

"I'll send out a search party if you're not back by dark." Mrs Rossett winked as she measured out flour to make pastry.

"Oh, never fear. If I am stuck, I will summon Wycliff. My mother has enchanted my wedding ring." Hannah held up her left hand with its plain gold band. While Wycliff's matching ring would vibrate if Hannah needed him urgently, she would still need to rely on the silver peacock feather wrapped around her smallest finger to get a message to either her mother or her husband.

The housekeeper stared at Hannah as though she had sprouted a second head. "Well, I imagine being the daughter of a mage comes in handy at times."

"It certainly does. I promise I shall return by dinnertime." Hannah patted Sheba and told the spaniel to stay with the housekeeper.

Then she fetched her small ensorcelled mushroom lamp to provide light and stood in the grand foyer, taking a moment to consider where to begin. Wycliff had said there were parts of the house that were quite old, but how to find them? Logic dictated that she start on the ground floor and examine every room in a sequential manner, until she arrived back at her point of origin. Except ancient whispers called to her from above. Murmurs like dancing will-o'-the-wisps that lured travellers deep into the forest, but in this case urged her to climb the stairs to find them.

She placed one hand on the head of a griffin, stared up the sweeping stairs, and made a decision. "Up it is."

Hannah followed the curve of the staircase and then stepped out on the semicircular balcony that looked down on the foyer. A vague pattern tried to emerge from the tiles, but the muted colours and lack of light kept the overall design hidden. Scrubbing tiles was a task that could wait for another day.

The corridor presented her with two options, left or right? She tapped the mushroom and the top lit up a deep yellow. With eyes closed, Hannah asked the shadows what direction to take. A chill brushed over her left side. Did that mean she should go in that direction or avoid it? Never one to steer clear of the darker side of things, Hannah struck out to the left.

What little daylight that managed to filter through the dome above was soon lost as the corridor closed around her. Hannah grabbed a brass door latch and pressed it. The door gave with a creak and swung open to reveal an empty room. Not a single piece of furniture remained, except for ghostly marks where once rugs had covered the floorboards. Goosebumps ran along her arm, as though a trapped ghost had slipped past her to escape.

Shutting the door, Hannah crept farther along the dark corridor. Doors revealed more empty rooms. In some cases, they were firmly locked. At one point, a cold gasp of air brushed over her cheek and she raised the mushroom lamp, searching for the source. A piece of trim on the wall sat a fraction of an inch away from its companions on either side.

"Has damp made you swell and pull free?" Hannah pushed on the strip of wood in an attempt to tap it back into place and a creak sounded against her fingertips. Curious, she traced a finger along the rail and found a vertical crack that ran all the way to the floor. Her nails slipped into the split and when she tugged, a panel sprang open.

"Oh," she whispered. She had found a secret door, albeit a short one, as it stopped about chest height where the panelling ended and the plaster wall began. Something for children, perhaps, or pixie staff?

She extended her arm as far as it would go to shine the mushroom into the space behind. A narrow corridor angled upward, but she couldn't see where it went. Part of her wanted to strike off along the hidden passage and see. Another part of her cautioned that it was foolish to follow the narrow corridor when no one knew where she was. What if she became trapped?

Light glinted on her wedding band. If the door closed behind her and she could not open it, she could summon Wycliff by rubbing her ring. Both he and Mrs

Rossett knew she was exploring and they would search for her in the gloomy house. Then a moment of doubt gnawed at her. Would Wycliff respond? With all the work he had to do, if his ring vibrated would he drop everything to find her, or continue about his day?

No. She must push that thought aside. In the worst-case scenario, all she had to do was bang on the door and *someone* would hear her. Eventually.

If Wycliff had been half as rambunctious as a child as Mrs Rossett claimed, he would know of the secret door and whatever lay behind it, and might head in this direction. In case more people roamed the halls to find her, Hannah cast around for an object with which to wedge open the door as an additional clue to her whereabouts.

In a corner where another corridor intersected the current one, Hannah found a knee-high unglazed pot. She dragged it along to the hidden door and placed it in the gap. Pleased with herself for thinking through the possibilities, she bent her head and stepped through.

The corridor slanted upward and as she walked, hunched over, the ceiling rose and soon she could stand upright. Not long after that, Hannah emerged in a space about ten feet square and flooded with light from a large square window. What drew her attention wasn't the view outside, but the one within. Before her was the curve of an ancient stone wall with an arched door-way. A set of worn stone spiral stairs beckoned, the light from above casting them in a pale pink glow.

"I say, how did you end up here?" She rested a

hand on the smooth stonework and peered up. Someone had walled up a tower and constructed the newer building around it. The rounded wall before her called to mind ancient forts that had once dotted the countryside, with thick walls to withstand any storm— whether thrown by Mother Nature or a mage.

When she peered out the window to try to orient herself, the exterior stone of Mireworth showed no hint of the tower hiding within. As though someone had tried to erase its very existence. If they didn't like it, why not pull it down instead?

"No point in turning back now," she said to the empty room, as she began the next leg of her journey.

The steps pulled her upward until they opened upon an airy room. Hannah walked to the middle and turned a slow circle, while her mind spun wondering about the history of the odd tower. The circular room had a timbered ceiling that soared to a point in the middle. A wrought-iron chandelier hung from a chain, its many branches empty, the candles gone long ago. Windows on one side looked back over the roofs of Mireworth; the other side allowed a view overlooking the drive. A fireplace opposite the door was plainly constructed and set into the curve of the tower, the surrounding stones stained black by centuries of smoke seeking escape.

No furniture remained to give any hint as to the former use of the space. Odd scratches and grooves in the walls could have been from bookcases...or the fingernails of prisoners. While this room lay above

Mireworth's roof, she had entered the spiral stairs on the first floor. From what she recalled, the stairs didn't extend in the other direction to the ground.

The fireplace drew her. She had to stretch her arms wide and still barely grazed either side with her fingertips. The mantel sat at her eye level, giving an excellent view of the accumulation of dust on the stone. Inside, thick black soot clung to the bricks and indicated that once, the room had been much used. Had it been a solar for the lady of the house? Or like her mother's turret, used for study?

In one spot on the left, a thick layer had peeled away and revealed scratches in the brick. Hannah leaned closer but couldn't make anything out. Searching her pockets, she found her small knife and used the blade to scrape away at the soot and resin. As she worked, she discovered the marks ran vertically.

Scratches formed into images and Hannah let out a gasp. "Impossible!"

Her work had revealed a vertical edge of stones inscribed with hieroglyphics. Her hands itched for the ensorcelled translation paper her mother had made. When the sheet was held over hieroglyphics, the images would transliterate and then translate themselves. If she had known the magical paper would be needed at the old manor she would have packed it, instead of leaving it tucked inside a book on her desk.

"Why would a tower hundreds of years old have stones inscribed with hieroglyphics in the fireplace?" She looked around, but of course no one answered. The most likely scenario was that a roaming ancestor of Wycliff's had removed the plaques from somewhere in Egypt and carried them home.

With one side revealed, Hannah tackled the other and discovered that it too bore a vertical line of ancient script. Careful knife work found the edges of the rectangular stones. There were four in total, each a foot high and about six inches wide. Two were laid on either side of the fireplace. She sat back to survey her afternoon's work. Soot coated her hands as though she had worked a twelve-hour shift down a coal mine.

The light outside dimmed and reminded her there was little more she could do today. Her knees protested as she rose and, resisting the urge to wipe sooty hands down her skirts, Hannah put away her knife and retrieved the mushroom lamp. Once she retraced her steps, she headed straight for the kitchen, where Mary and Mrs Rossett prepared dinner.

"Where on earth have you been? You look as though you fell down a chimney," Mrs Rossett said.

Hannah dropped the glow lamp on the table and peered at her blackened fingernails. "You are close. I was exploring a fireplace with unusual stones laid into it."

Mrs Rossett gestured at Hannah with a large knife. "Well, lady of the house or not, you must wash up."

Mary poured hot water from the kettle into the sink. Hannah picked up the soap and a brush to scrub her hands. Now that she'd started cleaning one spot, she itched all over. She probably had soot in her hair, too. "I will take the worst off here, but do you think a bath would be possible before dinner?"

"Anything is possible, but I doubt you want to bathe in the kitchen in front of the range like I do when I'm here alone." Mrs Rossett filled a large pot at the pump and set it on the range.

Hannah preferred a modicum of privacy in which to have a bath, but didn't want to stray too far—they had to cart the hot water. She had yet to test Wycliff's hellhound ability to heat a bath, even if he had been available for the task. "What if we set up a tub in the conservatory? That's still fairly close to haul the hot water."

Mrs Rossett nodded and peered under the bench to find two more large pots. "Mary can fetch the slipper tub. It's in the larder."

Hannah gathered a robe and clean chemise, and when she returned, Mary was dragging a small copper tub through the door. The two women placed it the conservatory next to the pool.

"It's not very big, but at least it won't take much to fill." Mary placed a chair next to the tub for the towel and soap.

"It's big enough to allow me to wash my hair." Although Hannah would need to stick her legs out and duck under the water to rinse off. Would she be finished before Wycliff returned? And if she was not, what would he do if he discovered his wife in the tub?

10

THAT EVENING, Wycliff sat at the head of the kitchen table and basked in a sense of accomplishment and contentment. Long days and honest hard work were making a difference on the estate. Next year, the merino fleece would increase the revenue earned from wool. He sipped his wine and stared at his wife. Thinking of Hannah made his heart swell. Everything he did, he did for her, and for the future he wanted to build with her.

Hannah turned to him with excitement and curiosity simmering in her eyes. "I found a round tower today in my explorations. It was hidden behind the walls and struck me as being very old."

Wycliff's thoughts tumbled back over twenty years to when he had made the same discovery. "The tower? Good grief, I had forgotten all about that. How on earth did you stumble upon it? As I recollect, it is rather well concealed."

She grinned as though they shared a childhood secret. "The hidden door wasn't quite shut and a draft blew through a crack. Having discovered the door, I then followed my curiosity."

Wycliff huffed a laugh. He remembered his excitement on finding the hidden door as a child, and creeping along the dark and narrow passage that opened out at the curved wall and spiral stairs. Having climbed to the top, anticipation hadn't met with expectation when he had found only an empty room. "When the house was rebuilt last century, my great-grandfather simply bricked up the tower and closed it off. I think the old stone and curves clashed with his plans for modern and elegant straight lines."

A slight frown marred Hannah's brow. "What an odd way to treat a piece of the estate's history. Almost as though he couldn't bring himself to tear it down, but sought to conceal it instead."

A curious young Wycliff had asked his father about the tower, but his only reply was that he was never to go there again. Then his father had removed his belt and soundly lashed the child for his discovery. He had only returned once after his father died, as an act of rebellion. In hindsight, he wondered why his father had reacted so violently to Wycliff's exploring the ancient tower. "From what I can remember, the tower is unremarkable and the room empty."

"I found it beautiful in its simplicity, and ideally situated to catch the sun. Add carpets on the floor and a comfortable chaise and I can envision it as a solar retreat for a lady." A wistful look entered Hannah's eyes.

Wycliff had forgotten all about the secret hidden in the walls of Mireworth. "I doubt you would get a chaise through the door or up the narrow passage if you wished to use it again. Unfortunately, there are no records that might show its original purpose. Given that the spiral stairs start on the first floor, I would assume it was once attached to a castle that stood here. The ground floor most likely housed animals over winter."

Hannah took a sip of water and Wycliff found himself entranced by how she licked her bottom lip afterward. "Did you know there are stones within the hearth engraved with hieroglyphics?"

Wycliff shook his head and tried to keep his mind on the subject of the tower rather than his wife's mouth. "No. I don't remember sticking my head into the fireplace."

"Oh." Hannah's excitement deflated. "I thought you might have known how they came to be there."

Wycliff stared at the ceiling and considered the approximate age of the tower and how the inscription might have come to be there. "Let me see...the Crusaders fought a campaign in Egypt in the twelfth century. It is possible that whoever owned this land back then may have acquired the stones and had them installed when he returned home."

Her eyes shone with excitement again. "Yes! That would fit, don't you think? And is it not rather coincidental that a small piece of Egypt found its way here, when that country and her magic is much on my mind lately? Not to mention the statue of Ma'at in the conservatory, although hundreds of years separate the two items."

Hannah and her mother were digging into Egyptian magic to find a way to halt the Affliction and to release the women held in its grip. Now that she had pointed out the connections, it did seem odd that she had found two traces of Egypt at Mireworth. Or not odd at all. Many travellers brought back things they found in other countries. "I'm sure many old houses have pieces of antiquity prised away by travelling sons. Do you know what the hieroglyphics say?"

Her nose wrinkled in a most delightful fashion. "Not without the translation paper that Mother made for me, which I left at home. I plan to go back to the tower with paper and charcoal to make rubbings of the stones. Are there any books in the library about your ancestors? There might be clues as to the origins of both the stones and the statue, and who knows, there might be other pieces of Egypt hidden elsewhere."

After a day of hard labour, Wycliff would rather put his feet up and sip a brandy while he read a book. Or take his wife to their makeshift bedroom and hear her whisper his name again. *Jonas.* He couldn't recollect the last time anyone had called him by his Christian name, and never with the breathy hitch of desire in which Hannah whispered the syllables. But perhaps if he found her a book to satisfy her curiosity, he could request a boon from her in return. Yes, that seemed a most excellent plan.

"We can look after dinner, if you like. It's a dark room even in the middle of the day, so it won't make any difference whether it is evening or morning, if we have a few lanterns to aid our search."

After dinner, Mrs Rossett dug into the Aladdin's cave of a storeroom she maintained and found a few lanterns. "They're not magic ones like yours, Lady Wycliff, but a good honest wick and a bit of oil throws a decent light."

Mary trimmed the wicks and refilled the oil before lighting them. Wycliff carried two and Hannah the third as they ventured into the gloom to find the library. He led the way to double doors tucked under one of the curved staircases. Wycliff placed the lanterns on the ground and stared at the doors. When had he last ventured into the library? It seemed a lifetime ago that he had packed away the last books of any value, to be sold in London. He could imagine what Hannah would think of the picked-over shelves—the volumes traded for coin to pay Swift's wages.

He slid a door to one side. It protested on its tracks and squeaked like a mouse, but yielded to a constant pressure. Wycliff picked up a lantern in each hand and entered the room. The dim room absorbed light and a faint musty odour greeted him, but at least he could detect no aroma of damp. The library occupied a high and narrow slice of Mireworth, as though someone had cut a piece from the manor house. A window over nine feet high and three feet wide at one end looked out over the garden. Or it would have, if anyone could penetrate the dirt on the glass.

Shelves ran the length and height of one long wall and then along over the double doors, where they terminated abruptly. The doors themselves hunkered close to the wall, their placement out of balance with the room. A set of steep wrought-iron stairs led to a narrow gantry that raced the length from door to window.

The wall opposite held narrow shelves that seemed out of place. Wycliff remembered they had once housed curiosities and treasures the viscount had acquired on his travels. Now they contained only dust and mummified flies. Few books remained, most sold long ago. The odd escapee hunkered down flat on a shelf, having escaped Wycliff's attention when he packed the others away.

Only one section remained with an almost full complement of books. These volumes were unique to Mireworth. Histories of the estate, penned by previous lords. Ledgers that tallied up the income and expenses of the house for decades. Diaries written by the masters and mistresses who called it home. Gardening notes, left by long deceased gardeners for their replacements who were never hired.

"What an...oddly shaped library." Hannah turned a slow circle.

"My grandfather was many things, but a reader he was not. He cut the library in half to enlarge the billiards room and give it a double-height gallery. Which is why there is no fireplace and the doors seem off centre." Wycliff waved to the wall opposite the bookshelves and the offending room beyond that stole the library's territory.

Hannah's eyes widened and one hand went to her chest. For a bibliophile, Wycliff couldn't have chosen a more horrific tale to tell. "What a monstrous thing to do. It is as though he cleaved the library's soul in two."

Wycliff agreed with her. He would much prefer a fine library than an ostentatious billiards room. "One day, I would like to remove this wall and restore the symmetry to the library, along with its missing shelves, rolling ladder, and fireplace. But I rather think a water-tight roof is our priority now."

"You will need to acquire a number of books when that day comes." Hannah moved along the room to the only area with dusty tomes shoved in a haphazard manner.

"Do you think me a monster for selling the books that once sat here?" He tried to inject humour into his question. But the state of the library seemed to reflect how he felt about himself. Depleted. Neglected. Abused. In desperate need of a tender touch to restore him.

"No." Hannah set down her lamp on an empty shelf and walked toward him. The lamplight caught in her eyes and lit the amber sparks within. "I see an opportunity to rebuild, and to restore this room to the grandeur she deserves. A situation is only ever irrevocable if you give up. It might take us years of budgeting to fill every shelf, but we will find a way. Together."

His heart swelled and he swallowed the lump in his throat. He reached out with one hand and drew her to him for a slow kiss. Then he released her before he forgot their task. "Many of the books sold were boring and in Latin anyway. As a boy, I remember being terribly disappointed there wasn't a single tale of pirates among them. We can start anew and create a collection that is to our particular tastes and interests."

Hannah laughed and left his embrace to walk closer to the remaining titles. "I'm surprised the rapscallion spent any time in the library at all."

"Well, I would have if it had contained books about pirates," he huffed.

Wycliff dragged over an old ladder-backed chair and set a lantern on it, close to the shelf. The other he placed in an empty spot among the books. "These are accounts left over the years by various residents of Mireworth."

"Which do you think are the earliest?" Hannah stood close to him and reached for the ledger in front of her nose. She opened the book and a puff of dust rose from it.

"They are not in any order, unfortunately. Nor do I recollect any that would be of a similar age to the enclosed tower. The most we can hope for is some bored ancestor who researched the history of this estate." He scanned the diaries and ledgers, and tried to guess by the bindings which were the oldest.

"Bother. This handwriting is terrible and the lack of light makes reading the script difficult." Hannah held a book at an angle beside the lantern.

"Perhaps we look for dates? Then we can take them to the study and you can examine them by daylight in the kitchen. Swift ensures the skylight there is kept clean for Mrs Rossett." He returned one diary and selected another, scanning yellowed pages looking for any indication of a date.

"It must be lonely for her here, with the house empty and no other staff to enliven her days." Hannah placed the book on the shelf and pulled another free.

"I offered her a cottage, but she wanted to retain control of her kitchen. We can afford to take on another staff member, especially if you wish to return here. Each time we stay at Mireworth, we can breathe a little more life into her." Should he tell Hannah of his hopes —that he longed for her to call the musty, crumbling old pile her home? That it was more than desire for her that burned through his veins?

"Potatoes, leeks, and pumpkins should be planted to see Mrs Rossett through the winter." She ran a finger down a page of script.

"Potatoes?" He stood on the cusp of stuttering out he loved her and she wanted to discuss potatoes?

"Yes, potatoes." She tapped the ledger against his arm. "We are too late for spring plantings to be harvested in autumn. We will need to put in hardy vegetables that can be bedded down to survive winter. Does it snow here?"

The conversation moved from potatoes to snowfall as they worked and continued to examine the books, and Wycliff realised he had lost his opportunity.

After half an hour, Wycliff found something that might solve at least one mystery. "Here is the diary of the Wycliff who built the current house in the early seventeen hundreds. There is a date here of 1701. While it is earlier than the rise of Georgian style architecture, this house, with its symmetry and simplicity, is not like the fanciful baroque buildings preferred at that time."

"Perhaps that Wycliff was before his time in his tastes? If he did construct the house, his journal might offer some clue about the mysterious tower." Hannah placed the current book she held on the discard shelf and leaned in to peer at the straggly writing.

"Now that I think about it, there should be drawings here somewhere. Even if his diary does not· mention the tower, it will be obvious on the original plans." Wycliff gazed at the shelves and tried to remember anything concerning the construction of Mireworth. His information was second- and third-hand at best. He had never met his grandfather, who might have known more. His father had little interest in the origins of the house, his priority being only to spend the money generated by the estate. A vague memory nibbled at him of drawings rolled up in a leather case. But they could have been for the house, the gardens, or the wider estate. "I seem to remember plans rolled up somewhere. Possibly in the crates in the study, or in storage in the billiards room."

"Oh! That would be marvellous if we could find them. Tomorrow I shall tackle the library window and remove some of the dirt to let a little more light in here. Then I can continue my search during the day while you are occupied elsewhere." Hannah picked up a lantern and paced the shelves, peering at each one.

The flickering yellow light made him think of women lighting candles in the windows of their homes for husbands lost at sea. That thought led to another— he had yet to make good on his promise. "I am sorry I have not yet had the opportunity to teach you to swim. It is a valuable skill, living so close to the sea."

"I wonder that I need the ability. It seems the ocean chooses whom it will claim regardless of whether the person can swim or not." The ghostly light swung over the corkscrew of wrought-iron stairs that led to the gantry and the next level of empty shelves.

He ran a hand through his hair and considered what to say to alleviate her concerns. "Perhaps when your mother is here we could ask her for a buoyancy spell to keep you afloat?"

Hannah's next comment was murmured so quietly, it could have come from a ghost. "Mrs Rossett said you knew Lisbeth Wolfe."

A spectre rose from his past. One with haunted eyes. Wycliff blew out a long sigh and tossed a journal back on the shelf. "Her father was the previous estate manager. Since we both lacked siblings and were of a similar age, we spent much time together."

"I am given to understand she was a great beauty." Hannah spoke to the empty shelves, her back to him.

He conjured up his memories and picked them apart objectively. Lisbeth had certainly been a beautiful child, and she had grown into a stunning woman. But it was the deep vein of mischief that had made them firm friends, not her appearance. It had also been she who had dared him to stick his head through the railing. Lisbeth had convinced him that at a certain angle he would see a different image in the patterned floor tiles below. "She would have been much in favour during the Renaissance, with her pale skin and black hair."

"Do you know the circumstances of how she came to drown?" Hannah turned and leaned against the shelves.

Wycliff swallowed and an old ache resurfaced in his chest. He had failed to help Lisbeth when she needed him most. If he had been at Mireworth that summer, could he have saved her? He wiped his hands over his face. "Her cottage is perched near the end of a promontory where the winds howl past. It is thought she lost her footing, or possibly the cliff gave way—they are quite chalky here."

"How terrible." On silent feet, Hannah approached him until she stood before him.

"Enough of maudlin thoughts. Shall we take the journal you found to the study, where the light is better?" Ghosts stalked his every footstep and Wycliff wondered what it would take to be free of them. Or was he stitched to events from his past, as Frank was attached to the souls of the bodies used to construct him?

11

THE NEXT MORNING, Hannah sipped her hot chocolate as snatches of conversation swirled through her mind. She thought of her first day in the village and the phrase that had snagged her curiosity and wouldn't let go. *Don't start with that old nonsense.* She glanced at Mrs Rossett, who had a battered recipe book propped open before her. Would the housekeeper be able to shed any light on the odd phrase, or would she think Hannah terribly nosy for asking?

With another sip, she made up her mind. Wycliff's boldness rubbed off, and Hannah had learned that if one sought information, one had to ask questions to extract it. "Mrs Rossett, have you always lived in Selham?"

"Oh, yes. Born and bred. As I told you, I entered service here as a girl and have never left." She beamed over the top of the book. She had done well to rise through the ranks to her position in command of the staff. Not that Mireworth had any in its current state.

Hannah placed her cup in its saucer and turned the handle to one side. "I am curious about something I overheard the other day. In reference to Sarah's tragic death, one of the village woman was about to say something when her companion said, *'Don't start with that old nonsense.'* Do you know what they might have been referring to?"

Mrs Rossett hummed and placed a dried flower in the book before closing it. "That *is* old nonsense. Practically as old as I am. When I was a youngster, our elders used to frighten us by saying sea creatures would drag us into the water if we were out after dark. There was a summer when men drowned and stories flowed about mermaids, selkies, and such-like."

Hannah's curiosity sat up and paid full attention. *Mermaids, selkies, and such-like?* Did the village have a problematic Unnatural lurking beneath the waves? "Do you remember any of the circumstances of the drownings?"

She shook her head. "It must be fifty years ago now. It was two men, I think, and I seem to recall one was a fisherman whose empty boat washed ashore. The other was a shepherd. I'm sure all villages across England have some story of bogeymen to scare children into obedience."

"Yes. I'm sure you're right." Two men had drowned fifty years ago. It did seem nonsense to connect that to recent tragic events.

After breakfast, and despite her reservations about the man, Hannah decided to call upon the apothecary and assess the range of herbs and potions he offered. There were things her mother required for the renewal spell if it was to be performed at Mireworth. On the off chance that Seraphina didn't bring everything with her, it would be prudent for Hannah to examine what the apothecary carried.

An image drifted through Hannah's mind of her mother conducting the ritual in the ancient turret, and the hieroglyphics bordering the fireplace glowing with a soft purple and silver light. The floor under Hannah turned inky black, as though her body hung suspended over a void.

An odd imagining, but her discovery was much on her mind. Hannah had spent the morning making rubbings of the stones, but she could do no more to decipher them without either her mother's assistance or the ensorcelled translation paper. A comparison revealed both sides of the fireplace bore the exact same inscriptions, but she could discover no clue as to whether their placement had a deeper meaning or if it were merely ornamental.

Needing the fresh air and exercise, she walked to the village accompanied by Sheba. Mrs Rossett had advised her that the apothecary was the last cottage on the end of a row, past the shops. Hannah slowed as she approached. It was a fine-looking building with two storeys, sparkling windows, and a plaque on the door urging customers inside. She tied a length of string to

Sheba's collar and attached the dog to the white painted fence.

"I'll not be long, girl." Hannah patted the dog's head. Mrs Rossett had slipped Hannah a bone and she placed it before the spaniel, as an offering to keep the dog occupied while she was inside.

Lavender overhung the path and brushed against Hannah's skirts, releasing a soft fragrance. She stopped to draw a deep breath. When she pushed open the front door, she found the two front rooms converted into a combination of shop and workroom. A square and solid bench stood before a wall of shelves and separated it from the rest of the room. Rows of bottles with neat cream labels and black lettering were arranged according to size. Large bottles were on the bottom shelf and they diminished in size as they neared the ceiling. The top shelf held bottles no bigger than Hannah's finger and a ladder was the only way to access them. Bunches of herbs hung from the ceiling and Hannah recognised lavender, rosemary, and thyme.

Mr Seager sat behind an enormous desk on the side of the room opposite the shelves, and with his back to a small, round window. Before him sat brass scales and he tapped a black powder from a tiny vial into one pan. He looked up and frowned. "Lady Wycliff, I did not expect to see you here."

Hannah braced herself for rudeness. He walked his own path, but that did not preclude her from remaining civil. "Good day, Mr Seager. I thought to peruse your available herbs and potions, in case I have need of them while I am at Mireworth."

He grunted and returned his concentration to his work, plucking the pan from the scales and tapping the contents into a mortar. "You may look, but don't touch anything."

For him, that probably passed for civil. Hannah decided to start on the other side of the room, farthest away from him. She wandered behind the bench and examined bottles. The labels were all written in the same neat hand. Many of the herbs she knew. Ground white willow for aches and pains. Dandelion extract to cleanse the liver. Chamomile to assist sleep.

One shelf at eye level held a pretty display of soaps scented with rose, lavender, jasmine, and other fragrant flowers. Hannah picked up a pale pink bar with flecks of rose petal trapped in the soap and sniffed. If she closed her eyes, there could have been a fresh, dewy rose in her hands.

"I *said* don't touch anything," a voice barked from behind her.

Hannah jumped like a startled schoolgirl caught in the act of committing a grave offence. She turned and held out the piece of soap. "I'm sorry, I couldn't resist smelling the soaps."

"I assume you will buy that one, since you have put your fingers all over it." Mr Seager dropped the pestle into the mortar and pushed back his chair with a scrape.

"Of course." She set the soap down on the bench

and noticed that underneath ran rows of drawers with curved brass pulls. One sat open a few inches, revealing notebooks stacked inside. A name on the book at the very front, which looked as though it had been hastily shoved back, caught her attention. *Sarah Rivers.*

Why had the deceased woman done business with the apothecary? The purchase of scented soaps or salves for her skin wouldn't require a journal. Unless Mr Seager kept a record of every purchase made by each person.

"I assume that since you attended Mrs Rivers' funeral, you were acquainted?" Hannah cast a line to see if the fish would bite.

"Selham is a small village. I know all the residents." He picked up the soap and plucked a square of cream tissue paper from a basket sitting on the counter.

"I am sure such a tragedy touches everyone who knew her. Such a terrible way to die." Hannah watched him wrap the soap.

He twisted the top of the paper and then selected a length of string from the same basket and tied it in a bow. "She was a kind and gentle woman who kept her nose out of other people's business. She will be missed."

Hannah stared at the ceiling and counted to ten in her head. Once, Wycliff had been as rude and abrupt. Time had revealed the loyal and honourable man under the gruff exterior. Would a deeper acquaintance reveal a softer side to Mr Seager? Perhaps he was like a long-neglected sheep and one needed to penetrate the outer floof to see what was within. No, that analogy didn't work, as floof was an excess of fluffy wool that created a dense and impenetrable shell. He was more like a crustacean with sharp pincers.

Since he appeared to be predisposed to a foul mood, Hannah decided she had nothing to lose by making another request of him. "Might I see your garden, Mr Seager? I am most interested to see what you grow, even if I am not much of a horticulturist."

He glared at her and looked on the point of refusing, when he let out a sigh. "I suppose you cannot do too much damage out there, so long as you stay on the paths."

He led the way through a door that opened into a short hallway with a set of stairs to one side, and then through the kitchen to the outside door that revealed the walled garden. Mr Seager walked down the steps and placed his hands on his hips, as though daring her to stand on any of the precious plants.

"Oh, my," Hannah murmured as she walked along the crushed shell path.

Stone walls eight feet high kept the harsh winds out, and heat-loving plants grew against the sun-warmed stones. The path led through regimented beds with neatly clipped, bright green hedging to stop the crushed shell invading the soil, and stopped the plants from escaping to grow wild.

Black painted wooden spires helped the ramblers to grow straight and true. Everything had a label at its base denoting its common and Latin name. The apothecary might have a prickly exterior, but his care of the garden revealed a deep love for horticulture. Hannah wondered what conditions would be required to make love bloom in the grumpy specimen before her. Or even civility.

Out in the warmth, some of the tension eased from Mr Seager's shoulders and his pose relaxed as he followed her. Hannah pointed to a leafy green plant with tall white spires. The tag at its base read *Black Cohosh*. It grew next to the purple flowered chaste berry.

"I am familiar with chaste berry, but not with Black Cohosh. What remedies do you make with it?" Hannah reached out and her hand hovered above its flowers.

Mr Seager stopped beside her and bent to pull a weed that had grown to obscure a label. "It assists with issues relating to the reproductive organs. I make it into a syrup with chaste berry, cinnamon, and a few proprietary ingredients, for those wishing to conceive. I have some already brewed if you want to buy a bottle."

Those wishing to conceive. Of its own accord, her hand went to her flat stomach. "No. Thank you. I am not in need of such a potion."

"Are you already carrying, then?" He narrowed his eyes and the action pulled a line along his brow.

"No." She turned back to the plants, taken aback by a question that no gentleman would ever dare ask a lady.

He grunted. "His lordship will need an heir. There's no shame in taking my brew. A dead mage cannot create life, if you think to seek your mother's assistance."

Hannah bit back a retort. Her fertility, or lack thereof, was nobody's business. Wycliff had known her condition when he offered marriage. He said it did not concern him if they had no offspring, as he did not want to risk creating another like him, bound to a hellhound.

Ignoring the apothecary's impertinent remarks, Hannah walked to the next bed that contained what appeared to be weeds, but the dandelions and ragwort were tended with as much attention as the herbs on either side. "I understand two other women lost their lives to the ocean over the last year. So much sorrow for the village to bear. I imagine your potions are sought after, to ease the pain."

He strolled down a different path and bent to prune a few dead flower heads from the chamomile. "Sorrow is like the ocean. It ebbs and flows. Some feel the pull of that tide more keenly than others."

A poetic interpretation from such a gruff man. "If one suffered an aching heart, would you have a remedy?"

He glanced at her. "Of course. I only wish some had sought a remedy from me earlier, rather than..." His voice trailed off.

Hannah recalled the few details she knew of the other two women. Since Amy Miller had had an offer of marriage, she didn't think she would have sought a cure for a broken heart. Mrs Rossett said Lisbeth kept herself apart from the other women and that the childhood teasing had never really abated. "I understand Lisbeth Wolfe walked a lonely path."

"I have much work to do, Lady Wycliff. Are you going to pay for your soap, or ask me to extend you credit?" With that, he strode back inside the cottage.

Hannah paid for the scented soap and placed it in her basket. Outside, she untied the spaniel, who barked and bounced as though she had been sitting in the same spot for days, rather than a handful of minutes. Since she was in the village, Hannah's next visit was to the hall. Word had spread, and a few women were present to sweep and clean the space. Two were on their knees, scrubbing the floorboards.

"Oh, my!" Hannah exclaimed at the industrious activity. "You have all been so busy."

"The dance is giving us something to look forward to, milady," a heavily pregnant woman said. Then she dropped an awkward curtsey. "I am Libby Tant. Since I can't see my knees to help scrub, I am supervising and making garlands."

"Good morning to you, Mrs Tant. Do you need to sit down?" Hannah reached out to steady the woman's arm as she wobbled. She recalled the woman from the day Sarah had been retrieved from the ocean. She had cried out Sarah's name and stood with the family at the funeral.

"If you don't mind." The woman blushed and with Hannah's help, lowered herself to a chair. From the size of her belly, she either carried twins or was due any day. Libby rubbed her stomach. "This one was supposed to have made an appearance by now. How I wish Sarah could have met him or her."

Hannah took the chair next to the expectant mother and guessed at the relationship between the two. "Was she your sister?"

"Yes." Libby looked away to watch three children at play. A young boy and a girl built a tower from pieces of driftwood, while a smaller child toddled around them. Sheba trotted over and sat down, much to the delight of the children, who immediately included the young dog in their games.

"I'm so sorry for your loss. I hope you do not think us insensible to your grief, holding the dance so soon after the funeral." Hannah plucked a shell from the basket beside her and ran her fingers along its smooth inner side.

The other woman flashed a sad smile at Hannah. "Not at all, milady. Truth be told, it gives me something to keep myself occupied. Otherwise I would be sitting in our cottage, fretting over what happened to Sarah."

"Would you tell me about her, if it's not too much of an intrusion?" Hannah said.

"Of course not. I'd like to talk about her." The heavily pregnant woman rested her work on her stomach as she threaded shells onto the string. "Let me see. Sarah and I were similar in age, with less than a year between us. Once, we were as close as two peas in a pod."

"What happened?" Hannah asked.

Libby placed a finished garland to one side and then cut off a new length of string. "I fell in love and married my George. I still saw Sarah as often as I could, but...well, when you're newly married and in love, nothing seems so important as being with your man. Then she married Jim, and I thought we would raise our families together."

Hannah scooped up a handful of shells as she listened. The story contained echoes of herself and Lizzie. They, too, were as close as two sisters could be, but Hannah feared married life and the demands placed on the duchess would pull them in opposite directions.

"We had our first child a year after we married. I swear I've never been as busy as I was then, what with a young one to care for, the house to keep, and making sure George had a hearty meal to look forward to at the end of his day." Her hands stilled and she gazed off into the distance.

"It's not so easy, settling into a routine after marriage." Hannah had adjusted to her husband's being a hellhound, although that didn't impose any particular demands on their relationship. It wasn't as though she had to clean paw prints from the rugs or provide souls for him to consume.

Libby scooped up more shells and laid them out on her stomach. "Then I had number two the next year, followed by our third. Each time I thought Sarah and Jim would surely be blessed like we were, but life can be cruel sometimes. I remember how sad Sarah looked at Christmastide, when I told her I was pregnant again. I truly did not do it to cause her pain. Her husband is away long hours minding those sheep, and a little one would have been such a comfort to her."

Hannah closed her eyes and placed herself in the dead woman's shoes. She imagined Lizzie with a brood of children and the busy life of a duchess. Wycliff away until all hours with either the needs of the estate, or his work for the Ministry. The chill inside Hannah crept along her limbs like a freezing river. How lonely Sarah's days must have been. Did she imagine that those she loved had no time to spare for her?

"I'm sure she knew that you still loved her." Hannah touched the other woman's arm. Fertility was an invisible and unpredictable blessing. Even her mother's magic could not coax life into being, if Mother Nature decided against it.

"The night she disappeared, Jim said they argued and she set off to spend some time alone. I wish I had said something to her. There was a look in her eyes the last time I saw her that I cannot explain." Libby sniffed and put aside her work to find a handkerchief.

Hannah tried to find words of comfort for the bereaved woman, but as she clutched the shell a little tighter, imagining that it could keep her afloat in the ocean churning inside her, no words came.

12

THE TODDLER DETACHED herself from the playing children and wandered toward Hannah. She picked a starfish from a basket, then waved it at Libby as she tried to climb up her mother's legs.

"You won't fit in my lap, Esther—your new brother or sister is taking up all the space." Libby brushed a hand over the toddler's cheek.

"She can sit with me, if she would like." Hannah smiled at the girl with her pudgy arms and blush pink dress with dark pink smocking on the front.

The child tugged a length of string free from another basket. She held starfish and string aloft in her fists, and a question burned in her young eyes.

Hannah put the clues together. "You want to make a garland featuring the starfish? What an excellent idea. It will hang from the ceiling like a star in the ocean." Hannah opened her arms to the child and took the string in one hand.

The child climbed up on Hannah's knee and assisted as they attached the starfish to the end and then found shells to thread on after it. Apparently it was serious business, and the girl often slid to the ground to search all the baskets for the exact shell to go next.

"Thank you, milady, for being so patient with my little one," Libby said as her daughter set off to find the next piece of decoration.

The other women finished scrubbing the floor and used cloths to wipe it dry, before any of the children slipped on the excess water. There was still much to do. Tables and chairs were piled in one corner and the light fittings were covered in dust cloths and swung like ghosts watching over them.

Hannah held out her hand for the shell selected by little Esther. "I think Esther is doing a fine job. Helping her is lightening my heart, and I am sure a small ray of joy will aid everyone."

Libby rolled to one side to pick up another handful of shells. "It's been hard these last few days, and I do find great comfort in my little ones. They miss their aunt, but Mr Hartley has explained to them that God called her to his side and that she will always watch over them."

"I wonder that the village can take any more tragedy. I understand that there were two other women who lost their lives to the ocean in the past year." Hannah tied a knot in the string to keep the shells from sliding down into each other.

Shells clacked together as they bumped one another on the strings. The irregular noise was not unlike that of knitting needles and the faint scent of salt-laden sea air rose off them under Hannah's fingers.

"The paths are narrow and treacherous in the dark, especially if you're upset and not seeing clearly. We lost Amy at Christmas, and then Lisbeth before her." Libby placed a finished garland in another basket and stretched her arms up over her head.

The deaths fascinated Hannah, not in a morbid kind of way, but in a way that sought a logical explanation for why they had happened, and under what circumstances. "Did you know them both?"

One of the other women carried over a tray with cups of tea. She dipped a curtsey and offered one to Hannah with a shy smile, and then Libby. Another chair was dragged over, its wooden seat serving as a side table as they continued to work and talk.

Libby took a sip of her tea before answering. "Lisbeth was a familiar figure, but we rarely saw her in town. Amy was in our circle. I think Sarah was a great comfort to Harvey, after Amy died."

"Were Sarah and Harvey close?" Did married women often form friendships with single men? Hannah considered the men in her circle and her dealings with them. Single men in service didn't count. The closest was Doctor Husom, but she wasn't sure how to classify her acquaintance with the Immortal.

"We were all close, once. There's not so many children out here and you find friends where you can. Got ourselves into a bit of mischief, we did, as youngsters." Libby plucked a plain biscuit from the plate.

Hannah thought of the tales Mrs Rossett had told of the young Jonas and Lisbeth. Noble or common, young people had a natural affinity for mischief.

Libby's other two children grew tired of their game and wandered over to sit at their mother's feet and sneak biscuits. "I thought they might marry, but then she fell in love with Jim Rivers. The heart wants what it wants, and there's no way for others to predict or understand it."

"No. Love is a mysterious thing." Never could Hannah have imagined that her heart would one day find itself given to the brooding Viscount Wycliff. Or worse, that she would experience the stirrings of a love that went unreciprocated.

Hannah spent a companionable afternoon with the women, making garlands, tidying the hall, and considering how to arrange the chairs and tables.

"You have done amazing work," Hannah said as afternoon lengthened and the spaniel grew restless, rather like the children who grizzled and needed a nap. "Later in the week, we will sort out the placement of tables and finalise the decorations." Then she picked up her basket and took her leave with her canine companion. As she walked the roads back toward the estate, myriad thoughts churned through her mind like a school of fish.

As she turned onto a narrow lane not far from Mireworth, up ahead a man moved a mob of sheep with the aid of two black-and-white dogs. The woolly sheep stopped often to eat the lush grass on the waysides and a dog would give a warning *woof* to get it moving again. The man wore a cloth cap and carried a stick taller than he was, using it to reach out and wave at sheep that got confused and tried to go back the way they had just come.

Sheba crept closer to the sheep, imitating the low crouch of the working dogs. Hannah wondered if these sheep were like Wycliff's merinos, or some other breed. She didn't want to offend by getting the breed wrong. Perhaps there was some sort of sheep identification book she could carry in her pocket, like the ones bird-watchers possessed.

When the man turned and touched the brim of his cap, Hannah thought there was something familiar about him. Yes, now that she placed his face, he had been at the cemetery and laid flowers on a grave after Sarah's funeral.

"Good day to you, Lady Wycliff," he called out.

Hannah waved and tried to put a name to the face, but in the moment couldn't recollect whether Wycliff had murmured the man's name into her ear. "I am sorry if we have been introduced. I do not recollect your name. I do promise I will learn everyone's names soon."

He used his crook to pull a wayward sheep back into line. "Harvey Cramond, milady."

"Mr Cramond." How fortuitous to encounter him, after her conversation with Libby Tant. Hannah fell into step beside him as the mob took off at a trot with the dogs padding behind. Now she knew his name, or at least the whispers of it. The last person to have seen Amy Miller alive. Her feet trod the road, while she wondered at the truth of the rumours. "I was sorry to hear of the loss you suffered, Mr Cramond."

He nodded and kept his attention on the sheep. "I'm glad I'm not in the village much these days. I couldn't stomach seeing Jim go through the same thing. I have nothing to say that would ease his pain."

Hannah gripped her basket more tightly, seeking a polite way to solicit his opinion on the deaths. "It is a great tragedy that three women have met a watery end in the past year."

Mr Cramond whistled and one of the dogs set off after a sheep heading in the wrong direction. "Amy's death is no mystery to me, milady, even though the magistrate refused to investigate when he came here. We would have been happy, me and her, if not for that selfish brute of a grandfather."

"You do not think her drowning was an accident?" The line of enquiry Hannah sought presented an opening. While she gathered whispers to her, she trod carefully so as not to offend the villagers with her questions.

"No, milady, I do not. Miller has an ugly temper. When I last saw Amy, I had proposed and she said yes. But she had someone to tell privately, before we announced our engagement to the village. She set off for home looking right worried, she did. Next time I saw her, we were pulling her from the ocean and anyone could see the bump on her head." He paused for a moment and wiped his face on the sleeve of his shirt.

"I'm sorry, I did not mean to pry. Of late, I find myself seeking justice for those who cannot speak for themselves. If someone did Amy harm, they must be made to pay for their crime." Especially if they had also taken the lives of Sarah Rivers or Lisbeth Wolfe. Rumours circled the village like seagulls. Three women drowned in the span of twelve months was surely an unusually high number, even for a coastal village? If they had been no accident, that meant a deliberate choice. But were the women so unhappy with their lot they could no longer bear to walk this earth, or had another hand snuffed them out? There was the delicate line Hannah tried to distinguish.

Mr Cramond fell silent and his shoulders slumped. Then he took off his hat and scratched his hair as he stared along the lane. "Something's not right here, Lady Wycliff, if you ask me."

A prickle at the base of Hannah's skull made her think the same thing. "If Amy never made it home that night as her grandfather claims, was there anyone who might have wished her harm?"

He huffed a soft laugh and his eyes shone when he turned to Hannah. "No. Everyone liked Amy. She was the kindest, sweetest woman."

Hannah took the opportunity to ask her next question. "What of Sarah or Lisbeth?"

He wet his lips and wedged the soft hat back on his head. "See? Something's not right. Good women, all three of them. God-fearing women who would never risk their immortal souls like some whisper. If you ask me, I'd look to Seager. Who knows what he puts in those potions he sells. What if he gave them something he shouldn't that made them fall in the dark?"

"Why would he do that?" The man struck Hannah as abrasive and rude, but those qualities didn't automatically mean he was capable of murder.

"I think he was jealous and the man is quick to anger. He used to visit Lisbeth, out at that remote cottage of hers. Old man Miller said he used to call on Amy, even when she was stepping out with me. Then I saw him staring after Sarah. What would a thirsty man do if a cool drink of water was denied him?" He clutched his crook tight in two hands.

This was quite the accusation, implying Mr Seager had courted all three women. But then what? In the grip of a jealous rage, did he stalk the women and push them, or concoct a potion that caused them to stumble while out at night?

"You have given me much to consider, Mr Cramond."

"I feel better having said my piece to someone. Thank you for listening, milady." He waved his arms to get the sheep moving, the animals having stalled while they talked. "I'm right grateful to Lord Wycliff for the opportunity he has given me, if you would tell him for me. These sheep are for the farm and I shall roll up my sleeves and fix the place up in memory of Amy."

Hannah managed to smile at his kind words. "Of

course I will tell his lordship." *When I manage to lay eyes on him.*

She returned to Mireworth to find the kitchen empty, but the beginnings of dinner on the range. Sheba flopped onto her blanket, exhausted by playing with the children and the walk home.

Hannah placed the kettle on the fire and then fetched the journal they had found the previous night in the library. She would set aside gloomy thoughts of possible murder and turn her mind to a puzzle of a more architectural nature. She sipped a quiet cup of tea while she read the tight script under the kitchen skylight. It took her a few pages to become familiar with the author's handwriting and how they formed their letters. She scanned pages, looking for anything about the construction of the house.

The references she found were vague, only mentioning that the architect had been engaged and his outrageous fee. How odd that a simple house with pleasing symmetry was more expensive to draw up than a baroque explosion with gargoyles and multiple turrets. The writer referred to the plans and Hannah wished she had them to hand to fully understand the layout of the house.

She flicked over the page, when a turn of phrase leapt out at her. Returning to the previous page, she drew a line down the middle with her fingertip until she found the right paragraph. She read aloud to the empty kitchen, as Mrs Rossett and Mary spent the afternoon in the walled garden. *"I give no import to ridiculous rumours, but since the tower cannot be torn down I shall at least conceal the damned thing."*

Hannah leaned back in her chair and stared up at the skylight. *Don't start with that old nonsense.* And now *ridiculous rumours* about the tower. "This village seems teeming with ridiculous rumours and nonsense, although I can't imagine a sea creature hiding out in a tower this far inland."

With renewed vigour, she tackled the rest of the journal, but found no more mention of the tower, nor any hint as to what the lord of the manor had heard about it. The light above had faded by the time Mrs Rossett and Mary returned, the housekeeper carrying a basket with the floppy greenery of carrots dangling over the side.

"How goes the study, milady?" Mrs Rossett placed the basket on the table and Mary crossed to the range to feed it more fuel.

Hannah closed the journal and gulped the last cold mouthful of tea. "Frustrating. The Lord Wycliff of last century was vague in his references. Are you aware of any old stories concerning the hidden tower? Would they at all connect to the old whispers of mermaids and selkies?"

Mary collected her empty cup and carried it to the sink.

Mrs Rossett emptied the basket of carrots, potatoes, and a pile of plump strawberries. She huffed a silent laugh. "Never heard of any mermaids at Mireworth, and I doubt that pool in the conservatory is big enough to hold one. Old houses like these carry all sorts of stories about things hidden in the walls or stuffed up in the attic. It's usually naughty children or troublesome wives bricked in, though, not towers."

"Is there anyone you can think of who might know more about the history of the area, or any old stories?" What Hannah needed was an ancient gossip who collected whispers and myths. There was normally one in every village who knew everyone's business stretching back numerous generations.

"You could try Mr Hartley." Mrs Rossett selected her favourite knife from the solid wooden block.

"Isn't he new to the area? I recall Wycliff saying he only took up his position some two years ago." At least the vicar had a far more pleasant demeanour than Mr Seager. It would be no hardship to call upon him to ask if he had information on the subject.

"He is, but his grandmother was born in the village and moved away when she married. I think that was one of the reasons why he wanted to move here, to *return to his roots*, as he put it." Mrs Rossett commenced chopping off the ends of the carrots.

"Thank you, I shall call upon him tomorrow. Could you also tell me how to find Lisbeth Wolfe's cottage? I am curious to see it, since it sounds like a beautiful spot." The more Hannah followed the strands of the other women's lives, the deeper her curiosity pulled her. Like a fish on a hook, she couldn't let go of the bait.

13

On her quest to find the tower, Hannah prowled the lower floor of the house all afternoon. While she knew roughly where the tower hid, deduced from the view afforded from its windows, not a single clue hinted at its presence from the outside. Her explorations to find a hidden access to the ground level of the turret were fruitless. Wycliff shook his head when she asked, but she refused to be defeated. Her brain knew the tower was there and there simply had to be a way to find its lower level, even if she had to take a hammer to the plaster and brick to reveal it. So, she would apply to the next most likely person to know.

"I shall visit Mr Hartley today, and see if he knows anything about the history of Mireworth," Hannah said over breakfast the next morning, determined to uncover any information that might assist her search.

"I have a woman coming today to look at the kitchen garden and to talk about duties. She's a sensible thing, and her children are grown and moved on." Mrs Rossett spoke as she moved around the kitchen and gathered the items needed for whatever she planned to make.

Mary placed a wicker basket on the table and then filled it with pastries, followed by slices of meat, a cloth-wrapped cheese, and a loaf of bread.

"Where are you off to, Mary?" Hannah asked as she sipped one last cup of fortifying tea before her walk.

"I'm taking a picnic out to Frank." She added a few apples to the available space left. Then she glanced up and added, "And Lord Wycliff, of course."

"Of course," Hannah murmured. She exchanged a smile with Mrs Rossett.

The housekeeper clucked her tongue and shook her head. "Even a blind man could see how smitten you two are with each other, Mary."

Mary tucked a tea towel over the top of the contents to keep everything secure and then a sigh heaved through her slight frame. "I am ever so fond of him. But I do wish he would propose. A woman does get tired of waiting."

Mrs Rossett barked her sharp laugh that startled the spaniel from her blanket by the range. "If you want to marry that one, you will have to do the proposing. Despite his size, he seems far too timid to ask the question."

Mary paled and dropped into a chair. One hand

went to her chest. "Me? Ask him?" Her bottom lip trembled.

"If you don't want to take that bull by the horns, you could always wait a few more years and see if he gets around to it." Mrs Rossett sliced a lump of butter from the pat.

Hannah reached across the table and took Mary's hand. "You know Frank has trouble articulating words. I imagine he cannot express what he feels in his heart and needs a gentle prod in the right direction." At least, Hannah hoped the gentle giant harboured feelings for Mary in his *own* heart. The man bore an ugly scar down his chest and who knew, Lord Dunkeith might have inserted another man's organ. But that didn't alter the fact that the entirety of Frank's pieces agreed in their obvious devotion to Mary.

The maid's eyes widened and her mouth made a silent *oh*. "I might find enough patience to wait a bit longer," she managed to say after a long silence. Then she fetched her shawl and bonnet, before grabbing the basket and leaving to find the men at work.

Hannah followed the maid's example. She carried a smaller basket to hold anything of interest she found on her walk. She tied her bonnet firmly under her chin, to stymie the wind blowing off the ocean that seemed determined to steal it from her head. "I will return later this afternoon, Mrs Rossett."

Sheba bounced through the grass as Hannah headed for Mr Hartley's cottage on the edge of the estate. It took her nearly an hour to walk the distance, but she didn't mind, as the wind died down and the sun held a pleasant warmth. The walk gave her time to mull over many different strands of thought. The history of the tower fascinated her. The deaths of the women worried her in that they might be connected. The growing void between her and Wycliff caused a coldness to seep inside her.

By the time she found the cottage, she was ready to talk to someone about at least *some* of her many problems. The house nestled into a rise and overlooked a sheltered bay with a glorious view of the ocean. She found Mr Hartley sitting in the shade under a spreading tree in the middle of the grassy expanse before his home.

He rose on spotting her and bowed. "Lady Wycliff, how fortunate I am to have your company this glorious day."

Sheba snuffled around the garden and Hannah approached the wrought-iron table with two matching chairs. "Good day, Mr Hartley. What a wonderful spot you have here."

He waited for her to seat herself before resuming his own. "I should live in the vicarage, I suppose, and not have such a walk to church. But I find I cannot bear to be so closed in, and since my curate is content to live upstairs and keep it up, then I am content to occupy this place. It is marvellous to sit and watch the ocean from here and I find it does much to stimulate my thoughts. Tea? The pot is still warm."

"I will not intrude, since it appears you are

expecting guests." There were two cups set out next to the blue teapot, and a plate of biscuits, as though he waited for someone to join him.

He smiled and she couldn't help but return it. "I am always prepared for company, in case someone seeks me out. It would appear that today, that someone is you."

"Tea would be lovely, thank you." Sheba dragged over a stick and sat in the grass at Hannah's feet to chew on the end.

"The upcoming dance is much talked of in the village. Everyone is keen to welcome you to this community. It is kind of Lord Wycliff to share his bride with us all, when you are not long married." Mr Hartley poured tea into the cup and his hand hovered over the milk and lemon as he made the cup just the way Hannah liked it. Then he passed it across the table.

Hannah took a sip and let warmth flow through her in the hopes it might ease a little of the ache in her heart. She spent her days cold and alone, her nights in Wycliff's heated embrace. How she wanted a little of the passion they shared in the dark to seep into the sunlight hours. Not that she could broach *that* particular subject with the reverend. "Everyone has been most kind and I am overwhelmed by how many people are helping to decorate the hall."

"Might I enquire if there is any particular reason you sought me out today? I find most travellers have a destination in their minds when they undertake this journey." He leaned back with his teacup in his hands. His attention moved to a gull circling out over the water.

There was something in his quiet manner that urged a person to fill the silence. She imagined he was an easy man to unburden one's woes to. Hannah plucked at a simpler topic to begin. "I seek your help, Mr Hartley, in a mystery concerning Mireworth."

He turned back to her with a sparkle in his sage green eyes. "A mystery? How delightful. Do elaborate."

Hannah played with the handle of her cup, rubbing a finger along the delicate silver painted line. "Hidden inside Mireworth is a tower that I believe is hundreds of years old. No one seems to know anything about the edifice, nor why it was bricked in when the house was built over a century ago. Mrs Rossett tells me your grandmother was a local and that you know something of the history of the area."

"Indeed. Grandmother gathered many stories to her. She was fascinated by history and passed that trait on to me. I do recollect something about an old tower. It caught my attention as a somewhat unruly boy—I was known for disappearing into the woodland to find old ruins to explore." He laughed at the memory of youthful antics.

It conjured images in Hannah's mind of a young Jonas adventuring over the estate, with Lisbeth as his constant companion. Had they discovered the tower together? "Did your grandmother live here long? I understand her husband was not a local?"

Mr Hartley offered Hannah the plate of biscuits. "No. Grandfather was a travelling man who met Grandmother when he passed through this area. They married and she moved away to settle inland with him. I think she missed the ocean terribly. In fact, this cottage was once hers."

On a calm day like today, the sea resembled a blue-green velvet blanket stitched with sparkling diamonds. Hannah could understand how some people could grow to love its changeable nature and the constant company created by the sound of waves caressing the shore. "Did she ever make it back here?"

He shook his head and a moment of sadness dropped over him as he remembered his grandmother. "No, sadly. She lived a goodly span and her stories are what made me seek out a position here. In quiet moments, I have been writing them down as an unofficial history of the area. As a child under her spell, I must warn you, I never knew which of them were true and which were embellished."

On impulse, Hannah asked, "Did your grandmother tell any tales of mermaids and selkies in this area?"

A smile pulled at his lips. "This is a remote village perched by the ocean and I believe she did spin a few such tales. But surely, Lady Wycliff, given your association with the Ministry of Unnaturals, you would know far more about such creatures than I?"

Hannah watched the waves purling against the sand. "There is not much mention of selkies or mermaids in London apart, I think, from a preserved mermaid presented to King Henry the Eighth. The poor creature sat on display in the palace for two hundred years, until she was given a decent burial last century."

He laughed. "Perhaps they do not make it so far up the Thames as to be commonly discussed? Returning to the tower, I think it is one of the earliest tales my grandmother told. It is over five hundred years old and was once part of a castle. It was built by the first lord to reside here, de Cliffe, who followed the Pope's call to the Fifth Crusade in Egypt in the twelfth century."

"Yes!" Hannah nearly leapt to her feet in excitement. "That would fit with what I have been able to discern about the structure, and Wycliff's impressions of it." She kept the presence of the hieroglyphic stones in the fireplace to herself, to avoid any questions about why they were important to her. Their existence gave her something against which to judge the truth of Mr Hartley's story. Had his grandmother known what the tower hid?

He leaned back and tossed a piece of biscuit to the spaniel, now hiding under the table. "Hmm...if I remember correctly without consulting my notes, that ancestor of the current Lord Wycliff distinguished himself and was given a parcel of land where Mireworth now stands upon which to build his castle. With its location near the cliffs, it would have been a defensive structure against an attack from the sea."

"Did your grandmother hear anything about why

the tower endured when the castle did not?" Hannah perched on the edge of her seat, waiting for the vicar to drop the pivotal information.

"No." He rubbed his chin and the light caught on a deep blue gem in the ring on his pinkie finger.

Her heart sank and she sat back in her chair.

The finger moved to tap his chin in a slow rhythm as he thought. "It is not uncommon for castles to fall into disrepair—England is littered with such ruins. Look at Corfe Castle, not far from here. Stones are often pulled down and reused in other buildings or walls. I imagine that due to its shape, the tower lasted longer. Although I do remember one tall tale, that I am sure is purely a work of my grandmother's mischief, about the tower being haunted. Perhaps it was left alone so as not to disturb its unquiet resident."

Now Hannah simply had to find the lower level. What if, rather than housing cattle and other stock over winter as Wycliff had suggested, someone had been buried there, in unconsecrated ground? The idea perked her up. "The stone masonry is exceptionally smooth and well made. I can imagine the tower weathering the test of time while the rest of the castle fell down around it."

"I have some letters from my grandmother and my own notes of her stories. I shall re-read them in case there is anything further I can impart about the tower's history." Mr Hartley dropped his hand back to his teacup.

With that information tucked away, Hannah

moved on to a more current issue. "You gave a lovely service for Mrs Rivers."

His smile dropped away, replaced by a solemn expression. "The ocean is as cruel as she is beautiful," he murmured.

"I understand hers is not the only such death in the last year, and that Amy Miller and Lisbeth Wolfe also drowned." Hannah broke a biscuit into small pieces and wondered how to ask if Mr Hartley harboured any suspicions as to how the trio died.

"Yes. I buried them, too. I believe Mr Cramond may have been rather taken with Lisbeth, but then she was taken from us. If so, it was a double tragedy that his heart managed to love again with Amy, only to lose her in the same manner." He spoke to the ocean, his words drifting on the breeze.

Hannah considered the new snippet, yet it didn't fit with her own version of Mr Cramond. He said it had been Mr Seager who had been enamoured of Lisbeth. Was the reverend simply mistaken? Then she recalled Libby's comment about her sister—that she had offered comfort to Mr Cramond after Amy's death. How far had such comfort gone? "Are you sure it was Mr Cramond, and not another man?"

Mr Hartley pursed his lips. "Perhaps I am mistaken. I am not one to rely upon for such gossip."

Hannah accepted the gentle rebuke, but it did not stop her. "I understand Amy had quite a wound to her head. Did any such injury exist on Lisbeth when she was found?" Hannah ate the broken biscuit while she wondered if the religious man would have been privy to such information.

He turned to her and clasped his hands together on the tabletop, a slight frown on his brow as he met her gaze. "Now, Lady Wycliff, you wouldn't be trying to connect two terrible events together at the expense of poor, unfortunate Mr Cramond, would you? I rather think he has suffered enough."

"I merely wish to understand how such tragic deaths could have occurred." She cast her eyes downward, feeling rather guilty for the aspersions the vicar believed she cast against a hard-working man.

"I wonder if perhaps you see a little of yourself in these women, that you have taken such an interest in their deaths? In the last year, I have buried a number of elderly members of this community, two fit and hale men who were struck down, and, most sadly, those children who did not walk this earth for long. Yet you have not enquired about their deaths." There was no rebuke now in his tone or expression, merely a gentle probing of her true motives.

Hannah stared at her hands in her lap as she absorbed his words. One image stuck—that of a tiny coffin being gently lowered into a small grave by a bereft parent. *Children who did not walk this earth for long.* How had it escaped her notice that tragedy could strike a community in many different forms?

Was it her empathy for the women that drove her to ferret out how they had met their ends, or did learning about their lives hold up a mirror to her own, and show a similar solitary reflection? "You are right, Mr Hartley. Perhaps I am struck not by the manner of their deaths, but by the substance of their lives."

The rest of Hannah's visit passed with the convivial company and she found Mr Hartley a thoughtful conversationalist. Soon the spaniel grew restless and it was time for the return walk. Clouds gathered out at sea and the wind carried a chilly edge.

"Looks like rain is coming in," Mr Hartley said.

Hannah tied her bonnet more securely and slid her basket handle along her arm. "I must head back before it turns. Thank you for your time and information, Mr Hartley. You have assisted me greatly."

He took her hand and held it between his, his gaze warm upon her. "A pleasure, Lady Wycliff. I do hope you will visit me again. I have much enjoyed our discussion."

Hannah set off for Mireworth at a brisk pace as the sky darkened overhead. Soon large droplets of rain fell around her.

"Blast." She would be soaked before she reached the house.

At that moment, she saw a sturdy horse trotting along the road, pulling a cart with Frank at the reins. He drew the horse to a halt and jumped down with a thud that travelled up Hannah's shins.

"Master...say...find you," he hissed.

"Excellent timing, Frank." Hannah placed her basket on the seat of the cart.

The large man scooped up the puppy and placed

her in the back. Then he picked up Hannah and deposited her on the seat. When he climbed in, an overcoat rose from the back. When Hannah lifted it, she found Barnes underneath.

"Thank you, Barnes." Hannah snuggled into the overcoat as the rain continued to fall.

Rather than finding answers with Mr Hartley, Hannah found more questions crowding into her head. Was the tower truly haunted? Had it been Mr Cramond or Mr Seager who had courted Lisbeth? How had Amy bumped her head?

Would tonight be the night that she found the courage to tell Wycliff she loved him?

14

THE ONSET of rain called a halt to Wycliff's tasks for the day, and he decided to concentrate on one particular task he had been putting off—tackling the estate's account books. As he entered the kitchen, he glanced through the open doors to the conservatory. Hannah had worked to clear the overgrown beds and scrubbed the reflecting pool. Frank had moved fresh soil into the beds and now they needed seedlings and plants to bring the space back to life. He thought he might enquire with their neighbours about cuttings, or ornamental fish to place in the pool. Although that would leave Mrs Rossett to tend both fish and plants when they left.

The more time he spent at Mireworth wresting her back into working shape, the more he found he wanted to prolong his stay. The roots he'd grown as a boy had been cut off when he reached adulthood. Now he wished to drop new ones and entwine them with Hannah's.

"Where is Lady Wycliff?" he asked when he did not find her in either kitchen or conservatory. Had she returned to the tower? An odd sensation rippled through him. He would like to be the one to guide her explorations through the house, like an adventurer armed with a torch and a machete.

"She set off this morning to visit Mr Hartley," Mrs Rossett said, poking up the fire.

The vicar occupied a cottage at the edge of the estate and a good hour's walk away. He couldn't settle on his work with the accounts knowing she was out there with the threat of rain in the air. "She will get caught if this weather turns. I shall send Frank to find her."

With Frank on his way, Wycliff retrieved the largest ledger and a stack of invoices from the study. Since Hannah used his desk as a dressing table, he didn't want to disturb her brushes and ribbons. Instead, he sat at one end of the kitchen table, while Mrs Rossett rolled out pastry at the other end. The kitchen had the advantages of a large work space, light, and the warmth of the range. Not to mention the delicious aroma of dinner coming from the oven. Besides, Mrs Rossett kept sliding him still-warm biscuits as though he were a lad again.

The rain thrummed against the skylight when the door opened and Hannah and the spaniel burst in. Sheba rushed to him and Wycliff dropped a hand to pat the dog, as his wife removed the large overcoat Frank had taken to keep her dry. Mary took the heavy coat and hung it on a hook while peering out the door, no doubt waiting for Frank.

"Thank you for sending Frank—we would have been soaked without him." Hannah rubbed her hands together and stood close to the range.

"I am glad you did not get too wet." Heat flared inside him as he stared at Hannah. Her cheeks were flushed from the chill outside and her eyes sparkled. The kitchen had a cosy intimacy that would be unheard of in London. He could almost imagine this being their life...if they hadn't been confined to only two rooms in the house and a deadly curse was not frozen inside her ready to still her heart. There was also his work at the Ministry that awaited him. It was only a matter of time before his weather cube turned red and Sir Manly summoned him back, or his secretary, Higgs, flew in through an open window clutching an urgent missive.

He let out a sigh and rubbed his hands over his face. The harder he worked to make it viable for Mireworth to be their home, the more it slipped from his grasp. Like trying to catch the greased pig at the fairs he remembered as a boy.

"Might I ask what you are working on?" Hannah pulled out the chair next to him.

Wycliff moved an invoice from one pile to another. There was no need to hide the situation from Hannah —she had only to look around to see what years of neglect had done to a once grand estate. "I am totalling up invoices for the farm and trying to predict wool and beef prices. I spoke to a man yesterday about repairing the roof, and wanted to see if I would be able to afford it before next winter."

"Is a roof such a great sum?" Hannah pulled the teapot closer and poured the steaming liquid into a cup.

Wycliff found the note from the builder and slid it toward her. Any amount was a great sum when you had very little.

Hannah turned her head to read the notations. "My word. I had no idea. But then, I suppose it is rather a large roof."

"Exactly. We may have to live with the leaks for a few years longer, which unfortunately means more water damage spreading through the house. I am hoping to get up into the attic and check for any new ones. It may be possible to repair the worst areas for now."

What kind of husband was he that he could not even provide an adequate roof over his wife's head?

"I will pay for the roof." Hannah spoke over the rim of the cup in her hands.

"It is not possible, Hannah. I do not have sufficient funds for it. Not without seeking more financing, and I do not want to borrow more than I can repay and risk losing everything." If only it were as simple as instructing that the work be done and hoping the bank would honour the debt.

Hannah took a buttered scone from Mrs Rossett

and nodded her thanks. "You might not, but I do. I shall use my dowry to pay for the repairs."

Wycliff snorted. He had been adamant that he neither wanted, nor expected, a dowry for marrying her. No one would say their match had been motivated by money. "I did not require a dowry when we married."

"No. But my parents gave me one for doing so." She bit into the scone with enjoyment, her rich brown eyes watching him.

"What?" Her words carved a path through his brain and Wycliff narrowed his gaze at her. *There* was a blow to his ego, if a purse had been dangled at *her* to accept *him*.

Humour simmered in her eyes, no doubt as she understood his reaction. "*After* we married, my parents decided I should have a dowry that I could apply to my new life. The funds are sitting, untouched, in the bank. There is sufficient there to repair the roof and most likely, for new glazing for the broken windows."

His inner boy let out a whoop of joy, but the adult hushed the child. Hannah was a marvel to throw him a lifeline he desperately wanted to accept. "I cannot let you do that. It is a significant amount."

"We are married, are we not?" Hannah arched one eyebrow and licked a trickle of butter from her finger.

"Of course we are." He had wedded and finally bedded her with no regrets about either decision.

"Which makes me mistress of Mireworth, does it not?" She continued her questions.

"Yes. You are mistress here." The idea warmed his insides more than Mrs Rossett's fresh scones.

A smile tugged on her lips. "As mistress and lady of Mireworth, am I not responsible for the running of our home?"

"What is your point, Hannah?" He had a suspicion he was about to run afoul of his wife's machinations.

Hannah leaned toward him and spoke by his ear in a demure tone. "My point, dear husband, is that you cannot stop me from spending *my* money to repair *my* home."

A cackle of laughter came from the end of the table. "You married a smart one there, milord. Best leave the mistress to take care of her domain, while you worry about the rest of the estate. Lady Wycliff will have the old house watertight and dry by winter."

Hannah beamed at the housekeeper. "Quite right, Mrs Rossett. Matters pertaining to the house are my domain. I suggest, Wycliff, that you stick to broken walls, blocked drains, sheep, and the like."

He swallowed his pride. Truth be told, it made his blood sing that she thought of the house as her home already and wished to see the place restored.

"Thank you," he murmured. Then he took Hannah's face in his hands, and kissed her thoroughly. That put more colour in her cheeks and Mrs Rossett let out another laugh of delight. "If you are certain, I will let the builder know he can assemble his workers and begin. As Mrs Rossett says, it should be done before winter."

An image of Christmas in the house sprang into his head, with an enormous tree in the grand entrance and strategically placed boughs of mistletoe so he had more excuses to kiss his wife. Hannah had wrought a miracle over him. For the first time that he could remember, Wycliff looked forward to what the future would bring.

THE STORM GREW in intensity outside and the sky darkened prematurely. Frank left straight after dinner to sit in the stables in case the thunder and lightning frightened the horses, and Mary and Barnes joined him. Wycliff hoped the fragile roof would hold. Should he take a lantern now, rather than waiting, and poke around in the attic to see if there was anything he could do? Hannah's generous offer would put him years ahead on restoring the estate even though it grated, somewhat, that he hadn't raised the money through his own efforts.

Tired muscles from long days of hard labour and the charged atmosphere from the storm made a headache press behind his eyes. All he wanted was to drop into bed and listen to the rain fall outside. It seemed Mrs Rossett also sought shelter from the storm in her room, and everyone said their good-nights early.

In the study, Wycliff peered into some of the crates stacked in the corner, wondering if he might find the missing drawings of the house among them. He had seen them *somewhere*, but the headache wouldn't allow him to remember where.

Hannah undressed and then, wearing her dressing gown, sat at her impromptu dressing table and brushed out her hair. "Do you not find it odd that three women from the village have lost their lives within the space of a year?"

He shrugged off his jacket and draped it over a chair. He could imagine what ideas ran through her head; that said, it did seem that murder had become a regular part of their conjugal conversation. "Life is different here, Hannah, and much harsher than what you are used to."

Her hand stilled on the hairbrush. "Three women drowned. How is that the harshness of life? Or do you mean the cruelty of the ocean? None of them died in childbirth, or a fire caused by an upset candle, nor were they struck down by disease."

"The village is situated by the ocean. All the women were last seen at night, one of them in winter when paths are slippery. As tragic as it is, they most likely lost their footing in the dark and fell into the water." He stripped off his cravat and waistcoat next, treating them more callously than the jacket. The items were tossed to the seat of the chair. The pressure inside and outside his skull reached a crescendo as thunder cracked above their heads. He spent his days trying to wrest the estate into better order to secure their future, and dowry notwithstanding, Hannah spent her time chasing silly rumours.

"Three young, healthy, and able-bodied women all fell? Amy wasn't even that close to the water." She laid down the hairbrush and pushed back her chair.

Wycliff raised a hand, on the point of snapping at her, but pulled himself under control and ran his fingers through his hair instead. His shoulders dropped before he spoke in a low tone. "Hannah, leave it be. No good will come from you stirring up old sorrows. There are whispers that the women took their own lives."

That stole the breath from her lungs and her mouth opened in an O. Then she frowned and Wycliff could practically hear her marshalling her thoughts to sally forth again. "That doesn't make sense. Why would Amy Miller take her own life when she had just accepted a marriage proposal? She had so much to look forward to."

Wycliff dropped to a chair to tug off his boots. "Perhaps she wandered off the track and fell then, but the other two jumped."

"Sarah had a minor disagreement with her husband, nothing worth such a horrible ending. Why are you so closed to the possibility there is something more sinister happening here?" Hannah had to speak louder to compete with the boom of thunder from above.

"Why are you so determined to find foul play?" he shot back.

Hannah's shoulders sagged and she turned to the bed and fluffed her pillow.

Wycliff regretted his outburst. In truth, the deaths

gnawed at him. One in particular kept him awake at night, wondering if he could have done more to prevent it. He let out a sigh and sat on the settee at the end of the bed. Leaning forward, with his forearms resting on his thighs, he stared at his hands.

"I grew up with Lisbeth. Apart from me, I think she was rather lonely and suffered bouts of melancholy. I remember a terrible day some seven years ago, when we were both not much older than twenty. I caught her about to throw herself from the cliff into the ocean below. I snatched hold of her hand as she overbalanced and was able to pull her back onto the grass. She cried in my arms that she couldn't bear the ache inside her any longer. I made her promise to seek help from somebody. After that, I thought she was much improved."

It had caused him pain to know his dear friend suffered in such a fashion and he was powerless to help her. He thought Lisbeth had much to live for, and the fault lay with the villagers who couldn't see all she had to offer behind her sad eyes. Many thought that like other men, he appreciated her beauty, but as a young boy it was her witty personality and throwing arm that had drawn him to her.

Slippers shuffled on the rug as Hannah approached and sat beside him. "I am sorry. I did not mean to...stir up old sorrows."

Hannah placed a hand on his thigh and Wycliff took hold of it and kissed her knuckles.

"And I am sorry for shouting. It is, as you no doubt have surmised, a delicate topic for me and I blame myself for not seeking more help for Lisbeth. I berate myself that if I had returned here last summer I might have done...*something* to ease her pain. As to the other two, I admit that I do not know for sure. If you believe there is more to these deaths, then I shall assist you. But tread gently, Hannah, in case you are mistaken. It is hard on the families left behind when a beloved member leaves them too soon by their own choice."

She leaned against him and rested her head on his shoulder. "I think that of the two of us, I am the one best known for quietly eliciting responses to delicate questions."

He huffed a soft laugh. If anyone could reveal the true cause, it was Hannah, with her quiet but determined way. "Indeed you are."

"I saw Mr Hartley today, and he implied that Mr Cramond had been rather fond of Lisbeth. Yet when I spoke to Mr Cramond, he said that it was Mr Seager who spent much time with her." She spoke quietly and he strained his ears to catch her words over the storm.

Two men interested in Lisbeth? He hadn't known and it struck him as odd. Lisbeth had guarded her heart fiercely. "Lisbeth never mentioned either of them the last time I saw her, nor would I have imagined either as being to her tastes. But what of Sarah Rivers? How does she fit into whatever theory you are brewing?"

"Mr Cramond is a handsome and affable man. Sarah's sister said Sarah offered comfort to him after Amy died. Perhaps he sought more than comfort and she refused? Although again, Mr Cramond said that

Mr Seager was often in Sarah's company and that he had called on Amy," Hannah said.

Both men could have touched the lives of all three women. Wycliff let out a sigh and stood, pulling Hannah to her feet. "If you are determined, I shall make certain discreet enquiries about both men myself. But walk softly, lest you do damage to their reputations and lives if you are wrong."

"I would never do harm to an innocent man. I shall be the soul of discretion," she murmured. "There is one other thing. Mrs Rossett mentioned that some fifty years ago, two men drowned, and rumours swirled at the time of a mermaid or selkie being responsible."

That was the old memory that had itched in his mind when Miller had ranted about Cramond dragging women into the ocean. Some villagers clung tight to old ways and beliefs. Wycliff made a noise in the back of his throat. "Do you suspect a sea creature who must be at least seventy years old, who emerges from the ocean every half century to claim victims?"

Humour sparkled in her eyes. "If it is, at least this investigation won't end with a chase. I assume an elderly sea monster wouldn't run very fast."

Then she tilted her head and parted her lips in an invitation he could not refuse.

15

THE NEXT DAY DAWNED CLEAR, the storm having passed overnight. After breakfast and some time scrubbing the window panes in the conservatory, Hannah sat at the table and twisted her hands together, pondering what to do next. Mr Seager may have had a valid reason for calling on each of the deceased women. Or he may have used his position as apothecary to mask the true reason for his visits. Ever since the visit to the village where Hannah had glimpsed the notebook with Sarah Rivers' name on the front, she had itched to know what remedy Sarah had sought from the man. However, he possessed an eagle eye and she couldn't simply rummage through his drawers unnoticed.

Not unless she had an accomplice.

Mary, while a most excellent maid, was terrible with secrets and subterfuge. The Miles family even had to hide their Christmas presents from her, or she would blurt out what they had purchased for one another.

That left Hannah with one other person who might indulge her.

"I wonder, Mrs Rossett, if I might pose a question of you." Hannah steeled herself for disapproval from the housekeeper.

"Oh? That sounds serious." With no immediate tasks calling for her attention, the housekeeper sat at one end of the table with her knitting.

"There is something I wish to accomplish, but I cannot be seen. I require someone who can...divert another person's attention." Hannah chose her words with care.

The older woman's eyes widened. Then she scooted her chair closer to Hannah. "Do tell, milady. I love a bit of mischief."

At least this was not an outright refusal. "It's not so much mischief as...well, actually, I don't know quite what it is."

Mrs Rossett patted Hannah's hand and poured a cup of tea. "Why don't you tell me everything? I may not know your ladyship that well yet, but I have wondered if something was preying on your mind."

Hannah heaved a deep breath. Better out than in, her mother would say. She would confide in Mrs Rossett and take things from there.

"It is the deaths of Sarah Rivers, Amy Miller, and Lisbeth Wolfe. Something about them does not sit right with me." Hannah glanced at the older woman over the rim of the cup. Would she think Hannah terribly nosy and officious, prying into the tragedies?

Mrs Rossett blew on her tea before taking a sip. "You wouldn't be the first. We were all terribly shocked when Lisbeth drowned. Some said she were a selkie and had found her skin to return to the ocean...until her body washed up. Then when Amy died, some folk whispered that the deaths were no accidents. But if they weren't, how did they die?"

Hannah hypothesised that if the deaths had not been accidental, something would bind the women together. Either motive or opportunity would be present, if she could find it. Mr Cramond was one possible common thread, although Wycliff did not think he had courted Lisbeth as Mr Hartley had said. Mr Seager was another person the women might have had in common.

"I am looking for any connection between the three women and what might have bound them together. The other day at the apothecary's, I happened to glimpse a notebook with Sarah Rivers' name on it. I wish to see what cures she sought from Mr Seager."

Mrs Rossett's eyes lit up with understanding. "Oh, yes, he has those drawers with all the little notebooks in them. He writes down whenever he makes a potion just for you. You might find the other women in there, too. Lisbeth was a sad thing, out in that desolate cottage all on her own, but in the last few weeks she had seemed much happier."

"Perhaps a tonic perked up her mood? But Mr Seager is so rude and unhelpful. I doubt he will let me see them if I ask." Hannah tapped her fingers against the cup, thinking of ways to sneak a look in the drawers. Wycliff might assist, if she could tear him away from his labour on the estate and convince him the matter required investigation.

Mrs Rossett chuckled. "He won't let you rifle his drawers. You'd think that one was keeping secrets for the Crown, the way he protects his potions and salves. Do you think he did it, then—killed them?" Her eyes widened and her voice trailed away to a whisper on the last two words.

Hannah nearly choked on a mouthful of tea. She certainly didn't want to make any allegations until she dug deeper into the women's lives and deaths. She had promised Wycliff she would tread carefully. Now that she turned the idea over, she wondered if more might be learned from Mr Seager's notebooks. "Oh, no, but I do wonder if perhaps all three saw Mr Seager for some reason? People can react differently to herbs and potions. For all we know, each may have ingested something that caused her to become dizzy, or lose her footing while walking the shoreline. We might avert another such tragedy if that is the case. Such is my theory. Now I need a way to test it. Will you help me, then?" Hannah hardly dared hope that the housekeeper would be complicit in what she intended to do.

Mrs Rossett winked. "Oh, yes. I must say, you are an excellent match for our rapscallion."

Hannah wondered what that meant. She had never deliberately misbehaved or broken the law. Not until Wycliff came into her life. "I never used to search through people's private papers until recently, and I was a very obedient child. My mother once observed that she thought Wycliff would embolden me, even as I smoothed off some of his rough edges."

The housekeeper let out her loud laugh that could have served as a foghorn in a storm. Then the two women plotted what they would do. After tea, Frank hitched up the cart and Hannah took the reins as they headed for the village. Once more they left the horse and cart with the blacksmith, and then walked along the main road to the apothecary's cottage.

"Lady Wycliff. Mrs Rossett." He addressed them from high on a ladder, as he placed a small vial among its fellows on the very top shelf. He climbed down and then moved the ladder along to a corner and out of the way. "Do you need more cough syrup, Mrs Rossett?"

"Yes, I have nearly run out. Thank you, Mr Seager." Mrs Rossett wandered over to the square desk with the tiny scales in the middle. Two chairs sat in front of the desk and she clutched the back of one. She fanned herself with her hand and then dropped into the chair. "Oh, I say, I feel ever so faint."

"You do look rather flushed, Mrs Rossett." Hannah rushed over to the housekeeper. "Could you fetch her a glass of water, please?" she said to the apothecary.

He narrowed his eyes at both women, tensed his shoulders, and held his ground. For a moment, Hannah thought he might refuse and throw them out of the shop instead. Then he blew out a snort that reminded

Hannah of an indignant horse asked to do something beneath it. "Very well. Stay right there, the pair of you."

When he disappeared through the door to the rear of the cottage, Mrs Rossett grabbed Hannah's hand. "Off you go. I'm going to follow him and get him to take me outside for a breath of fresh air. You won't have long. Five or ten minutes at most."

Hannah wasted no time. She hurried to the counter with the drawers and pulled open the one she remembered being ajar on her last visit. She found Sarah Rivers' notebook, no longer at the front but toward the middle of the row. Hannah turned the pages and scanned the neat notations. For a period of six months, the woman had visited the apothecary once a month for a tonic containing chaste berry, Black Cohosh, and cinnamon. All ingredients in the syrup he said he brewed to assist fertility.

Time ticked by. What of Lisbeth Wolfe? Moving as fast as she could, Hannah pulled drawers and scanned names. Five minutes passed with no luck, when a bottom drawer revealed the first dead woman's notebook. With shaking hands, Hannah found the last entry. Lisbeth had been dispensed a tonic containing St John's wort.

"Good for melancholy," Hannah murmured. She thrust the book back into place and shut the drawer just as Mrs Rossett's voice came from behind the door. She barely had time to scurry to the window and made a show of peering out and watching the passers-by.

"There is nothing wrong with you that wouldn't be

aided by more vigorous exercise, losing some weight, and drinking less port of an evening," Mr Seager said as he propelled Mrs Rossett back into the room.

"I'm an old woman, Mr Seager, and my nightly port is one of the few pleasures left to me in life. But I shall take your advice." She returned to the desk.

Mr Seager made a noise in the back of his throat, then walked to the shelves and scanned the contents. He fetched a large, dark green glass bottle and then a smaller blue one. He turned to the drawers and opened one, muttering under his breath as he found a notebook and pulled it free. On his return to the desk, he collected a small empty bottle from a box. Once seated, he set down his armload of things. With a funnel from one corner of the desk, he measured differing amounts from the two bottles into the smaller one.

"Sixpence, Mrs Rossett, if you please," he said and held out his hand.

Mrs Rossett pressed coins into his palm and took possession of the bottle. "Thank you, Mr Seager. Now that we have Lady Wycliff at Mireworth, I shall enjoy her company on our walks across the estate to get more exercise, as you recommend."

The apothecary grunted and took up his pen to make a notation in the notebook with *Mrs B Rossett* on the front. Being ignored was their cue to leave.

Once outside the cottage, the housekeeper glanced over her shoulder before tipping her head closer to Hannah. "Well? What did you discover?"

"Mr Seager was indeed dispensing a tonic for

Lisbeth to assist with her melancholy." St John's wort wouldn't have made her stumble into the ocean, though, unless it made her sleepy? If only Hannah could consult with her mother! But the mage was unreachable while in the Fae realm.

"Did you find Amy Miller's book in those drawers?" Mrs Rossett asked as they walked back toward the blacksmith's.

"I didn't see her name, but I only managed to flick through a few drawers before you came back in." The state of Amy's health notwithstanding, it seemed unlikely that a potion for lifting a mood and a fertility aid could cause symptoms severe enough to cause a woman to fall into the water.

Mrs Rossett made a noise in the back of her throat. "When I told Mr Seager I needed fresh air, he told me to go for a five-mile walk. The cheek of him. With a disposition like that, the fellow will never marry."

"People used to say the same of Wycliff." Perhaps the apothecary donned rudeness as armour, to protect himself. "He might have a reason to act like that. A broken heart, perhaps?"

Mrs Rossett chuckled and pulled on Hannah's arm. "Now, that would be a juicy piece of gossip. Yes, I can see him giving his heart to some woman who treated him cruelly, and so vowing to treat others the exact same way."

"I am sure Mr Seager is not a lost cause. He simply hasn't found the right person to worm under his armour. Now, shall we see how the decoration of the hall is coming along?" Hannah steered the housekeeper toward the squat building next to the tavern.

Much to her delight, many more women and children had volunteered to help make the seashell garlands to use as decorations. Completed ones had even been dropped into baskets left outside the hall. Two women draped the garlands from the hanging lanterns, under the watchful eye of Libby Tant.

"It's going to look marvellous," Hannah said after she greeted the women.

"The paintings are not far away. Moira is making them on stiffened cloth that we can attach to hooks." Libby rubbed her belly with one hand.

"I do appreciate the work you are doing, Mrs Tant. I hope you are not overtaxing yourself?" Hannah worried the woman might give birth to child number four right there on the floor.

She laughed. "Oh, no, this one's a week away yet. A woman comes to know when the time nears. With any luck, I will still be able to attend the dance."

Hannah decided that the ability to sense an impending birth was one mystery she didn't need to understand. "If you are sure, your help is most appreciated."

"From what I remember of you as a youngster, Libby, you and Sarah were always organising the other children." Mrs Rossett touched a dangling starfish and it rotated on its string.

"That we were, Mrs Rossett. Always better to be busy." The children abandoned their play and encircled their mother, clamouring for her attention. "There is one thing we need to organise, Lady Wycliff. Mr Cramond has some old fishing nets we can use, if someone could fetch them from him. He doesn't need them anymore since he has taken over the Miller farm."

Hannah spied an opportunity for a quiet conversation with Mr Cramond. "I don't mind going. Shall I return you to Mireworth first, Mrs Rossett?"

"Yes, milady. Mary and I have dinner to start." The housekeeper gave the starfish another poke.

The two women took their leave and returned to fetch the cart. Hannah deposited Mrs Rossett back at the estate and turned the horse in the direction of the rundown farm, now the responsibility of Mr Cramond. Hannah slowed the horse to a walk along the road toward the house.

"Oh, dear," she murmured. She thought Mireworth appeared dire, but the former home of the Millers appeared to be inhabited by nothing but weeds, chickens, and vermin.

Mr Cramond straddled the roof, replacing slates. His shirt was rolled up to his elbows and a red handkerchief was knotted around his neck. He climbed down the ladder on seeing her, and approached as Hannah looped the reins around the brake and climbed down from the cart.

"Lady Wycliff." He touched the brim of his cap and then wiped dirty hands on his trousers.

"Good day, Mr Cramond. I don't envy you the job ahead of you." Yet, as Hannah looked again, she saw the signs of a man determined to wrest his holding back from the brink and make it profitable. Much like Wycliff.

The porch was swept, the windows cleaned, and broken panes had fresh wood covering the gaps as a temporary measure. Sheep grazed on tuffs of grass and weeds to bring the pasture back under control. The barn doors were wide open and an enormous pile of old hay and manure to one side indicated the interior had likewise received a thorough cleaning.

"Nothing wrong with a bit of hard work, especially when it will bring its own rewards when the farm is producing again." He stood with hands on hips as he surveyed his new home, but a sadness lingered in his eyes.

"I'm sure it will not take you long, given how industrious you have been. I am here to fetch the nets you kindly said we could use as decoration for the celebration ball." A chicken crossed Hannah's path, its head cocked as it stalked an insect.

"They're just over here. I'll load them into the back of the cart." He gestured to a neat pile sitting by the open barn doors.

"Will you miss life as a fisherman?" Hannah wondered which life was harder. Both were subject to the whims of the weather and nature.

He shook his head. "No. I turned my back on fishing after we pulled Amy from the water. His lordship's offer was providential—I couldn't bear to go out after that."

"I am so sorry. Such a tragedy when you were to be married." Hannah prodded the subject, curious to hear his version of events.

"Took me by surprise when she said yes, if I'm honest. For a time, I thought she was sweet on someone else." He carried the bundle of nets to the cart and fell silent as he placed them within.

"Oh? Was it Mr Seager?" Previously, he had intimated that Mr Seager had appeared keen on both Amy and Lisbeth.

"I don't know for sure. She never did say, but I saw the way he used to look at her." He clenched his jaw and his hands dropped to his sides.

"What do you think happened that night?" Hannah studied the cottage, wondering if Amy had made it back or not.

Cramond stared up at the sky and tugged the cap from his head. He turned it over in his hands, as thoughts might turn over in his mind. "That we will never know. It was close to twilight and bitterly cold. Depending on the route she took home, she might have missed her footing in the dark and slipped into the water. I'm also aware some think she turned me down and I did it. But those that know me know I would never raise my hand against a woman."

Hannah pondered that course of events. Previously he had said that Amy needed to tell *someone* of their engagement. What if it wasn't her grandfather, but Mr Seager she had spoken to, to decline his advances? It was quite true that some thought Amy had refused Mr

Cramond and he had struck her, or that her grandfather had flown into a rage. Which version was the true account?

Mr Cramond patted the horse. "Amy and I had talked about the future, and I said I would farm this land with her and make it productive again. Maybe, in time, I'll find another lass to share the road ahead, but I won't love another like I did Amy."

The young man's voice held such sadness that Hannah reached out and touched his forearm. "She will always have a place in your heart, but I hope that when you are ready, another will bring some sunlight into your life."

He swallowed and managed a weak smile. "Mayhap. One day. I have too much work to do first, and no time for love."

No time for love. The words echoed through Hannah as he handed her up into the cart. Was that how Wycliff felt? That the needs of the estate left no time for love?

16

THE NEXT DAY Wycliff had not needed Frank, nor Barnes, since he was tethered to the larger man. Not wanting to waste the opportunity of having Frank at her disposal, Hannah and the others decided to tackle the walled garden. A new maid, Charlotte, had been engaged to assist Mrs Rossett and to look after the vegetable garden. If Hannah and Wycliff were to spend more time at the estate, it made sense to have the kitchen garden productive once more.

They spent a busy morning pulling weeds and clearing beds, and Frank took charge of the wheelbarrow, dumping the rubbish on the growing compost heap. Another job for Charlotte would be adding horse manure from the stables, and turning the compost pile to create a rich fertiliser for the garden.

With sweat running down between her shoulder blades, Hannah rested in the shade for a few minutes. She watched Frank assisting Mary. The big man grinned constantly in Mary's presence, and she often giggled and swatted at him, her hand lingering upon him. A tug at her sleeve made Hannah look down. Barnes sat next to her on the bench.

"What do you think of your country excursion so far, Barnes? Are you enjoying yourself?" To date, the hand had stayed out of trouble and mostly within his range of Frank. Only once had Hannah spotted Frank stalking across the paddock with Barnes dragging behind him, pulled through the grass by the invisible tether.

The hand gave a thumbs up. Then he tapped on the gold ring on Hannah's left hand and pointed to Frank and Mary.

"Will they get married? I really don't know, Barnes. It is clear they have affection for one another, but I think Mrs Rossett is quite right. Frank won't ever be able to articulate the question, and Mary would faint dead away if she ever had to ask him." Hannah wondered if she should intervene and ask them their intentions, but that would remove some of the romance of having someone propose.

The hand was his version of silent, meaning he sat very still. Then he snapped his thumb and middle finger as though he'd had an idea, and jumped off the bench to run along the garden path.

THE NEXT MORNING, Hannah woke alone. As usual. More unusually, she had spent the night alone for the first time since she had come to Mireworth.

"Did Wycliff not return from looking at the sheep last night?" Hannah took her usual spot at the kitchen table and reached for a piece of toast.

"No, milady. The shepherds have gathered with their flocks for the summer shearing, and he camped out with them. Knowing those men, they were probably awake half the night telling each other tall tales around the fire." Mrs Rossett poured hot chocolate from the pot into a cup for Hannah.

"Oh." The days without his company were tolerable when she had their nights to look forward to. Now even those had been taken from her. "I might go for a walk after breakfast and explore a bit more of the area."

"Very well, milady. With Mary and Charlotte's help, I will start the baking for the big picnic tomorrow, when we all gather to help with washing and shearing the sheep." Mrs Rossett opened the doors to her cavernous larder.

"I will be back to help however I can later on. I find myself in need of a walk this morning." While Hannah had no direction in mind when she left the house and let the spaniel dictate their path, she had a purpose: to be able to think. The bright chestnut dog with her floppy ears chased a scent back and forth. As they walked, the crash of waves against rock and the call of seagulls replaced the chirp of birds and rustle of leaves.

When they reached the path worn along the side of

a hill, Hannah climbed over tussocks. Picking a spot at random, she sat on the grass. She pulled her knees up and hugged them as she stared out at the ocean. Waves foamed and slapped the rock below as though water and earth argued. A vast expanse of sea drew her eye to the horizon, the line smudged where ocean met sky.

Hannah had come to Mireworth with hopes and expectations that had erupted into joy when Wycliff took her in his arms on their first night. Then, the morning had dashed cold water over those dreams when she had awakened alone. She foolishly thought their new physical intimacy would be the missing piece to bring them together in a true marriage. Yet every day she found herself more alone, as Wycliff grew more distant.

Hannah's heart ached and it seemed the breeze picked up her dreams and scattered them over the unfathomable ocean. Tears rolled down her cheeks and were whisked away by the salty wind. Sheba huddled into her side and offered her warmth. One hand rested on the spaniel's head like an anchor point while her mind crashed with thoughts like a stormy sea.

She stared down at the dog. "I don't know what to do, Sheba."

Common sense dictated that she sit her husband down and tell him how she felt. An image appeared in Hannah's mind of a hen-pecked husband listening with deaf ears, as his wife read from a long scroll detailing his faults. She would never be such a wife. For truly, apart from their growing more distant every day, she had little to complain about.

Having discovered through introspection that she loved her husband, she found herself at a loss as to what to do with that knowledge. Life had seemed easier when they dealt with each other as colleagues with a mutual admiration. Love skewed the partnership and dropped a heavy weight onto one side of the scales if there were nothing to balance it. If there could be some tiny indication from Wycliff that he felt the same way, Hannah would consider speaking up and exposing her heart. Then, it would be worth the risk.

A figure in a dark, swirling coat walked along the narrow path. He stopped as he drew near to where she sat and touched the brim of his hat. "Lady Wycliff, what a pleasant surprise."

"Mr Hartley." Hannah couldn't smile, the sadness flowing through her body too deep to allow it.

He narrowed his gaze at her. "I say, is everything quite all right?" Before she could reply, he climbed up the hill and sat next to her. He stared out at the sea, painted in deep tones of green and blue with white crests. "You have chosen a lovely spot to think. But I wonder that the view alone is not helping sort through your troubles."

Hannah drew a ragged sigh and dashed the salt traces of tears from her face. "I am sorry, Mr Hartley, I am not good company at the moment."

He smiled and leaned closer. He sat on the side more buffeted by the wind and his larger frame acted as a shield. "I shall let you in on a secret, Lady Wycliff. I am rather good at offering a listening ear or a handkerchief to those in need. Some would say it is something of a vocation."

That made a small chuckle puncture her dark mood like the flash of a firefly. "I have so much to be grateful for, it seems churlish to bend your ear with my small woes."

Warmth simmered in his eyes that, combined with his tone, created a much needed offer of friendship. "I have a responsibility to all my flock. Anyone who is lost is deserving of my time, regardless of their station in life. And if you will forgive my impertinence, Lady Wycliff, you do look as though you are lost at sea without an anchor to steady you."

If she were lost at sea, an anchor would send her straight to the bottom. What she needed was a boat and a hand to haul her in. Rather than picking holes in the reverend's analogy, though, she laced her hands over her knees and stared at them. Her fingers made a kind of boat with the ocean in the background. If she raised her thumbs, they could almost be masts or sails.

Could she save herself from the ocean inside her? Where did one even start in unburdening such problems? Some were far too intimate to share with anyone, even Lizzie. Hannah doubted the duke rose early, abandoning his bride to awaken alone with only cold sheets beside her, and an emptiness within. No. Harden would sleep late with Lizzie in his arms and only rouse to seek breakfast for her. Which brought to mind another concern—Lizzie had still not replied to any of Hannah's messages, and she could not help but worry.

Hannah let out a long sigh and picked a mundane issue to share with Mr Hartley. "I was never born to this position. While my mother held a high rank when she was alive, my father and I lived a relatively quiet life in her shadow. I find Lady Wycliff has many responsibilities to both the tenants on the estate and the wider community, and I am unaccustomed to having such expectations held of me."

"It can be a lonely road to walk, if you do not have a companion at your side. But I am sure Lord Wycliff is helping you settle into Mireworth." His eyes pierced her and sought out a true answer.

Hannah swallowed. Wycliff had promised to teach her to swim, but she found herself drowning on dry land. "Wycliff has many responsibilities of his own. There is much to be done to revive the estate," she murmured.

Sheba squirmed at her side, their spot too cold for a snooze. She was growing impatient at the inactivity when there were rabbits to flush out of the long grass.

"You do not have to be alone, Lady Wycliff. I offer my services to share your burden. You have only to take my hand, as it were." A serious glint lit Mr Hartley's eyes.

Why couldn't her husband extend such an offer? How easy it would be to unburden herself to the reverend. But a tiny voice made her hold back. "Thank you, Mr Hartley, that is a generous offer. Perhaps you could offer your assistance in directing my efforts toward the tenants? I do not want to pry and they are somewhat reticent around me, but I want to help those who need it the most." Much could be made easier in their lives if leaky roofs were mended and empty tummies filled. Either pride or embarrassment seemed to be stopping the tenants from bringing their problems to the new Lady Wycliff.

The reverend smiled and a warm flush burst through Hannah. "It would be my honour. I was heading out to call upon Mr Miller, if you would care to join me?"

She knew that name. The grandfather of one of the drowned women. A perfect opportunity to at once sate her curiosity and enquire after his welfare. "Thank you, that sounds like a splendid place to start."

He stood and extended his hand. Hannah placed hers in his and found a warm grasp that washed comfort and support over her. The spaniel ran on ahead, bouncing across the path as scents caught her attention. Hannah and Mr Hartley chatted about the village and the forthcoming dance as they walked.

"You may need to take an extra pair of slippers. Many of the men are keen to dance with your ladyship and I doubt you will have much chance to sit down." Mr Hartley had placed Hannah's hand in the crook of his elbow and rested his hand over hers, to steady her on the uneven ground.

The more time she spent with him, the more at ease she found herself. "I am glad it has brought some excitement to the village. I had concerns about whether the sea theme was appropriate, given the recent death."

He fell silent, then cleared his throat before speaking. "Death walks arm in arm with life, and they are a practical sort hereabouts. Many rely on the ocean to support their families and they know she is a force unto herself."

"You speak of the ocean as though it were some type of deity. Is that not a conflict with your religious beliefs?" Hannah recalled her father's associates in the Society of Unnatural Scientific Study. In particular, Reverend Jones possessed a fervent belief that he could call down God to free the trapped remnant of soul in an Afflicted woman. His spiritual beliefs had been shattered when he failed. Hannah thought that particular religious man rather narrow in his view, with no consideration for other religions or types of deities.

Mr Hartley stopped and gestured to the tumultuous ocean. Waves crashed at their feet and foamy peaks rose and fell. "Does she not resemble a pagan goddess? Powerful, unfathomably deep, her arms wrapped around our globe and capable of the greatest mercy and the cruellest acts. Sailors have long referred to the ocean as *she*, and I think only a foolish man would try to downplay her true nature." Then he turned to Hannah with a sheepish smile. "But please don't tell the bishop I said that, if he ever visits. It's not the done thing."

Hannah laughed, genuinely this time and not the hollow mimicry she'd felt earlier. "I promise to hold my silence on your admiration of the ocean. My mother holds similar views and refers to the ocean as one of Mother Nature's handmaidens." The dead mage had an affinity for nature and the weather that remained undiminished by her passing.

They found Mr Miller at his new cottage, on the outskirts of the estate and an easy walk from the village and the tavern.

"Good day to you, Mr Miller!" Mr Hartley called as they approached.

A weathered bench sat in front of the cottage, the timber worn silver by time and the salt-laden wind. The dour man sat upon it, staring off toward the horizon. His face bore deep wrinkles and his hair was white and tousled like peaky waves. He leaned on a cane clutched in both his hands. A pottery jug sat at his feet and a whiff of stale alcohol and sweat tickled Hannah's nose.

"Who's she?" He narrowed his eyes until they nearly disappeared into the wrinkles.

Mr Hartley stopped by the bench. "Lady Wycliff, may I make known to you Abraham Miller. Mr Miller, her ladyship has come to enquire if you are settled in after your recent move and if you need anything."

"Good day, Mr Miller. How do you find the cottage?" Hannah dug inside her for a sliver of happiness and used it to fuel her smile and tone.

Mr Miller grunted. "His lordship threw me out of my own home."

"I understood you could no longer work the land,

which is a terrible shame, to be sure. But in this smaller cottage, you won't have to worry about all the chores going untended." Wycliff had ranted for some time about the state of the Miller farm, the pastures left fallow for too long, and the disrepair of the buildings.

"I was going to get around to mending things and buying sheep. I only needed more time." He cleared his throat and then spat a glob of phlegm in the dirt.

That wasn't the version of events Hannah understood. Wycliff had said Mr Miller was at least six months behind in his rent. From what she'd seen of the state of the old farm, it had no hope of generating any income without the sort of hard work Mr Cramond was prepared to put into the soil.

"I am so sorry that you lost your granddaughter— that must have been quite a blow." Hannah peered over his head and through the window. The cottage appeared orderly, but then he had only been a resident for a few days.

"It was that Cramond, I'm sure of it. He's a monster that dragged her into the ocean. Probably couldn't stand that she would rather help her old grandpa than cook his meals." He shot out the words and the colour rose in his face.

Hannah considered her next words carefully. From what she'd observed of Mr Cramond, he seemed a genial and even-tempered man, unlike the specimen in front of her. A sadness had lingered in the young man's eyes when he spoke of Amy. "Mr Cramond does not seem the type of man to fly into a rage, from what I have observed of him."

"You think it was me, don't you? I know they all say I killed her, but those nasty gossips are all wrong. I'll swear on the Bible that Amy never came home that night," he shouted. Spittle flew to the ground.

"Are you sure, Mr Miller?" Hannah bit her tongue before she asked how he could have known that, if he had been blind drunk that night. Rumour, after all, whispered that he had struck Amy in a drunken rage and thrown her body into the water when he sobered up and realised what he had done.

"I waited all night for her to come back. Always sat up, I did, to make sure she found her own bed safe. That's how I know he did it. I swear to God she never crossed my threshold." His eyes bulged and the whites shone brighter as his face turned deep red.

Mr Hartley placed a restraining hand on the old man's shoulder and eased him back down to the seat. "No one is suggesting otherwise, Mr Miller. Lady Wycliff is merely concerned for your well-being."

"Of course." Mr Miller might be old and drunk, but he seemed adamant that Amy had never come home. Mr Cramond was equally certain she'd left him that evening to walk home. That only left one possibility, and the certainty grew in Hannah that the *someone* Amy had to tell her news hadn't been her grandfather, but another. "Mr Miller, do you know if Amy was seeing anyone other than Mr Cramond?"

He coughed and when he caught his breath, his

colour returned to normal. "Maybe. Sometimes she would say she was heading out to see Cramond, but then he'd turn up on my doorstep and she weren't with him."

That was hardly proof of any other pull on her affections. Amy might simply have been distracted, or changed her mind. "Did she see Mr Seager for any potions?"

Mr Miller barked a coarse laugh that turned into a cough. "Oh, that one. Used to sniff around the farm with a face like a thundercloud, he did."

"Well, we shall leave you to your day, Mr Miller, if you don't require anything." Mr Hartley offered his arm to Hannah.

Hannah let herself be led away, her mind bounding through ideas like Sheba in the meadow. One in particular began to take shape, but she had more enquiries to make first. How she wished she could discuss this with Wycliff. She glanced up at the profile beside her. Although it had to be said, Mr Hartley made a fine companion for the walk home as he told her the history of the village.

17

THE ESTATE DEMANDED MORE than Wycliff's days; his nights also came to be given as sacrifice. The summer shear was a major event, and the farmers and shepherds gathered in the fields of Mireworth beside the river. The men worked together to bring in their flocks to run through the river and, once dry, to be shorn. Working alongside his tenants during the long days gave Wycliff an opportunity to hear their concerns and ideas.

Unfortunately, the evenings ran late, as the men sat around the fire to talk. That turned into a few celebratory drinks, either to toast Wycliff's marriage or to simply mark the end of a hard day. The first night, after consuming more ale than he could recollect, Wycliff fell asleep where he sat by the fire. The next night, he was determined to make it back to Mireworth. He was too old for sleeping on the hard ground when he had a comfortable mattress and a willing wife awaiting him.

By the time he slid off his mare, it was after midnight and the ground tilted and swayed under his feet in a way that reminded him of the miserable time in a ship during a rough sailing. His stomach rebelled and he clutched his middle waiting for the sensation to subside. Instead of crawling into a warm bed with his delectable wife in it, he stumbled to a pile of hay, collapsed, and awoke at dawn to...Barnes.

The hand stared at him from a spot on his chest that made Wycliff go cross-eyed trying to look at him. The hand had one finger tucked under another in a gesture that mimicked a person with their arms folded in disapproval.

"If you want to be useful, fetch me a clean shirt and a coffee," Wycliff grumbled as he sat up.

The hand slid to the ground, saluted with his fore-finger, and then scurried from the stall.

Wycliff hauled himself to the trough outside the stables and immersed his head. Cold water dribbled down his spine and revived his senses. He scooped up handfuls of icy water and scrubbed his face. Stubble clung to his chin, but he would shave later. A sniff of his armpit confirmed that the horrid smell was indeed coming from him.

The rancid shirt was pulled over his head and tossed to the ground, then he plunged his torso into the water trough. He experimented with calling the hound forth and was delighted when the frigid water warmed around him. He stopped when it became tepid, not wanting to harm the animals who wouldn't realise the water had changed temperature.

Snippets of conversation from the previous night emerged from the fog in his head. A group of farmers with a few ales in them gossiped more than women. There was one strand that stuck out—all the men mentioned that Seager possessed the magic potion to cure a pretty woman's ailments. From the accompanying winks and nudges, it was clear what they meant by *magic potion,* and it wasn't anything that came in a vial.

Wycliff had agreed to keep an open mind about the drownings of the three women, but it pained him to linger on the death of Lisbeth. He berated himself for not doing more for his friend. There was a comfort in believing an accident had taken her life. That she must have slipped while watching the storms hit the promontory where she made her home. The alternative placed the fault at his door, for not reaching out earlier to ensure she had the help she needed.

But if Hannah's instincts were right, he did his childhood friend no service by failing to investigate the possibility that another hand might have pushed Lisbeth to her death. It was time for him to have a quiet conversation with Seager and discover how many women of the village he *treated* for their problems. The apothecary displayed a foul temper. Who knew what he would do if provoked? Had he conceivably struck out at one, two, or all three?

Frank lumbered across the yard carrying a folded

shirt in one hand and a tin mug in the other. Barnes trotted ahead.

"Taking a supervisory role, Barnes?" Wycliff asked as he took the mug and shirt from Frank. "I thank you both." He gulped the hot brew, and then balanced the mug on a post while he donned the clean shirt and buttoned his waistcoat over the top. "Shearing begins today, and we have more sheep to swim to wash the fleece. Feel like riding a ewe through the river, Barnes?" Wycliff finished the strong coffee.

Stitched monster and hand had stayed at the house yesterday to assist Hannah. Today they followed Wycliff out to the field, where years ago a sheep-wash had been constructed along the river that bordered Mireworth. At a narrow point sat a bridge with low arches that allowed the water to flow, but stopped the animals from swimming away. On the flat ground next to the river stood a pen to funnel the creatures into taking a dip. Stone walls ran down into the pen and created a narrow corridor where they drove the sheep.

The shepherds used their dogs and crooks to direct the woolly creatures into the top of the funnel, channelling them into the pen. Wycliff stripped off his jacket and rolled up his shirtsleeves to wade out into the water to help the washers. As the sheep sprang from the pen into the river, they were dipped under the surface and the wool cleaned before they were released to clamber out on the other side into another stone-enclosed yard.

By the time they had dipped the last of the sheep

on one side of the river, the first few out the other side were dry and ready to be clipped. One at a time, a worker grabbed a sheep from the pen and herded it to a shearer. The day lengthened as they worked. Everyone had a specific task to perform.

The shearers' backs were drenched with sweat from the hard labour as they wielded the shears, two lethal-looking blades, with expert precision. A sheep would lie on its back between the man's feet as he removed the heavy fleece. Then, once righted, it would bounce away as though reliving its youth as a lamb. Shepherds gathered the shorn flock to graze, waiting to be driven back to pasture.

The midsummer shear of the sheep was a gathering of the community, as many hands were needed to tackle the job. Women threw the fleece onto boards for inspection. Any remaining debris or loose locks were snipped off. Children collected the offcuts, which were stuffed into bags to be used in their homes. Next the fleece was rolled and bundled into sacks and loaded on large carts.

For two days Wycliff worked as hard as the men, taking his turn to drag out a sheep for the shearer. He watched the man flip the creature onto its back, then Wycliff decided he had earned a break. His own back protested the time spent hunkered over and he arched his neck to let his joints pop to ease the ache.

He grabbed a water bottle and stood in the shade, conveniently close to where Seager inspected the bags of loose locks.

"What do you do with the fleece clippings, Seager?" Wycliff asked as he gulped water down a parched throat.

"I remove the lanolin from the wool to make hand creams and lotions that are much in demand by the ladies." The man spoke without looking up as he crammed more snippets of wool into a bag.

"What else do you offer the ladies that they enjoy?" Wycliff pitched his question low so that it would escape the ears of the children running around the pasture. Hannah thought Cramond might be the common link between the three dead women, but Wycliff preferred Seager for that role.

Seager straightened and met Wycliff's gaze. He narrowed his eyes and seemed to chew each word before speaking. "I am the apothecary. I offer many cures for the ailments of the villagers—man, woman, and child."

"Let me speak more plainly, since you seem determined to misunderstand. Were you tending to Lisbeth, Amy, and Sarah?" A gentle breeze stirred and Wycliff tugged on the neck band of his shirt to allow his skin to cool.

"I don't have to tell you who sought my cures." Seager turned his back and opened the next bag of offcuts.

For a moment, Wycliff wondered if this was how Hannah had felt early in their acquaintance. Seager was deliberately obtuse and Wycliff suppressed a strong urge to seize the man by the collar and shake some civility into him. "You can either talk to me here and now, or I will drag you off to the Repository of Forgotten Things until your tongue loosens."

"You cannot do that." Seager turned and his nostrils flared like those of a bull about to charge.

Wycliff took another long drink. "You're an aftermage. That gives the Ministry of Unnaturals dominion over you. I could find you a nice cell next to the Afflicted incarcerated because they cannot control their urges. They rot on their feet, oozing bodily fluids that heal when they are given their allotted slice of *pickled cauliflower*. The stench is stomach-churning, but I'm sure as an apothecary you will find it a fascinating chance to study them up close."

Seager yanked on the bag's drawstring, pulling it tight before kicking it to one side. "I treated all three women. The only one whose condition might have led to her death was Lisbeth Wolfe. But you already knew that, didn't you?"

Wycliff's hand tightened around the water bottle. He wanted to believe Lisbeth had found a kind of peace on the promontory, not that loneliness and desperation had made her end it all. "So your potions didn't help her?"

"Lisbeth was much improved. Ask anyone." Seager spat the words.

"Were you intimate with her?" He had no romantic claim on Lisbeth, but the idea of her rolling around with Seager turned his stomach. As her lifelong friend, he thought she deserved far better.

The other man's eyes widened. "Of course not! One can offer a woman friendship and advice without bedding her, or is that a revelation to you, my lord?"

Wycliff ground his teeth. While he wrangled his own temper under control, he indulged in imagining how satisfying it would be to smack his fist into Seager's chin. If for nothing else, he deserved it for his continued rudeness to Hannah. Another part of Wycliff wondered what deep scar Seager covered with his prickly exterior. One porcupine recognised another. Thankfully, Hannah had worked her way through Wycliff's quills to find the man underneath.

"What of Amy and Sarah? What ailed them?"

Seager fisted his hands and for a moment, Wycliff thought he would be denied the information he sought. "Mrs Rivers sought assistance to conceive. Amy Miller sought relief from constant headaches. Although she refused to hear my advice that the biggest cause was that drunken grandfather of hers."

"Did you offer them anything else, aside from the relevant potions?" The more they spoke, the more Wycliff sensed the other man was hiding something. He only needed to run it to ground.

"No. As difficult as that is for you to believe, I did not offer to cure them with my *magic wand*." He flung his arms up into the air.

Wycliff grunted. The apothecary might have tried and been rebuked. Who knew? Dead women couldn't recount what had happened in their last moments.

"What of the potions? Was there anything in them that might have affected their balance?"

"I am most careful of my ingredients and customers are warned if there are side effects such as dizziness. None of the women took anything that would cause them to lose their footing in the dark. You will have to find another party to blame." Seager bent to pick up his sacks.

Not wanting to waste any civilities upon the man, Wycliff nodded and stalked away. Movement on the brow of the hill caught his eye and soon a cart appeared, drawn by a solid horse. Hannah held the reins with Mrs Rossett beside her, Mary and Charlotte in the back. Wycliff wiped a handkerchief over his brow and headed in their direction as Hannah pulled the horse to a halt.

"It is a pleasant surprise to see you here." More than that, he had not seen her face or held her form for two days, and he missed her closeness, her faint lavender fragrance, and the twinkle in her eye when she considered mischief. Most of all, he missed the way she murmured his Christian name when they were alone and he kissed his way up her neck.

"Mrs Rossett has commanded her troops for the last two days. We have worked hard under her direction and, I hope, brought enough to feed everyone," Hannah said as she clasped his hand.

In the back of the cart were crammed numerous boxes and baskets with cloths tucked into the tops and a delicious aroma wafting from underneath. His stomach growled and reminded him that he hadn't had breakfast.

Wycliff kept possession of Hannah's hand and raised it to his lips. "You are a marvel," he murmured against her skin. He would thank her more fully later.

A becoming flush raced over her cheeks. "Mrs Rossett said the summer shearing was a big gathering of the villagers. I don't need magic to know that men who are working hard will be hungry."

Children swarmed the cart like rats on cheese, no doubt drawn by the odours dancing across the meadow. Eager hands unloaded the boxes and baskets and laid them out on a makeshift table.

Wycliff let go of Hannah to summon the workmen. They tugged their caps and thanked Hannah as they dove into the spread of meat pies, savoury pastries, and biscuits the women had made.

Wycliff and Hannah sat on a blanket in the sun, although she put up a parasol to shade her face, and cheerful conversation flowed around them. While he worked hard and barely had time to spend with Hannah during the day, it made the quiet moments in her company all the more valuable. Each day brought a greater sense of satisfaction at what he could achieve. He even proudly displayed a blister on his palm, something that would make the fops in London faint.

After their meal, he took Hannah's arm while they strolled along the river in the shade of the weeping willows. He wanted privacy to tell her what he had discerned so far. "I spoke to Seager. He was indeed dispensing cures for the three dead women."

"Oh? I found Lisbeth's and Sarah's records among his notebooks, but not one for Amy. Did he say what he treated her for?"

"Apparently Amy suffered headaches. Seager also said that none of the potions he dispensed would cause the women to be dizzy or lose their balance." The potions might be blameless, but that didn't absolve the man. Not yet.

"Then if we continue with the hypothesis that their deaths were not accidental, we must consider what else might have bound the women." She reached up to snag a leaf to spin between her fingers. "Although, from talking to those left behind, the only thing I can find they all shared was loneliness. Lisbeth was isolated by the community, Sarah's husband is a shepherd and spent long hours away from home, and Amy was somewhat alone in dealing with her grandfather. Having met him, I am not surprised to learn she endured headaches."

"We may have some fiend with a demented sense of how to cure them, or possibly a spurned lover who tried his luck with all three. But I agree, if we pursue this line of thought we are grasping at what links them and why they were targeted." While he still struggled to believe the deaths anything other than terrible accidents, he approached it with an open mind for Hannah's sake.

A whisper from long ago snaked through his mind.

Hannah had stirred up the old story of two men who had drowned one summer fifty years ago. He waved a hand across his face to brush aside the tale. How many people had drowned in the village over the last fifty years? Probably fifty, since the ocean claimed roughly one a year. Sometimes a fisherman's boat was caught out in a storm and overturned, or a child was snared in an undercurrent while swimming alone. Or someone walking the cliffs stumbled and fell.

They had seen too many unnatural murders in London over the preceding months, and were jumping at shadows.

Hannah let out a sigh and turned to face him. She twisted her fingers in the linen of his shirt. "There is another option. I may have to concede that my husband is right, and I am seeing murder where there is none."

"I have a suspicion that such a concession may be a rare occurrence. I might start a diary when we return to Mireworth, to record such events." He tried to school his features into a stern expression, but the sparkle in her eyes undid him. So he kissed her instead.

18

Later that week, Hannah spent the morning scrubbing yet more panes in the conservatory before deciding she needed an afternoon off. Given she held the title of lady of the house, she worked harder than a new scullery maid. She removed her apron, and washed off the grime that had run from the brush down her fingers and arms.

"I'm going for a walk to find Lisbeth's cottage." For some reason, she had put off finding the isolated cottage. Perhaps she was even worried that Lisbeth's spectre might still cling to the stones and whisper of carefree days spent with Wycliff. Hannah fetched her warmest pelisse and a bonnet. Sheba began running in circles at the signs of an imminent walk.

"You take care out there, milady—it's exposed to every gust of wind and the paths are narrow. I'll send Frank to fetch you if the weather turns." Mrs Rossett wore a worried look as Hannah prepared to leave.

"I promise to be careful. The dance is not far away now, and I don't want to miss it." Hannah waved to the housekeeper and set off.

Sheba barked and shot away through the grass. Hannah called the spaniel, to ensure they both walked in the right direction. Today she had a purpose more investigative than emotional—to find the remote spot where Lisbeth, Wycliff's childhood companion, had once lived.

By the time Hannah laboured up another hill, she was starting to question her determination to walk. Her breath came short in her lungs and her calves protested the constant exercise. While she was no riding enthusiast, a horse might have been a better mode of transport.

Then she reached the brow of the hill and found her exertions almost over. The promontory ran out before her like a finger pointing at the horizon, as the land mass narrowed and thrust itself into the water. Waves crashed on either side and there, near the end, perched a sturdy little cottage with a most determined tree growing next to it.

"Oh, I say." Hannah stood for a moment and soaked in the view that possessed a wild and lonely beauty. "Come on, Sheba." Hannah began her descent and trod a worn path that created a spine down the point to the cottage.

The land flattened out as she approached, revealing that the cottage didn't perch quite so precariously on the edge as it appeared from above. One side of the point had a gentle roll down to the water and even a crescent of sand. The other side fell away sharply, with rocks far below. Was this where Wycliff had caught his friend about to hurl herself into the ocean? In her mind's eye, Hannah saw Wycliff galloping down the hill on his horse to pull Lisbeth back from the brink.

Tears burned behind Hannah's eyes, as she imagined the dead woman driven by an utter sense of hopelessness. Did the vast ocean before her echo her loneliness, or had a voice on the wind promised to end it?

Hannah stepped back from the edge and the pull of another woman's memories. Instead, she contemplated the tree deformed by the action of the wind—its very existence a sign of life determined to survive despite adversity. She couldn't discern the species of tree, other than *hardy*. A trace of salt spray had dried to the bark and the few needles it sprouted were narrow and a deep green. Branches spread over the roof of the cottage as though it offered additional protection against the elements. Perhaps to repay the shelter and companionship the cottage provided to the tree.

The cottage where Lisbeth Wolfe once lived remained untenanted, its grey stone walls weathered by the action of wind and salt. Hannah peered in the windows, indulging her curiosity to the fullest since there was no one to witness her pressing her nose to the glass. On impulse, she banged on the door latch and surprise surged within her when the ancient piece of timber creaked open.

She paused on the threshold, unsure what to do.

Violating a dead woman's home seemed a step too far, nor could she bring herself to rifle through the belongings that might remain inside. Instead, she ensured her boot tips stayed firmly on the outside edge of the door frame and craned her neck. The cottage comprised one well-sized room. An enormous fireplace dominated one end, the hearth large enough to swing a pot from the hook embedded in the blackened stones. A cast iron plate sat to one side that could be swung over the embers to become a cooking surface.

Cupboards were built into the wall on either side of the fireplace. A bench ran under a window overlooking the sea. The wall opposite the fireplace held a bed, the mattress stripped of its bedding. In the middle of the room sat a square table with four wooden chairs. A worn but comfortable-looking armchair occupied a spot close to the fire. A small footstool huddled close, ready for the owner to rest their feet after a long day.

From the outside, Hannah thought the cottage would be a bleak and lonely thing, but when she cast the interior with a golden hue and imagined a blazing fire in the hearth, instead she saw it as a quiet retreat. The sort of place a woman could be alone with her thoughts while sheltering from the storms outside.

Mrs Rossett said Lisbeth had a gift for predicting the weather, and the cottage was certainly bombarded by everything nature could hurl at it. You didn't need an aftermage gift to watch a storm heading for the shore, but it was the unseen change of weather that would catch the fishermen of the village unawares.

High-pitched barking caught Hannah's attention. She yanked the door shut and hurried to find her little dog. The noise came from the inland side of the cottage, where the tortured tree spread its boughs. Sheba's tail wagged, a bright chestnut splash against the drab grey of the stone and the gnarled bark of the tree.

"What have you found, girl?" Hannah knelt next to the dog.

The spaniel's upper body had disappeared into a hole and she scrabbled with her front paws. A rabbit, perhaps? A metallic *clunk* caught Hannah's attention and she used both hands to haul the eager dog from the burrow. Dirt coated the spaniel's nose and face, but she sat on the grass as asked and tilted her head to watch.

Hannah stuck a hand in the hole thinking she would find a scared rabbit, but her fingertips scraped cool metal. Grabbing the object, she freed it from its earthly prison. The dog had uncovered a small metal tin buried at the base of the tree. It was roughly square and no longer than her palm, and the sides were dented and the metal laced with red ribbons of rust.

With the tin on her lap, she contemplated what to do. She assumed it had been placed in the hole by the resident of the cottage, otherwise it was a dashed odd hiding place for anyone else to use. To confirm her idea required her to open the box and peer inside. That seemed at odds with her decision not to violate Lisbeth's memory by searching the cottage.

But surely it was fate that made Sheba dig here? A small voice in her head gave a dissenting opinion.

"Well, I walked all this way to see if I could learn something about Lisbeth Wolfe, and this might be the clue I seek." Decision made, Hannah prised the lid open against protesting hinges. Within sat a bundle of letters, tied with a faded red ribbon, the name *Lisbeth* written on the uppermost one in a neat and restrained hand.

"Whose letters were you hiding?" Hannah murmured as she picked up the bundle.

"Lady Wycliff! Is that you? Is everything all right?" a familiar voice hailed her.

With her back to him, Hannah shoved the collection of letters into the interior pocket of her pelisse. Then she closed the lid of the tin.

She turned to find Mr Hartley, a coat buttoned up to his neck and a short top hat wedged firmly on his head to prevent the wind snatching it away. He held a gnarled walking stick in one hand and had a battered leather satchel slung over his shoulder.

"Mr Hartley. What a surprise to see you here. I am quite well, thank you. Sheba disappeared down a hole —I thought in pursuit of a rabbit, but she dug out this tin." Relief tinged with guilt washed through her that she no longer had the dead woman's private letters clutched in her hands.

"I often take a constitutional out this way. There is something beautiful about this spot, as though from here I can more easily commune with our Creator." He knelt next to her and stared at the tin. "May I?" he asked with a hand extended.

"Of course," Hannah murmured and passed the box to him.

The reverend held it by his head and shook it. "Sounds empty." He flipped the top open with his thumb and stared within before turning it upside down.

"That is a relief. At least Sheba has not disturbed a pirate's buried treasure." Hannah brushed the remains of dirt from her pelisse and skirts.

"Nor was it something of great value that belonged to Miss Wolfe." Mr Hartley stared at Hannah. On closer inspection, his sage green eyes contained grey flecks, like moss that clings to a tree's bark.

He has a soulful gaze, filled with kindness. She needed to watch her words in case she blurted out too much. The letters weighed down one side of her pelisse, but she held her tongue. Instead, she sought another topic. "I found myself most curious about this cottage. It seems such a desolate spot to make one's home, don't you think?"

Mr Hartley slid the tin back into its hiding place, and then offered a hand to Hannah to help her rise. She accepted his gentle touch.

The reverend kept hold of Hannah's hand. "Miss Wolfe chose it quite deliberately, I am told. She had a slight gift for predicting the weather and wanted to be closer to the ocean to sense the storms and winds that rolled off her."

"That is what our housekeeper told me. Did you

know Miss Wolfe at all?" Hannah cast one last look at Lisbeth's refuge against all that the world hurled at her.

"She came to services on a regular basis and possessed a lovely singing voice. She is much missed during the hymns," he said as they strolled along the spine of the promontory.

"I understand she lost her life out here." Hannah plucked at a strand in her mind.

"Yes. A terrible tragedy. No one knows what happened. While I do not like to indulge in village gossip, some whisper that she was much enamoured of a gentleman and that when he rejected her, it was too much for her heart to bear. And so, she threw herself from these cliffs." Mr Hartley used his walking stick to brush aside a piece of wood on the path.

Had someone broken her heart, or had a spurned lover lashed out in anger? So many possible scenarios could have played out with only the silent cottage and tree as witnesses.

"I am most curious, Mr Hartley. Do you have any clue as to the identity of this callous lover?" Hannah waited for his response, certain the name of Mr Seager would be spoken next. The man's rude demeanour might have its root in guilt at being the cause of Lisbeth's death.

Mr Hartley stopped and faced Hannah. "Yes, but I do not wish to cause you distress, Lady Wycliff."

Tendrils of doubt wriggled into her mind. "I am hardier than I appear, Mr Hartley. Having made such a comment, you are now compelled to tell me, or I shall imagine far worse."

He cast his gaze downward and spoke in a low tone. "I believe that his lordship had been close to Lisbeth for some years. She had a wild kind of beauty that some men find irresistible. Keeping such an isolated cottage allowed them to maintain their privacy when he was at Mireworth and away from the prying eyes of the village. I do not know what transpired between the two of them, but to this day, I blame myself that I did not do enough to ease her suffering."

Wycliff. A chill wind swirled through Hannah's soul. Had Lisbeth declared her love for him, only to be rejected? How horrible, to love someone who did not return such affection.

Worry creased the reverend's brow. "I'm sorry if I have upset you by repeating such a rumour, Lady Wycliff. I only wanted to give you a full account of what might have happened here. Besides, such is the way with nobles, is it not? They rouse women to admire them, only for the lord's ardour to cool and their paramours to be abandoned. Lords are not like us more common men, who give our hearts only once."

He would give his heart only once. The words made a sigh heave in her chest. Hannah placed what she hoped was a kind smile on her lips. "I am not concerned, Mr Hartley. I am aware that his lordship and Miss Wolfe were childhood friends." Had childhood friends become young lovers? Despite being married to Wycliff, Hannah had no inkling as to the state of his heart.

Her husband certainly roused Hannah's admiration, but at times she wondered if Wycliff loved the estate and his sheep more than she, or any other woman, for that matter. She rubbed her chest but it did nothing to ease the ache there. How she longed for Lizzie's advice. Yet again, and in a somewhat louder tone, the sensible part of her mind argued that the easiest course of action was to confront Wycliff and demand to know outright the depth of any emotion he felt toward her. But the quiet and reserved part of her that preferred to hide in a library shuddered at the very idea.

If he declared he admired her but would never love her, how would she go on?

Far better to hypothesise possible scenarios, but never validate the experiment with cold, hard truth. That way, she could exist in two worlds simultaneously. In one version, Wycliff swore his lifelong friendship but no more, leaving the cold void inside her to fester and consume her over the years. In another marvellous world, her husband declared his most ardent love for her.

With only a sliver of her attention, she chatted with Mr Hartley on the return journey and they parted company at a fork in the road, where one arm of the milestone pointed to Mireworth and the other to the village of Selham. Back at the estate, and needing time alone with her thoughts, Hannah sought out the library.

The poor room, cut in half by Wycliff's grandfather, possessed only one window to illuminate its soaring wall of shelves that should have been crammed with books. Once, a grand chandelier had lit the room and protected the books from the ravages of sunlight. Now it resembled a tomb, the solid desk like a sarcophagus left in the middle of the stripped floor.

She padded across the floor to the window. The built-in seat offered no comfort, its padded cushions removed long ago, but she didn't mind. Tucking her feet up under her, Hannah huddled in the corner and pulled the bundle of letters from her pocket.

First, she closed her eyes and offered a silent apology to Lisbeth for what she was about to do. Then Hannah untied the ribbon and pulled free the first letter. Angling it to what light came in through the window, she read the declarations of love it contained, the restrained and tidy hand at odds with the outpouring of emotion. The writer confessed to an ocean of love for Lisbeth, if only she would return his affection.

"I am lost without you. Say you love me, otherwise alone, I will drown in my despair," Hannah whispered the words to the empty library.

Then she closed her eyes and rested her head against the cold wood, the letter clutched to her chest. *"Alone, I will drown in my despair,"* she repeated. Tears welled in her eyes. Had Wycliff penned those words to his childhood sweetheart? Although that would be at odds with the tale Mr Hartley told of Wycliff breaking Lisbeth's heart. In these letters, the writer asked Lisbeth to declare her love.

Melancholy rippled through Hannah's body and her fingers tightened on the paper. Then she sat up and stared at the letter. When on earth had she decided to cast herself as the heroine in a badly written gothic romance? Honestly, she had created a wallow of self-pity for herself almost as large as the ocean.

"Where did you leave your common sense, Hannah?" she chastised herself.

Yes, she loved Wycliff. Yes, the way he slipped from their shared bed before dawn and left her alone hurt. But unless she grew a spine and tackled the issue head on, it would never be resolved. The loneliness would fester until she, too, flung open her arms to welcome the ocean's fatal embrace.

"No. That's not right." That idea snagged on another in her mind and the two combined into a larger idea. Hannah jumped down from the window seat and knelt on the floor to arrange the letters around her to study them.

Surrounded by words of love and despair, Hannah sat back on her heels and reviewed what she knew. Three women had drowned, but the more she learned of their lives, the less she believed the gossip about their shared fates.

Amy Miller had accepted Mr Cramond's proposal, but seemed troubled and had gone to break the news to *another*. Sarah Rivers was married, childless, and alone —that created parallels to Hannah's own marriage. What if she had sought solace and understanding from another, but no more? Lisbeth Wolfe had supposedly been spurned by her lover and taken her own life. But that didn't match the content of the letters—what if she had refused him?

The more Hannah considered the lives and deaths of the three women, the more she began to see another hand at work. One that did not respond well to being rejected.

What if Amy dreaded telling another man that she was engaged to Mr Cramond that night, and would see him no more? What if whoever wrote these letters and claimed not to be able to live without Lisbeth chose to end her life instead? That left Sarah Rivers, who had argued with her husband and stormed off to think. Or had she sought a shoulder to cry on that night? Someone who might have seized a moment of vulnerability, only to be spurned?

"Oh, I see you now," Hannah whispered. "And I will find you."

19

A NEW SENSE of determination flared into life. Hannah *would* uncover the truth about the women's deaths. That meant another conversation with Libby Tant, to determine if she knew of anyone her sister may have confided in. Hannah also decided the hidden tower would yield its secrets to her—which would require a more corporeal plan.

"Do you know where Mrs Tant lives?" Hannah asked Mrs Rossett that morning. Wycliff had found a gardening book for Hannah, and she flipped the pages looking at brightly coloured illustrations. She found herself anticipating her parents' visit. Her mother would know what to plant to breathe new life into the conservatory.

"Oh, yes. They have a lovely cottage up above the village. It will soon be rather cramped for them, I imagine, with the new one about to appear, if it's not here already." Mrs Rossett stood at the bench, a limp pheasant before her as she plucked feathers from the creature and dropped them into a bucket.

"She did look imminent last I saw her." Hannah wondered what she could take along for the new mother—it wouldn't do to turn up on the doorstep both uninvited and empty-handed. One of the crates in the study contained wooden soldiers and horses. She would ask Wycliff if any could be spared. Mrs Tant might appreciate a diversion to keep her children occupied.

"When the man dropped off the milk this morning, he said his wife—she's the midwife—had been fetched to attend Mrs Tant." The denuded bird was placed in the sink for a wash and the housekeeper wiped fluff from her fingers.

"Probably not a good day to visit, then." Hannah had little experience with babies, but she should probably wait at least a day or two before imposing on a woman who had just given birth.

"If you ask me, she's probably popping the babe out now so she can attend the dance." The washed pheasant next had its internal cavity inspected.

Hannah stifled a laugh as she watched the housekeeper at work. Given how Mrs Rossett called autopsies a *city thing*, she was doing a fine job of conducting a similar examination of their dinner. "Well, perhaps I might return to the tower today instead, and examine the stairwell. There may be a doorway leading down that I have overlooked."

The housekeeper patted the bird dry and then

picked up a bunch of herbs, tied with string. "Oh, speaking of that, his lordship said to tell you he remembered where the plans are, and that you would find them in the Oriental cabinet in the billiards room."

"Oh, brilliant. Thank you." Hannah gulped down the last of her tea and then returned to the study to fetch her glow lamp.

Armed and ready, she pushed into the billiards room and bit her lip to stop herself from crying out. The room wore half the library like a beautiful animal skin draped around the shoulders of a hunter. The marble fireplace remained, but the wall on either side had been demolished, leaving the chimney exposed. Likewise, the bookshelves were gone, but the metal gantry remained as a spine that stretched on either side of the solid brick chimney.

Hannah placed a hand on the cool mantel. Veins in a silvery grey swirled through the marble and tiny specks shimmered. "One day, you will be restored."

The billiards table squatted on the other side of the fireplace and claimed more space than Henry VIII's monstrous bed. Probably its size had saved it from being sold. Hannah couldn't imagine how it had originally been squeezed in through the doors. A sheet covered the felt and Hannah peeked underneath at the green surface so similar to closely mown grass. She recalled the table in Baron Medwin's house; thankfully, this one was free of bloodthirsty puppets.

"The Oriental cabinet," she murmured to herself as she surveyed the rest of the room.

Sideboards, paintings, rugs, and chairs had all been stripped from the room, but a dark wood cabinet that hunkered in a corner drew her eye. It was easily eight feet tall and six feet wide, and closer inspection revealed scenes had been carved over the entire surface. Pagodas stood before flowing rivers. Cranes waded out into the water, and ladies in kimonos fanned themselves from where they lounged under spreading cherry trees.

Deep red tassels hung from the doors and they swayed as Hannah pulled them open, to find the cabinet might once have been a wardrobe. The shelves in the upper half were empty. The lower half comprised drawers of various depths such as a lady might use for rolled stockings and underthings. She pulled the top drawer open and papers fought to escape. She plucked a few at random and found the pages covered in drawings that seemed to be sketches of gardens, plants, and water features.

"Oh, I wonder if you will show me what the grounds used to look like. The conservatory pond and statue might be among you." Adventures in horticulture would have to wait for another day. Her current mission was architectural in nature.

A middle drawer housed numerous long leather cylinders fastened with buckles. Hannah rolled one over and a label read *Farm cottage*, and another said *Stables and outbuildings*.

"Please all be properly labelled as to your contents," she whispered.

The next one rotated in slow motion and read *Mireworth 1701*. She only hoped her luck continued and the actual plans were within and not a drawing of the sheep-wash. She unbuckled the top and held the lamp close to see tightly rolled paper within. Glimpses of a wall with windows confirmed it did indeed seem to be a house plan.

Carrying her booty to the kitchen, Hannah tipped out the plans onto the table directly under the skylight. Bottles of condiments held down each corner and fought the plans' natural urge to roll back up. The aged paper had yellowed in places, but fortunately the cabinet and the storage cylinder had kept it safe from hungry mice.

Hannah oriented herself, letting her fingers walk through the drawing. "Entrance, library...oh." On paper, the library was no longer sliced in half. Here, it possessed two windows overlooking the drive and, when she squinted at the squiggles, a spiral staircase up to the gantry. Those pieces now looked down on the slumbering billiards table. She tapped the lines of the desecrated room and repeated her promise that one day, it would be returned to its correct proportions.

"Where are you hiding?" she whispered to the tower. From what she had observed from inside, she knew roughly the space the tower occupied. While not quite on a corner, it was near one end on the northeast side.

Yet where she expected to find the twelfth-century construction, the plan showed only a void. Hannah traced corridors—one ran down one side of the empty space and on the other side was a narrow room with no apparent reason for existing. To make certain her finger trod the right spot, Hannah examined the other rooms on the lower floor. Here were the study that served as their bedroom, the library, a parlour, and the network of rooms that comprised the service areas, kitchen, and staff quarters.

"Now this is curious." She sat back and closed her eyes, seeing again the view from the south-facing windows.

"What is, milady?" Mrs Rossett asked from her spot at the end of the table. She had moved on from the pheasant and now rolled out dough to make biscuits.

Hannah opened her eyes and looked again at the spot where her brain said the tower had to be. But there was no door, no opening, not even a scribble saying *ancient tower*. "There's nothing here, only an empty space where it should be."

"So that tells you where it is." With the dough flat, the housekeeper picked up a star-shaped metal cutter. She pressed it into the dough, removed the raw biscuit, and placed it on a baking pan.

Hannah stared at the void left on the sheet of rolled dough—a perfect star shape remained. "Of course. The journal! The Lord Wycliff who built this house wrote, *since the tower cannot be torn down I shall at least conceal the damned thing.* That is what he did. It is not mentioned, nor does there appear to be any door marked to give away its presence."

"How will you get into the lower level, then?" More stars were cut out and placed on the tray, until only thin ribbons of dough were left to connect the empty spaces.

"I shall examine the corridor first, somewhere between it and the library. It is possible there is a concealed door such as I used to gain access on the second level." Now that she had an idea of what to do, excitement raced through her.

With her glow lamp in hand, Hannah headed for the library.

"I know where you are," she murmured to the room as she touched a griffin's head on her way past.

Behind the curved stairs, and running alongside the library, was a dark corridor. Hannah clutched the lantern more tightly. The inky darkness reminded her of how Wycliff had disappeared the day her mother asked him to search for a way to the underworld. A chill swept over her and she rubbed the heel of her hand up her arm to dispel it. She paced the length of the corridor that appeared to serve no purpose. At the end stood a slim doorway.

"Aha!" With a sense of triumph, she jiggled the door handle.

The metal protested and the wood seemed stiff in the frame, but the door swung open...to reveal a tiny sliver of a room with a large window overlooking the curved drive. A built-in seat on the wall opposite the window would afford a grand view of any arriving visitors. She could imagine children wriggling on the bench, waiting to be the first to spot their father's return.

Since the light was better in what she promptly dubbed the *waiting room*, Hannah took the opportunity to feel every seam in the panelling. None gave to her fingertips, nor did there appear any doorway to the space beyond, given the way the seat was attached to the wall. From idle curiosity, she lifted the wooden seat, to reveal an empty storage chamber beneath.

"Blast." As she went to drop the lid, she stopped.

A spot caught her eye, somewhat darker than the rest of the inside of the storage space. She propped the lid open. When Hannah moved the lamp closer, she found a rounded hole at the bottom of the wall and tucked under the seat. Reaching in, her fingers found nothing. No wall blocked their progress.

She perched on the side of the open seat and considered the implications. It could be a hole eaten by a very large and hungry rodent, but it edges were too smooth. But why make a tiny entrance to the space behind? What a shame only a hand fit within.

A hand!

Barnes would fit through the tiny doorway and could tell Hannah what he found on the other side. However, if it were as dark as the corridor, he wouldn't see much. Although he didn't possess eyes, for whatever magical reason he still required a light source to find his way about. There might be a way for Barnes to take a small glow lamp through with him. First,

Hannah would ensure there wasn't another way to the imprisoned tower beyond.

Inch by inch, she examined the panelling in the dark corridor. Every join in the wallpaper made excitement surge inside her, only to plummet when her fingernails found nothing but plaster behind. After some hours, she finally declared herself vanquished. If there was a secret door, it had won this round of hide and seek.

"Barnes it is," she said to the empty hall as she walked back to the kitchen.

Hannah returned to her work cleaning panes in the conservatory. Fortunately, Frank arrived for lunch with the hand perched on his shoulder.

"Master...no...need," Frank whispered in his stilted way. Then he dropped into a chair with a thud.

Wycliff might not need them, but Hannah would put them to use. "Excellent. Since I have you for the afternoon, Barnes, I have a task for you, if you feel up to a bit of solo exploration."

The hand jumped to the tablecloth and scuttled to where she sat. The hand sat on the heel of his palm and waved one finger in a *carry on* gesture.

"There is a hole I want you to venture into and report to me if you find anything beyond." Now that Hannah had the house plans, Barnes could draw on the empty space what he discovered.

The hand gave a thumbs up and then scuttled over the side and curled up on a chair to wait.

After lunch, Hannah led her team of explorers to

the narrow waiting room. With nothing to do except be an anchor in case something on the other side latched on to Barnes, Frank stood by the window and tapped on the glass at the birds flying past.

Hannah lowered Barnes into the space under the seat. Then she set her small travelling lamp down by the hole.

"I need you to go in there and tell me if there is an empty room beyond, or if you find the base of the tower." Hannah tapped the top of the glow mushroom. She had wrapped a piece of twine around it and then looped it around the wrist of Barnes.

He waved his index finger in a kind of salute and then set off, dragging the light behind him the way a horse pulled a plough. Little by little, the light faded away.

Like Frank, the only thing Hannah could do was wait. She didn't want to drop the lid to sit on the seat, in case Barnes rushed back through. Instead, she took up a vigil by the window. Beyond the dirty glass lay an uninspiring view. The once clipped lawn had transformed into a tangled mess of weeds and brambles. Even the gravel had succumbed to neglect and needed a good weeding and a new top layer. More tasks to add to their never-ending list. When the estate recovered its finances, they would need a team of industrious gardeners to wrestle the grounds back into shape. Thinking of pleasure gardens seemed so frivolous when the roof leaked and the windows were cracked.

After nearly an hour, the hand reappeared, dragging the glowing mushroom.

Hannah removed the twine from the wrist and picked up Barnes. "Well?" she asked, almost unable to voice her question with so much excitement pressing in her chest. "Is the tower beyond?"

Barnes wagged his first finger up and down in a *yes* motion.

Delight burst through Hannah. It was there! At least the builders hadn't cut the tower off at the knees, leaving the upper levels. She had only to make a hole in the wall to reach it herself.

Barnes tapped on her thumb and Hannah stopped imagining large holes in the plaster. He moved his finger back and forth, which meant *no*.

"No? No what? You did find the tower and not some other strange construction?" Hannah tried to interpret the gestures.

Yes, he waggled, he had definitely found it.

"But there is a problem?" That could be the only explanation for the no. "Is the lower floor full of rubble?"

No.

Sometimes, trying to communicate with a disembodied hand was remarkably frustrating. What could he be trying to tell her? Then her heart sank. "Did they brick in the bottom of the tower?"

He responded with a so-so motion, which meant she was close to guessing the correct answer. "There's no door?"

Thumbs up.

Bother. A tower with no door. How Rapunzel-ish. Or it might be there, but unclear in the dim light. She had sent Barnes in with only a tiny glow lamp, which might have missed a ground floor entrance such as a postern gate, or cracks if it had been bricked in at some point.

Wycliff had agreed that Lady Wycliff had dominion over the house. Did his newfound tolerance extended to holes in the walls? Hannah decided to wait until her husband returned at dinnertime to ask, before she directed Frank to knock through the plaster. Wycliff might even remember another hidden doorway that had escaped Hannah's explorations.

"There is another matter, Frank, while I have you alone." Hannah dropped the lid on the bench seat and sat. Then she patted the spot next to her.

The giant bent his knees and lowered himself. The wood groaned, but held under his weight. He faced Hannah with deep lines in his brow.

"I wanted to talk to you about Mary," Hannah said to alleviate his worry in case he thought he had done something wrong.

"Love...Mary," Frank whispered.

Barnes hopped onto the monster's knee and gave a thumbs up. Apparently he either agreed with Frank or was confessing his own affection for the maid. Hannah wasn't sure which, nor did she want to dwell on it for too long.

"Do you wish to marry her?" As Lady Wycliff,

Hannah decided to take matters into her own hands after all. There might be a way to prod Frank into proposing while making it appear spontaneous for Mary.

Frank nodded. Then he tapped his chest and pointed to his mouth. "Words. Hard."

Barnes bounced up and down on Frank's knee and waved his fingers in the air.

"Are you offering to assist, Barnes?" Hannah might have laughed at the idea, but she was already turning it over in her mind. A helping hand was *exactly* what Frank needed. "What do you say, Frank? Are you willing to let Barnes help you ask the question? If so, I would like to give you a ring for Mary."

"Yesss." Frank grinned and showed all the teeth crammed in his jaws.

She clapped her hands as ideas spun in her head. "Very well, gentlemen. Let us concoct a plan."

In the study, Hannah unrolled the piece of velvet containing her jewellery. She knew exactly which piece to give to Frank. The ring had often been admired by Mary and some impulse had made Hannah include it for this trip. A single pearl clasped in a deep pink enamel setting, it reminded Hannah of the dress Mary had admired in the village. Which gave her another idea.

She handed the ring to Frank. As he plucked it from her fingers, a tear welled up in his eyes and he leaned down and kissed her cheek.

The happiness on his face eased a little of the loneliness inside Hannah. Perhaps her forte in life was to organise fairy-tale weddings for Unnatural creatures? Although finding the perfect match for Barnes might prove to be quite a challenge, unless she stumbled upon an unattached lady's foot.

20

THAT AFTERNOON, Hannah bombarded Wycliff with questions as soon as he walked through the kitchen door.

He listened as he washed his hands, but shook his head as he dried them. "I'm not aware of any door to the bottom of the tower. I admit it didn't excite my curiosity that much to search for one. Since you will not be deterred, I cannot see any problem with making a hole in the wall to admit us."

Hannah bounced on her toes, then kissed Wycliff's cheek. "Thank you."

"Although I did think to *repair* Mireworth, not make her more dishevelled." He frowned, but ruined it with the laughter simmering in his dark eyes.

Ideas bubbled in her head as to how to knock through to the tower. They needed a large hammer, or possibly a metal bar, depending on how the wall was constructed. They would also need lanterns to reveal what Wycliff's great-great-(or however many greats)-grandfather sought to conceal. The little Barnes had managed to convey to her indicated that the space beyond sat in inky darkness.

"I assume you will want Frank for the demolition work and the tools you require will be found out in the stables," Wycliff murmured as he took the cup of light ale she passed him, to ease his thirst from an afternoon of work in the fields.

"Do you think there is time to start before dinner?" Hannah clasped her hands together to stop herself from rushing off.

Wycliff had returned from the fields early, and there was at least another hour of light before the sky dimmed.

A mischievous glint in her husband's eyes made Hannah's stomach turn a slow roll. Oh, how she loved him, even more as she glimpsed the rapscallion still hidden deep inside him.

Wycliff took her hand and kissed her knuckles. "I believe, dear wife, that if we do not make a start before dinner, you will be in peril of exploding from excitement."

Wycliff took Frank out to the stables to find what they needed. Hannah fetched the lanterns and arrayed them along the windowsill in the thin sliver of a waiting room. The men returned with tools and Frank stood with the enormous sledgehammer in his hands as he waited for instructions.

Hannah pointed to a spot above the built-in bench

and also directly above the hole through which Barnes had crawled. "Start there, please."

The smash of the first blow made her cringe, the noise echoing through her body in the cramped room. Hannah pressed herself to the wall by the window as chunks of plaster flew. Wycliff stood next to her, sheltering her body from the crumbly snow. As Frank progressed, the snow turned red as he smashed his way through brick.

"When I brought you here, I never imagined you tearing walls down," Wycliff said against her ear and over the noise of the hammer.

"I prefer to think of it as revealing the true history of the house. Don't you think the oldest part deserves to be brought into the light after so many years hidden away?" Hannah split her attention between her husband and Frank.

The constructed man proved able at deconstruction, and soon had a hole the size of his head made in the wall. He dropped the hammer to rest by his toe and stared at Hannah. "More?" he rasped.

"Let us see if this will work first, before you expend all your energy, Frank." Wycliff pushed off the wall and picked up one of the lanterns.

Hannah followed close behind him. Wycliff stood on the bench seat and held the lantern to the hole. After several long seconds, he turned and held out a hand to Hannah. "The wall is not so thick, if you wish to look."

If I wish to look? She bit back a laugh and balanced

on the bench next to her husband. The light from the lantern made her squint in one eye as it cast extra shadows through the hole. "Would it be possible to hold the lantern on the other side?"

"If you don't mind standing close," Wycliff said. He angled the lantern through the gap Frank had made, stretched his arm through, and dangled the lantern on the other side. He wrapped his free arm around her waist as Hannah pressed herself to him and peered into the space.

"Oh," she whispered, feeling like an explorer who has discovered an ancient burial mound.

The lantern cast a soft yellow glow over the room beyond. Approximately eight feet of space lay between the wall and the slumbering tower, which echoed what she had found on the upper level. The curved stone wall glowed a rosy pink. She followed the curve of the wall as far as she could see. Barnes was right. There did not appear to be any door, or at least none she could discern. Nor did there appear to be any windows or other routes in that she could see from the little light the lantern provided.

"What would you like to do?" Wycliff asked as she withdrew her head from the hole. He looked in for himself before withdrawing his arm and the lamp.

"I would like Frank to continue, please, and release the tower from its prison. If nothing else, it will increase the space here and turn this into a useable room." Removing the wall would make the tower visible from the drive, too, and give future visitors an intriguing glimpse as they descended from their carriages.

Wycliff lowered the lantern to the bench, then jumped down and caught Hannah around the waist to swing her to the ground. "You heard her ladyship, Frank—carry on and free the prisoner."

The tension of the last few days dropped away from his features and Jonas, the mischievous boy, smiled back at her. It transpired that Hannah had only needed to take a sledgehammer to his ancestral home to reveal his hidden heart. Now, could she claim it?

THE DAY before the village ball, Hannah set off to pay a call on Libby Tant. She clutched a basket with a selection of wooden soldiers, horses, and tiny cannon. Wycliff had so paled at her suggestion that she wondered if he snuck them out at night to re-enact war scenes upon the worn rug. After careful consideration, he agreed to let half the toys go to the Tant children. Then he insisted on selecting which of his wooden army could be spared.

Hannah left the horse and cart with the blacksmith and then walked up the hill to the cottages. One had pink ribbons tied to the fence railings, the ends fluttering in the wind and signalling the sex of the new arrival to the curious neighbours. Her knock on the door was answered by a woman with grey hair tucked under a cap and laugh lines etched around her eyes.

"Lady Wycliff, how do you do? I am Mrs Gallon, the very busy grandmother." Libby's mother gestured for Hannah to enter.

Esther toddled forward with her arms extended and Hannah knelt to receive a sticky hug. Then the girl pointed to the basket and cooed.

"This is for you to share with your brother and sister." Hannah offered the basket to the girl. With the same great care she used to select a starfish, Esther chose a horse and then held it high to show the room.

"Thank you, milady. New toys will keep that lot quiet for quite some time," Libby said from the window, where she cradled her newborn and had a view over the roofs of the houses below out to the sea.

"It's my pleasure. I thought a distraction would afford you some peace." Hannah passed the basket to Mrs Gallon, who carried it over to where the children played on a rug.

"Do come and meet my daughter, Sarah." Libby's voice caught on the name and she glanced away.

Hannah approached on quiet feet and regarded the baby asleep in her mother's arms. A tiny, red, screwed-up face was surrounded by wisps of pale gold hair. "What a lovely way to remember your sister. I am sure little Sarah will grow to be as kind a person as her aunt."

"Would you like to hold her?" Libby offered, and then sat forward to gently place the baby in Hannah's arms.

Hannah lowered herself into the chair opposite

Libby, and stared down at the little face. The baby twitched her nose in her sleep and a sweet aroma that could be described only as *newborn baby* drifted upward. The child trusted that she remained safe and protected with whoever held her. She also contained a world of possibility as to what she might become or do —if only the world allowed her to reach that potential.

"Babies are amazing to look at, are they not? I find each time my mind spins, wondering what sort of person the child will become," Libby murmured, as though she had read Hannah's mind.

The other children set up the soldiers and the horses while Esther circled them holding her horse aloft as though it were Pegasus. From the little Hannah had seen of the toddler, she exhibited a thoughtful and imaginative mind. What might she become in the future? Perhaps an enquiring investigator for the Ministry of Unnaturals?

"I hope you are both well?" Hannah asked.

"Oh, yes, thank you. She had an easy birth, and we are blessed that all four of our children have thrived." Libby turned to stare out the window.

They talked of the children and the dance for some time. Then the baby stirred and made an alarmed squawk. Hannah returned the babe to her mother to be soothed. "I have a question about your sister, if it is not too much of an intrusion."

Libby offered a sad smile as she rubbed the baby's back. "Ask away, milady—I trust your heart is in the right place."

Hannah gazed out at the crests of the waves and searched for the right approach to a delicate matter. "I am trying to discover whether anything bound Sarah, Amy, and Lisbeth together. Do you know if Sarah sought solace with another, or a friendly ear to share her burden, when you have been so busy?"

Libby rocked the child as the latter continued to make mewling noises, though they diminished in volume. "It saddened me how distant we had become in recent months, and she no longer confided in me as she once did. But Mr Hartley might know. Have you asked him?"

Mr Hartley. The name slammed into Hannah's brain. So obvious with his kind and generous nature. Then a cold finger stroked down Hannah's spine. What if he had counselled all three women? And yet...surely Hannah saw a monster where none dwelt? The shepherd of their flock was indeed a good listener, and had even offered his broad shoulder to Hannah if she desired to unburden herself of her problems. It seemed entirely reasonable that Sarah Rivers had sought the same patient counsel...and inconceivable that he might have had anything to do with her untimely death.

Objectively, he was a handsome and generous man who made it easy for a lonely woman to lean on him. Hannah argued back and forth with herself, and in the end decided it was a simple matter that could be cleared up by a conversation with Mr Hartley. Which reminded Hannah of another matter, long overdue for clarification through conversation. "Thank you, Mrs Tant, you have been a great help."

"Do you think something happened to her, other than what some say?" Worry swirled in the woman's gaze. Mrs Gallon approached with the same deep concern written over her features.

Hannah shoved all the horrid ideas clustered in her head to one side. "I don't know, but some force compels me to try and find out what exactly happened in the dark to Sarah, Amy, and Lisbeth."

Mrs Gallon rested a hand on her daughter's shoulder. "When I was a child, my mother used to tell us never to venture near the water's edge at night, in case some selkie or mermaid snatched us to serve in their watery kingdom. Two men drowned one summer and the locals hereabouts found it right odd. Both were strong swimmers. One was a fisherman plucked from his boat in a flat calm. Do you think the creature has returned and taken Sarah and the others?"

Hannah rose to her feet, having intruded long enough. She sought the words to reassure the women. It seemed highly unlikely that deaths separated by decades could be in any way connected, apart from the cruel sea being responsible. "I am sure that is simply a tale told to keep children inside at night. Drowning is an unfortunate risk when one lives so close to the ocean."

Back in Mireworth that night, the household ate a quiet dinner, as though they all preserved their energy for the dance on the morrow. Barnes sat on the table and kept tapping Frank's hand. The monster would brush him away, his entire focus on the plate before him. Hannah idly wondered what disagreement brewed between hand and constructed creature. Barnes was obviously picking at his larger friend over something. Perhaps it rankled that Frank had broken through to the tower without the hand assisting. Or perhaps the hand was merely reminding Frank that it was high time he took advantage of his help where Mary was concerned.

When the meal was over, Mrs Rossett and Mary cleared away and stood at the sink to wash the dishes. Hannah put things away, enjoying the quiet company in the kitchen.

Soon, they would return to London and the formality of lives separate from those below stairs. If only there was a way to keep the intimacy that the ruined house forced upon them. Perhaps she could tell Wycliff she didn't want to restore the house or increase their fortunes? But that seemed disloyal to both husband and Mireworth.

Barnes climbed up Frank's arm and tugged on his ear. The large man stared at Mary and heaved a sigh. Then he nodded to the hand. Frank reached into a pocket and removed something that he tucked between his fingers.

Hannah held her peace. With the antics between the two and the longing looks at Mary, her thoughts of what might transpire this evening were confirmed. The last platter was put away on its shelf and Hannah fetched down the teacups.

Mrs Rossett put the kettle on to boil and Mary dropped into her chair.

Frank cleared his throat with a ghostly rasping noise like the protest of antique hinges. "Love…Mary," he croaked.

She giggled and swatted at him. "I love you, too, you big lump."

Frank extended his hands, Barnes cupped in his enormous palms. The hand walked to the tips of Frank's fingers and bowed to Mary by swiping one finger in an arc. He pointed to Mary and then to Frank. Then Barnes did a sort of dance that made Hannah think of the display some male birds did when trying to impress a female. The dance came to a stop and Barnes sat back on his stump and held aloft the pearl ring.

"Oh!" Mary gasped. Her eyes wide, she stared from Barnes to Frank.

"I believe, Mary, that Barnes is proposing on Frank's behalf," Hannah murmured in case their honourable intentions weren't obvious to the maid.

"Yes. Marry. Frank. Please," the big man whispered in a much higher tone than usual, as though a case of nerves tightened his throat.

"Yes, yes!" Mary cried and flung her arms around Frank's neck. Frank's hand jerked upward and launched Barnes, who did a somersault in the air and landed on the table—still clutching the ring.

Frank took the ring from Barnes and slipped it on

Mary's finger. She held it out and stared at it. Joy sparkled in her eyes.

"Oh, milady, thank you," she whispered. Unshed tears glistened as she glanced at Hannah.

Hannah hugged her maid. "I am sure you and Frank will be very happy. You will have to decide whether you want to marry here at Mireworth, or back at Westbourne Green?"

Wycliff shook Frank's hand and Barnes strode up and down the table looking as pleased with himself as though the whole thing had been his idea.

"Well, that's a bit of excitement. Shall we have a drop of port with our tea, to celebrate?" Mrs Rossett winked at Hannah.

"An excellent idea, Mrs Rossett. It seems the old estate has worked her magic to bring this couple together." Wycliff gazed at Hannah as he said the words.

Would the old house work some magic for her, and finally bring them together in the way she dreamed?

21

In celebration, they toasted Mary and Frank, and wished them happiness. Hannah found a quiet moment to pick up Barnes. She carried him over to the conservatory doors and held him to eye level.

"Well done, Barnes. You are a true friend to both Mary and Frank." Then Hannah kissed the hand's knuckles, which she hoped was an approximation of kissing him on the cheek.

Barnes flopped to his back in her palms, his fingers in the air. Hannah suppressed a laugh—she had either slain him or he had swooned. Then she carried him back to the table and set him down.

Mrs Rossett poured a splash of port into a saucer and placed it before the hand. "Here, I don't know if you can eat or drink, but you deserve to be a part of the celebrations."

Barnes stood in the middle of the saucer and appeared to paddle in the liquor. He splashed around for a few moments, then went still. The body of the hand pulsed up and down on his fingertips, like a spider hovering over its prey. Oddly, the port disappeared from the saucer. Then the hand lurched to one side and toppled over the edge of the saucer to flop on to the tablecloth. He waggled his fingers in the air as though someone tickled his palm.

"How did Barnes manage to achieve inebriation with neither mouth nor stomach?" Wycliff asked Hannah, laughter glinting in his eyes.

Hannah watched Frank's friend roll around, attempting to get his fingertips under him. She really should start a journal about life with the disembodied hand for posterity. Few people would believe such a tale unless they saw it with their own eyes. "The skin is a type of organ and possesses the ability to absorb liquids. Somehow, Barnes has sped up or amplified that process. And, of course, he still has a circulation system, blood, and veins. We simply don't know how any of it works."

Her father would be fascinated to hear of this new turn when they visited. Hannah could imagine evenings spent with Sir Hugh experimenting on how much it took to get the hand drunk.

Due to the happy occasion, love and relationships were much on Hannah's mind as she preceded Wycliff down the corridor to their temporary bedchamber. She loved Wycliff and needed to know if she could ever have a place in his heart. She twisted her hands together, contemplating how to begin such a conversation.

"They are an odd couple, but no one can deny their affection for one another." Wycliff dropped his jacket over a chair and undid the buttons on his waistcoat.

"Indeed," Hannah murmured. She unlaced her gown and pulled it over her head. Shaking out the material, she draped it over the side of a cabinet to wear again the next day. Her bravery nearly deserted her. Then the glass of port she had consumed to celebrate the engagement steeled her spine, marshalled her resources, and yelled *Charge!*

She swallowed several times before managing to whisper, "Wycliff, can I ever hope to hold your affection in a similar way?"

"Whatever makes you doubt such a thing?" He paused in his undressing, his fingers on the placket of his shirt. For whatever reason, he chose not to answer her question.

Hannah stared at him and snapped her mouth shut before she caught a moth. How was it that for all men declared themselves the superior sex they could be so...*dense* about certain things?

Because you have never said the words I love you, she wanted to cry, but managed to hold on to a few shreds of dignity.

As much as it pained her, Hannah had to mention his first, and possibly only, love. She didn't blame her husband for loving a woman with fairy-tale beauty, whom he chased along the halls of Mireworth as the two got into mischief. Indeed, she entirely understood if his heart had broken the day the ocean snatched Lisbeth from his life, and he would never love another in the same fashion. The question was, could he create a sliver of room in his heart for her?

Her hands fell to her sides and she tangled her fingers in the soft linen of her chemise. "I walked to Lisbeth's cottage and found a stash of love letters, written to her and hidden in the roots of the tree. They are such desperate outpourings of emotion, speaking of a vast and deep love." The writer compared his love to the ocean and said he would drown if his love was not reciprocated.

The frown on Wycliff's face deepened and he took a step toward her. "Whatever you might have been told, Hannah, I did not write those letters."

On that point, at least, they agreed. Despairing that her husband loved a ghost, Hannah had stealthily opened the account ledger in order to compare the handwriting to that of Wycliff. While both had a restrained, neat hand, the unknown lover was not he. The author of the letters had a particular way of flicking the tails of his letters that Wycliff did not do. Although that only proved he had not written the letters Hannah found. It did not reveal the state of his heart.

"Are you denying you loved her?" Hannah whispered. Now that she had started down this dark path, she was determined to follow it to the end.

Wycliff pressed a hand to his temple as though the memory hurt him. "Of course I loved her."

Hannah's heart fractured at the raw emotion in his voice. She had opened an old wound and caused him fresh pain, and for that alone she was sorry.

Then he extended his hands to her. "As a sister, Hannah. Her father was the estate manager before Swift, and with no other siblings or children here, we often played together. I considered her my sibling."

"Mrs Rossett said that everyone thought the two of you would marry." Hannah couldn't stop herself—she had to keep picking at the old memory. As the daughter of a physician, she knew any wound had to be scrubbed clean before it could heal.

Wycliff fisted his hand and dropped it to his side as a heavy sigh made his shoulders heave. "I considered it, yes. I was fond of Lisbeth and she was good company. What more could a man ask for in a wife? But Lisbeth would not have me. Even though I was content to make a match without passion, Lisbeth was not. She announced she would only ever marry if a man truly and deeply loved her. Like the ocean, she used to say—boundless and wild."

"That was what she found, according to the letters. I wonder what happened?" Lisbeth had found the deep love she sought, so why had she tumbled from the cliff that night a year ago—had the lovers quarrelled?

Hannah walked to the window and stared out at the night. The inky darkness gathered up her worries that multiplied during the day. What wouldn't she give for an hour alone with Lizzie to pour out her heart! Perhaps she should take up Mr Hartley on his offer of a broad shoulder. Her instincts said the vicar would be sympathetic to the condition of a woman's heart. Hannah could not imagine she would be the first to cry on his jacket. That thought swirled through her mind and etched itself into her consciousness. There was something in it that she needed to examine more closely.

In the morning.

Returning to her current predicament, Hannah didn't know what to say to Wycliff. Her husband admitted that he had been prepared to content himself in a marriage without love, and that the most he aspired to in a wife was *good company*. Well, if that was all they had, at least friendship created a solid foundation for a partnership. Nor did his lack of love for her stop her from loving him.

A gentle touch on her shoulder made her blink away the tears and turn.

Wycliff stared at her, his dark eyes wide with concern. "Good lord, Hannah, do you not know that you are loved?"

She swallowed the lump in her throat and looked away. "I know ours was a marriage of convenience. But I thought since we came to Mireworth and with the change in things...that possibly...but then you never said anything..." She fought back more tears and couldn't finish her sentence.

"Damn wolf," Wycliff muttered.

"Wolf?" The disconnect broke her train of thought and halted the sobs building in her chest.

"At Harden's wedding I sought a quiet word with Sir Ewan Shaw, as the man seems to possess some magical ability in matters of love. Unlike me." Wycliff flashed a self-deprecating smile. "Shaw suggested that if I had trouble saying the words, I should *show* you the depth of my devotion through action. That if I wrapped you in my affection, it would seep through to you. Somewhat like damp rot. He should have mentioned that there are certain words that still need to be said out loud."

He placed a fingertip under her chin and lifted her face to his. With his other hand, he caught the single tear that had escaped and rolled down her cheek.

"I love you, Hannah. I'm sorry you ever felt overlooked and forgotten. The truth is the exact opposite. Thoughts of you drive me from our bed early every morning, and I have worked like a farmhand, all for you. I wanted to achieve something here, so that you might regard Mireworth as our home and not as an abandoned ruin fit only to be demolished."

She gulped a breath of air, her mind scuttling in several directions at once, as though Barnes had multiplied inside her head. "You truly love me?"

Wycliff smiled and caressed her cheek with his thumb. A heat shimmer drifted around his head as though the hound sought to take over his form. "I love you, Lady Hannah Wycliff, with all that I am and in a way I have never, nor ever will, love another. If you would still have a hellhound shifter with only a tarnished title and a rundown house to his name."

Hannah reached up and brushed her hand through his hair. The phantom smoke curled around her fingers and she wondered if, when Wycliff experienced high emotion, it allowed the other creature to break through from its realm. "Despite what you have imagined, I happen to be rather fond of Mireworth. I think there is an ancient magic at work and I find myself wanting to spend more time here. With you, husband. Always with you. I love you."

His smile turned into a very hound-like grin and he kissed her.

THE NEXT DAY, Hannah awoke with her husband's warm form curled around her and a sense of love and peace washing through her. Last night, matters had finally been resolved with Wycliff and the knowledge that she was loved lapped at her limbs like gentle waves against warm sand.

"Good morning, Hannah," he murmured against her skin as she stirred. "Have I told you today how much I love you?"

She bit her lip and tried very hard to make her tone somewhat serious as she replied, "No, my lord, I do not believe you have."

Wycliff then proceeded to whisper words of love as he kissed his way down the side of her neck. Hannah decided this was the most marvellous way to wake up. Far better than an empty bed and cold sheets, no matter how well intentioned.

Love as a topic remained much on her mind. After breakfast, Hannah retrieved the bundle of love letters written to Lisbeth and showed them to Wycliff. "Who do you think wrote these? I cannot help but think this is our clue to what happened to Lisbeth, and possibly Amy and Sarah, too."

He unfolded a letter and studied the handwriting. "It seems familiar, but I cannot place it."

"Mrs Rossett, do you have your tonic handy that Mr Seager makes for you?" Hannah wondered if the apothecary had penned the love letters. She tried to recall the entries she'd seen in his journals, but a stolen glance was insufficient to allow a comparison from memory.

"I have it here." The housekeeper opened a cupboard and produced the glass bottle. They compared the instructions on the label to the hand in the letters. It transpired that Mr Seager had a lavish hand with curls and flourishes, completely at odds with his dour personality.

"It's not him. What of Mr Cramond?" Hannah suggested.

Mrs Rossett returned the bottle to its home. "Unlikely. Not many of the men around here can read or write."

"Oh. Is there not a school in the village?" Hannah

pondered little Esther Tant and hoped the child might receive an education to fit her curious nature.

Wycliff picked up another letter and scanned the contents. "There is, but it's common for the lads to skip their schooling and head to work at an early age. When Cramond signed the agreement for the farm, he struggled to form his letters."

"Then who is our mystery lover?" Hannah sipped her tea.

"I know this hand. I only need to remember to whom it belongs." Wycliff refolded the letters and made a tidy stack.

"Let's worry about it tomorrow. Tonight is the village ball and there is much to do. We will need a quantity of hot water to ensure everyone is clean. Including you, Barnes, and under your fingernails, mind." Hannah pointed to the hand. Not only did he scramble through the dirt, but Sheba liked to lick him. He needed to be scrubbed twice as hard to ensure he was presentable.

For the first time in their visit, the old house seemed alive with the tingle of excitement. Mary danced around the conservatory clutching the dusky pink dress. Hannah had quietly purchased it on her last trip to the village, and presented it to the maid as an engagement gift. The men were banished to the stables to bathe in the water troughs heated by Wycliff's hellhound ability.

For the dance, Hannah selected a silk gown in a deep green. Mary piled her hair up on her head and then pinned a silver painted starfish among her locks. A shawl of blue and white echoed the waves of the ocean and Hannah felt rather nautical. Wycliff wore formal black pantaloons and a black tailcoat with an embroidered waistcoat in deep blue underneath.

Despite his challenging size, the three women had managed to cobble together a suitable outfit for Frank. He wore a cream shirt Mary had sewn for him, and a waistcoat Mrs Rossett had found in a trunk stored in one of the storage rooms, its tails removed to suit current fashion. Hannah wondered if a giant had previously lived at Mireworth, given that the enormous item fitted Frank perfectly.

"Don't think you are being left out." Mrs Rossett pointed to Barnes, summoning him. The hand scuttled across the tabletop and stopped before the housekeeper. From behind her back, she pulled out a tiny black collar with a miniature snowy cravat. She tied it around Barnes' stump and beamed at him. "Now you look suitable to accompany us."

Mary's eyes shone with excitement and she twirled in her new gown. "My first proper appearance in company as an engaged woman." She held out her hand with its ring and then compared the enamel work holding the pearl to the deep rose of her dress. The two were a perfect match for one another.

"You look very pretty, Mary. I'm sure many of the village lads will be disappointed to hear you are spoken for," Hannah said as the women found their shawls and wrapped exposed shoulders for the journey to the village.

Wycliff handed them up into the large carriage, then Frank climbed to the driver's seat and took command of the horses.

In the village, Hannah stepped over the threshold of the hall and hardly recognised the place, even though she had helped with the decorations. The old fishing nets were stretched across the ceiling and became the sky above. Starfish were dotted about like stars, painted with a phosphorus paint from Mr Seager that glowed in hues of soft orange and buttery yellow. Strands of shells hung everywhere, in some places making curtains that revellers had to duck through. The magical paintings of fish seemed to dart among the seaweed that swayed to an ocean current.

Lanterns were surrounded by sheer fabric tinted green and blue, and cast the room in water hues. Movement from the artificial sea creatures caused the light to flicker as though they were underwater.

"Oh, it looks marvellous." Hannah had seen it only by daylight, but now with the lanterns lit, it transformed into something truly magical.

A trio of men were seated at one end and took up their instruments to strike up a rousing country dance. Everywhere, people smiled and laughed.

Wycliff seemed in a rare good mood and called out to many of the men who hailed him. He kissed her hand. "Excuse me, Hannah, a small matter of business needs to be attended to. I want to ask Swift what price the fleece fetched."

Mr Hartley appeared at Hannah's side and bowed in a courtly fashion. "Lady Wycliff, might I have the honour of introducing you to the villagers you have not yet met? And if I could be so bold, perhaps a later dance?"

Hannah glanced at her husband's broad back. He had gathered a semicircle of men around him and laughter rose from them. She turned back to her gallant companion. "That would be most pleasant, Mr Hartley, thank you."

He extended his arm and she rested her fingers on his sleeve. He wore a waistcoat of sea green with an aqua silk cravat that increased his attractiveness. Hannah found herself wondering how Mr Hartley had managed to live in the village for two years and remain unmarried. He would be an excellent catch, with his good looks, easy manners, and intelligence.

"I cannot monopolise your time, though, Mr Hartley. Is there not a special woman here you wish to dance with tonight?" Since the dance had a sea theme, Hannah tried a spot of fishing to see where the reverend's affections lay.

His gaze caught hers and he stroked her gloved hand. "I am exactly where I wish to be, Lady Wycliff. I have not found such a kindred spirit in any other."

His low words rippled over Hannah. If she hadn't been a happily married woman, and if she were given to fanciful flights of imagination, it might almost seem as though Mr Hartley was expressing some type of romantic interest in her. Impossible. But perhaps a quiet word might be warranted, to clear up any misunderstanding?

"I have been reading the notes of my grandmother's stories and believe I may have unearthed a few tidbits about your tower," he went on. "Perhaps I could tell you later in a quiet moment?"

The musicians struck a chord, and Wycliff turned from his company to claim her for the first dance.

"Yes, please," Hannah said. The perfect opportunity would present itself later to both subtly remind Mr Hartley she was a married woman and advance her mission to uncover the tower's secrets.

22

Hannah took the floor four times—two dances with Wycliff, one with Mr Cramond, and last with Mr Hartley. Her heart hammered at the exertion and the room grew overly warm. Thankfully, the musicians stopped for a drink and afforded her a short break. She fanned herself as Mr Hartley escorted her from the floor.

"Could I offer you a glass of punch, and perhaps a few minutes outside in the cool air? I can tell you of my discovery before the dancing resumes," he said, holding out his arm.

Hannah searched the room for Wycliff, but couldn't see him in the press of people. Frank created a more prominent landmark, standing to one side with Mary. Barnes clung to a starfish above them, and swayed back and forth as though the music still played.

"That would be lovely, Mr Hartley. I could certainly do with a breath of fresh air." Hannah took his arm.

As they headed to the double doors that led outside, she glanced again at Frank and Mary. The maid looked up and waved, an enormous smile on her face. Hannah waved back and they continued on their way. For some reason, it reassured her that Mary had noted her departure. Not that she was in any danger from having a glass of punch with Mr Hartley, as she recovered from the exertions of dancing.

In the foyer, a table was set up, draped in a cloth of cream embroidered with lavender and vivid blue cornflowers. In the centre of the table, a wide glass bowl that appeared large enough to bathe a child in held a deep red liquid. Small glasses were arrayed on the cloth around it. Mr Hartley filled two glasses and handed one to Hannah, then they continued out the door. The cool breeze skated over her skin and brought instant relief.

"Shall we walk down to the beach? It's such a lovely evening," Mr Hartley said.

"Yes, it does appear magical tonight." Hannah found herself agreeing to his every suggestion. His words tugged at her, like the pull of the moon drawing the tides.

Moonlight reflected off the waves, their crests sparkling with silvery diamonds. The ocean was calm, the only sound the gentle murmur of water caressing the sand. The mage silver ring on her smallest finger sent a tingle up her arm. How odd. Perhaps it reacted to the moonlight.

"You have quite kept me in suspense, Mr Hartley.

What have you discovered about the tower?" Hannah sipped her punch, careful not to spill any on her dress as their footing changed from packed earth to loose sand.

He leaned in close. Flecks in his eyes glittered a soft green, rather like the soft glow of a cat's eyes, and she found herself staring as she contemplated their unusual hue. Under the night sky and by the ocean, his eyes seemed to take on a reflection of the salt water.

"I am sorry you are much ignored by your husband," he murmured.

Hannah frowned. They had come outside to discuss the tower, not the state of her marriage. Which, happily, had much improved. A prickle washed over her scalp, the one that warned of magic in use. She stared back at the hall, wondering what might have triggered that sensation. Some of the decorations inside had been created by an aftermage painter. No doubt the overhead enchantments made her head itch and she simply hadn't noticed due to the fun of dancing.

"Lord Wycliff has much to keep him busy, Mr Hartley." Hannah turned back to stare at the ocean. Only a slight breeze blew and the water seemed almost mirror-like and serene.

"We are alone, Lady Wycliff. You do not need to keep up the pretence for me. I am aware that your heart aches and loneliness laps at you." Mr Hartley led her closer to the waterline.

"You are correct, Mr Hartley, in that I was rather sad for a time. But an honest conversation with his lordship cleared the air. I can assure you there is no need for concern about the state of my heart." Apart from the curse poised to squeeze the life from it.

The tingle from her mother's ring edged farther up her arm until it tickled along her collarbone. The nettle-like sensation on her head rolled downward to meet it. Her thoughts struggled through a fog that had descended upon her, like a sudden sea mist that rolls over the shore.

"You stand in difficult waters, Hannah. Let me be your friend and support," he murmured quietly, like the lap of water against the shore.

"I do not think I should have any more punch," she whispered.

Mr Seager had been responsible for mixing the brew and it was supposed to be non-alcoholic. Had he made it potent without warning anyone? Had he similarly changed his potions for Lisbeth, or Amy, or Sarah?

Mr Hartley took the glass from her and a blue light shone through the ring on his right hand. "You deserve to be immersed in love."

Immersed in love. She shook her head, trying to clear the mist. She was loved—by Wycliff. She didn't want to be immersed, all cold and wet. She much preferred to be surrounded by hellhound fire, which was rather toasty. And why was her blasted ring acting in tandem with the blasted ability to sense magic? Her whole body scratched—at this rate, she would need a witch hazel tonic to soothe the irritation.

Rings.

She stared at his hand again. It wasn't the moonlight hitting the gem that made it shine. The gem itself
was glowing a deep blue. *Magic.* He was using magic
and her body and the ring were trying to protect her.

A single moment of clarity burst into her brain.
"You. It was *you.*"

He held tight to her hand, pulling her against his
chest. "I offer an ocean of love. Here, all your pain is
washed away. I will love you 'til death."

'Til death? Hannah snorted. She possessed a love
that went beyond death. Fear tightened its grip and
fuelled her mind's fight against the fog wiping away her
thoughts. She would get to the bottom of his murderous
ways. "How are you doing this to me?"

He grinned and held up his hand. "The ring has
many attributes. Surrender to me, Hannah, there is no
need to struggle anymore. I have you."

A cold weight wrapped around her legs and she
stumbled. The ocean surrounded her to waist level.
Somehow, Mr Hartley had walked her out into the
ocean and she hadn't even realised it.

Hannah rubbed her wedding ring and thought of
Wycliff. She was in rather a pickle.

WYCLIFF WANDERED the edges of the room, humming
a few bars of music under his breath. Hannah and her
team of helpers had worked a small miracle, turning the
plain hall into an underwater scene. The village came

together to celebrate the new Lady Wycliff, and many men shook his hand and wanted a few words in his ear. He brushed a curtain of shells aside and walked to the tables being prepared for supper. Set on the side of the hall closest to the tavern, the plates of food would be carried across and placed on the tables. Dancers could then either sit inside or out in the sheltered courtyard with their refreshments. He picked up a card bearing the order of events and idly stared at the neat hand.

The itch in his head exploded. He had found him— the author of the love letters to Lisbeth.

He waved the card at Mrs Rossett, who stood by the table. "Who wrote these?"

The housekeeper oversaw the arrangement of plates. "Oh, Mr Hartley did those for us."

A chill dropped over Wycliff. Hartley had been in love with Lisbeth. The reverend offered a sympathetic ear to those in need in the village, and appeared to have crossed the line with at least one woman. Wycliff tapped the card against his hand. He needed to talk to Hartley immediately.

Mrs Rossett moved a stack of empty plates to one side. "Milord, I have another bit of news. Mrs Gallon and I have had our heads together trying to remember who Mr Hartley's grandmother was. Why do you think he never said much about her?"

Why indeed allow it to be forgotten that his grandmother had been a local? "Who was his grandmother, Mrs Rossett?" Wycliff asked before she veered too far off course.

"Rosie Ferry. An odd one she was. Used to swim in the ocean no matter the weather. People used to laugh and call her a selkie, and warn her to watch out that some boy didn't steal her seal skin. She left the village some fifty years ago, the summer those two men drowned. We assumed she had a fright in the water, and that's why she moved so far away."

Ideas collided in Wycliff's head. Hartley's grandmother had married someone not from the village and settled inland, where she never saw the ocean again. Two men had drowned that long-ago summer, but they had had no more inexplicable drownings until Hartley came to them. What if Rosie *had* been a selkie or some sea creature, and her grandson had inherited her attributes and used them to lure vulnerable women into the water?

"Thank you, Mrs Rossett. That is most helpful." He had to find Hannah to tell her of his discovery. But where was she? Wycliff searched the dance floor, but couldn't see any sign of her.

Mary chatted to a group of women to one side, Frank standing guard beside them.

"Mary, where is Lady Wycliff?" An ache took up residence in his chest.

"She went for a walk with Mr Hartley, milord. She was looking right flushed since everyone wanted to dance with her," Mary said.

At that moment, his wedding ring vibrated and shook on his hand. Wycliff spun on his heel and made for the door, waving away the revellers who wanted to draw him into the festivities, and emerged into the cool night air. He ran toward the ocean.

Two figures were out in the water. Hannah was waist deep, the tide tugging at her skirts, which billowed around her. The moonlight cast the fabric in an eerie green like seaweed surrounding her. Hartley had hold of her arm and pulled her into deeper water.

"Hannah!" Wycliff shouted. He shrugged off his jacket and tossed it to the ground as he ran.

Hannah turned, confusion written over her features. She waved a hand in front of her face as though to clear something from her vision. A wave rolled into her chest and she staggered a step and nearly fell.

"Stay out of it, Wycliff. She has made her choice. She wishes to immerse herself in my embrace and wash away her sorrows," Hartley called.

Water rushed into Wycliff's shoes but he had no time to remove them as he waded toward his wife. "I love you, Hannah, beyond death. Whether in this realm or the next, my love will remain constant and unaltered."

Deeper Wycliff walked, forcing his legs through the water and trying to use his hands to cut a path. No matter how far he waded, Hannah stayed out of his grasp, as though an outgoing current had hold of her. She kept moving backward with Hartley and water now lapped over her chest.

"Beyond death?" Hannah spoke at last, as though she had not realised he was there. Now the water brushed under her chin and she tilted her head to keep her mouth and nose clear.

Hartley laughed. "That is ridiculous. Love is a temporary thing that ceases when your heart stops."

Hannah pressed one hand to her temple and struggled to pull herself free of Hartley's grip on her arm. "No. True love continues after death."

She spun and fought to take a step in Wycliff's direction, back toward land. Hartley released her and for a moment, relief soared in Wycliff's chest. He jumped forward to reach her, so close now. He pulled a brown object from his coat and shrugged it on. With a blue flash, he disappeared. A large brown seal lunged at Hannah and pushed her beneath the waves.

"No!" Wycliff yelled as Hannah disappeared under the water.

Rage and despair exploded inside him. Fire ignited along his veins and the water around him boiled as the beast crashed over him in an instant. He let out a howl and the hound dove beneath the waves, searching for Hannah and the selkie.

To his hellish vision, the water shimmered a pale aqua and appeared to be comprised of millions of tiny spheres. The specks parted around him yet supported his weight. A flash of silvery green caught his eyes and he struck out for it.

The monstrous seal had its flippers on Hannah and was pushing her downward. Easily six feet long and solid with muscle, it used its greater weight and driving force to propel her to the bottom. Her arms flailed above her head as she fought, but she couldn't dislodge him or swim away.

Because Wycliff had never found the time to teach her to swim.

Anger fuelled him. Through his own stupidity, he would lose his wife. He should have ensured she had some confidence in the water. He should have told her sooner how much he loved her.

No. Their time was not over. Not so long as any breath remained in his body.

The hellhound used its powerful legs to strike out. Inch by inch, he gained on Hartley. When he neared, Wycliff lunged and managed to grab a mouthful of Hannah's dress. He yanked her sharply to one side and out from under the flippers of her would-be murderer. Once free of the selkie's grip, he dragged her up to the surface. They broke free and she gasped for air, but in her panicked state she couldn't stay afloat.

Hannah grabbed at fistfuls of his smoky fur but they disintegrated in her hands and offered no purchase. Her eyes were wide and frightened as she battled her waterlogged clothing with no ability to swim, her head dipping beneath the surface with each surge of the ocean.

"Put your arms around my neck," he commanded, paddling to hold his position but careful not to strike her with his claws. The frigid seawater clashed with the heat flowing from him and the bluish-green spheres turned purple and popped like myriad tiny champagne corks.

"Wycliff!" She gasped his name with terror in her voice.

A stab of panic carved through his chest. He would not lose her. He barked and swam closer.

Hannah gritted her teeth and swung one arm, trying to secure herself over him. As her fingers slid around his neck, her head snapped back and she shot downward to disappear once more beneath the surface.

Around him, the ocean stilled, as though it had swallowed her and then closed its lips tightly against him.

23

WYCLIFF SCREAMED Hannah's name and plunged after her, using his powerful hind legs to search the depths. A faint green glimmer came from far below him. The seal had Hannah's gown in his mouth and pulled her deeper as it swam.

"Let her go!" Wycliff barked.

When Hartley had assumed the Mireworth living, the quietly spoken man had said he wanted a life by the seaside. Wycliff could never have imagined the smiling vicar was actually a murderous selkie who preyed on women whose only fault was in needing an ear to listen to their woes, or a friendly smile to lighten a dark time. Both well within the remit of a man of the cloth. Certainty flowed through Wycliff that while Hartley had killed three women already, Hannah would never join their number.

I failed you, Lisbeth, he whispered to his childhood friend. *But I will never fail Hannah.*

A silvery shape flashed past Wycliff, too fast for him to make out its shape. Another selkie, or a large fish? The last thing he needed was a shark drawn in by the turmoil. Not that it mattered if there was one or a thousand such creatures under the surface. None would take her from him. Hannah was far more than his love and his wife. She was his safe harbour. The reminder of his humanity when the dark void sang to him and sought to erase his soul. If he lost Hannah, he, too, would be lost.

Closer and closer, he gained on them. The seal might think the ocean its environment, but Wycliff dwelt between realms. The tiny water spheres boiled and popped around his mouth, and created an air pocket that allowed him to breathe. His heated form slid through the sea like a knife through butter.

As he neared, Wycliff opened his jaws and latched on to the seal's side. He stopped swimming and sought to use his weight to halt the selkie's downward plunge. Hannah reached out for him, her eyes wide as the ocean sought to claim her. The tiny luminescent spheres forced their way between her lips and down her throat.

Wycliff growled and closed his jaws. He wrenched his head from side to side, as the selkie thumped him with a solid flipper. Hartley curved his body to use his strong tail flipper to strike the hound, each blow like that delivered by a prize boxer.

In his mind, Wycliff imagined the void and tried to summon it forth. He needed a quick end to Hartley so he could save Hannah. Answering his call, the void opened within the water. The bluish-green droplets pushed up to the edges but did not enter the inky space. The voices flowed from the darkness, singing a seductive tune that could have been those of a mermaid luring a sailor.

Channelling his anger, Wycliff redoubled his efforts. His teeth sank into tough skin and pierced blubber. Then he hit something that oozed around his teeth like jelly. The water churned around them—spheres boiled and popped, blocking his vision like a sudden hailstorm. He fought blind, relying on instinct and the singing of the void to guide him.

Snapping down on the thick substance in his mouth, he worried the selkie's magical skin. Inch by inch, he pulled the creature's soul from its body. He gulped, to adjust his grip, and dug his teeth into the foul-tasting soul. Wycliff reeled Hartley's essence forth, to expose the true monster within that was neither man nor seal. Coated in slick black like eel skin, it possessed a long and sinuous form like a serpent. A short and rounded head contained multitudes of sharp teeth like a barracuda.

From the hovering void, black arms emerged and drifted on the current as they reached for the monster's soul. Clenching his jaw, Wycliff wrenched his head and shook the soul free. Then he tossed Hartley to the inky seaweed. The dark tendrils wrapped the monster in an embrace he would never escape no matter how hard he struggled.

A scream tore from the soul's being as the demons from the underworld dragged him to a different kind of depth. With a soft *pop*, the void closed in on itself and disappeared. Severed from its soul, the seal's physical remains twitched once before it fell motionless and floated away.

The water stilled around him as the agitated spheres calmed. His vision cleared and Wycliff cast around for Hannah. When he'd torn Hartley's soul free, the seal's dead form had let go of her gown. Its soft green glow came from far below him.

Then the silver flash wrapped itself around the disappearing green shape. The other creature had her in its grasp.

I have battled one, I can fight another to free her, he thought as he dove.

The merged colours created a new form as they entwined together. Moss green and silver alternated before his eyes. But...the creature had not only halted its descent, it was rising. Spinning round and round like a beautiful lure on a line, the two soon hovered close to Wycliff's paws.

A slender, translucent shade held tight to Hannah. As he drew a breath to strike out at the new threat, it let go of her and with a gentle push, propelled her body toward Wycliff. He snapped his jaws and grabbed hold of his wife's dress, careful to avoid clawing her as he paddled to hold his place.

The shade watched, floating on the current. Her dress was gossamer thin, the fabric merging with the spheres clustered around them. Long hair drifted around the spirit's face. She bobbed up and revealed her face. She smiled with a familiar tilt to her full lips.

Lisbeth.

The spectre nodded, then blew him a kiss. Her task completed, Lisbeth turned into thousands of tiny diamonds and dissipated in the water.

Wycliff sobbed in gratitude, then powered upward with Hannah in his jaws. Her body hung limp and unresponsive as he hauled her to the surface. He nudged his head under hers, to keep her face clear of the water, and manoeuvred his body under her until she rested along his back. Fighting back his fears, he swam for shore. Once they reached the shallows, he shoved the hellhound away and gathered Hannah in his arms.

"Hannah? Hannah?" He called her name as he walked free of the ocean and trod the wet sand.

A crowd had gathered, drawn by his rapid exit from the hall and concerns for Hannah's whereabouts. Mrs Rossett, Mary, and Frank stood at the front. Barnes had two fingers hooked into Frank's collar.

"Blankets! Fetch blankets!" Mrs Rossett commanded when he staggered from the sea.

Hannah's eyes were closed, her lips tinged blue, and no breath whispered from between her lips.

"Don't leave me. Not like this." Wycliff laid her flat on the sand and opened her mouth, checking her tongue didn't block her airway. With one hand holding her nose, he covered her lips with his, and blew. He forced long, deep breaths into her lungs.

"Is she alive?" Mary said from close by.

Wycliff couldn't spare the breath to answer. He concentrated on Hannah, pouring his love into her with each breath he took. After what seemed a lifetime of sheer agony...she coughed.

"Blankets," he called.

Wycliff rolled Hannah to her side as seawater spilled from her throat and she shook from cold and shock. He gathered her into his arms and held her close. Mrs Rossett dropped a blanket over both their forms. Here, at least, was one benefit of being a hellhound. He let the hound's fire heat his form and his chilled wife. Soon a fine mist drifted from the wool as water turned to steam.

"It was Hartley. He tried to drown Hannah as I believe he did Sarah, Amy, and Lisbeth." Wycliff spoke in a low tone as he cradled Hannah. His words carried on the still night and were relayed through the assembled people.

"What happened to him?" Seager pushed to the front of the crowd.

Wycliff shook his head. "We fought out in the water. I struck him, to make him let go of Hannah. Then Hartley drifted away. My only concern was Hannah. I have no interest in him. The ocean will decide his fate and will determine whether he returns to shore."

No need to mention the creature had died the instant Wycliff ripped the soul from its body and fed it to the ravenous void.

Seager snorted. "Never did like him. Thought he was too nice all the time. I was sure it had to be an act."

Frank shuffled closer and extended his arms. "Take. Mistress?" he rasped.

Wycliff held Hannah tighter. He couldn't let go of her and needed the reassurance of her breath against his skin. "No, I will carry her."

"We can take her to the tavern and tuck her up warm in a bed," the publican's wife offered.

Hannah stirred in his arms as he stood. She still seemed chilled, but he didn't want to boil her or expose himself by turning up his internal heat too much.

"Mireworth," she murmured. Her eyes were closed, her face nestled against his neck.

He didn't know if she was conscious, or merely whispered the word in a dream of a confused and watery world. Wycliff swallowed a tight knot in his throat. Whether she was aware or not, Hannah wanted to go home. Their home. "Fetch the carriage, Frank, instantly. She wants to go home."

The big man nodded and lumbered away with purpose in his long stride.

The crowd parted for Wycliff as he carried Hannah across the beach. Cramond stood to one side, his hands clenched and his eyes wide and sad.

Wycliff paused beside him. "I'm sorry. I didn't know. If I had acted sooner, I might have saved Amy."

Cramond shook his head and swallowed several times. "None of us could have known. While he took three souls, at least it wasn't four...or more."

The men shared a silent moment, then Wycliff nodded and carried on up the strand. By the time he reached the road, Frank had the carriage waiting.

Once back at Mireworth, Wycliff shooed away Mrs Rossett and Mary. The concerned women wanted to undress Hannah and tuck her up in a warm bed. His wife was even now returning to them, and her eyelids fluttered as her mind sought to surface from the depths of unconsciousness.

"I will tend her." Wycliff escorted the well-meaning housekeeper and maid to the door.

He stripped off Hannah's ruined gown and under-garments and helped her under the blankets. His own clothes were dumped on the floor in a careless fashion. Clothing could be repaired or replaced. Hannah could not. His priceless wife was his sole concern. He gathered her up and curled his body around her.

"Tell me again how much you love me," Hannah rasped against his chest.

His arms tightened around her and he placed a kiss on the top of her head. "I love you beyond death. Wherever our lives lead us, I will be your constant companion and lover."

She let out a sigh and settled against him. Then the looseness of an exhausted sleep swept over her limbs.

THE NEXT MORNING, Wycliff watched as the sunlight penetrated the study window. He had hardly slept, and had stayed awake to guard Hannah, terrified she might be taken from him during the night. Impossible as it was, he imagined Hartley bursting through the window and snatching her up. Wycliff couldn't contemplate losing her when he had only just come to realise how deeply she resided in his heart and mind. Once, his life had stretched empty before him. Now it was populated with possibilities, love, and laughter.

Only with the break of day did he allow himself a breath of relief that the nightmare had ended.

"Did you watch me all night?" She opened her eyes and reached up to stroke his face.

He captured her hand and kissed her palm. "Only when the terror of seeing you disappear beneath the waves stole over me. In those moments, I craved the reassurance of knowing you slept beside me. Your mother once told me to find a safe harbour, lest I be lost on this ocean I sail. I find it somewhat ironic that I first had to save my safe harbour from drowning."

Hannah sat up and pulled the blankets with her as she tucked herself closer to his chest. "What happened to Mr Hartley?"

He placed one arm around her and with the other, pulled free a lock of her salty hair and wound it around his finger. "The hellhound dispatched his soul to the underworld. The ocean will either surrender his form or keep it in her embrace."

"He knew exactly what to say to make a woman feel seen and wanted. I found myself looking forward to his company on our walks, but you were always in my heart." She splayed her fingers over his chest. "Both my magic-sensing ability and the mage silver ring tried to protect me from his enchantment. They sent warning tingles rippling over my body, but the ring wasn't powerful enough to fully protect me. His words clouded my mind. I didn't even notice he had walked me into the ocean. When he took my hand, I thought we strolled on the sand."

"He possessed a charming and intelligent facade that hid his deadly intentions. Mrs Rossett said his grandmother left the village that summer the two men drowned. I suspect she, too, was a selkie, and pulled those men to their deaths." He would have to discuss what had happened with Sir Manly when they returned to London. If all selkies harboured murderous intent, they would need to be strictly monitored.

Hannah's fingers drummed a slow beat over his heart. "He wore a blue ring that glowed. It must have fuddled my thoughts and perhaps concealed the skin that allowed his shift of forms. It chills me, how easily he must have lured the others into the water when most likely they only sought his advice as a clergyman."

"He said you had chosen to immerse yourself in his embrace and wash away your sorrows." Had Lisbeth walked out with him to ease her pain, or had she fought to survive? Amy had much to look forward to and had

had her chance at happiness snatched away. Sarah Rivers probably only wanted a shoulder to cry on after an argument, and found herself pulled to the bottom of the ocean.

"Compulsion is not a choice. Mr Hartley took away our free will to resist him and then took their lives." Her words skated across his naked chest.

"I saw Lisbeth," Wycliff whispered.

"No! Where?" Hannah pushed off his chest to face him, her eyes wide with questions.

"I was fighting the seal. He had let go of your gown, and you sank out of my reach. A silver flash caught you before you disappeared and brought you back up to me. I recognised Lisbeth's soul. She smiled and, I think, has found some measure of peace." It comforted him to think Lisbeth's soul had become part of the ocean, both of them wild and free. Now, his friend would never be alone.

"She must have been a remarkable woman. I wish I could have known her." Hannah kissed him. When he let her go, she glanced over her shoulder at the mottled light coming in through the window. "We must bathe and dress. The day is slipping away and we have much to do."

Wycliff grinned and waggled a finger at her. "I am going to insist, Lady Wycliff, that you stay right here. Mary and Mrs Rossett will be wanting to check on you and they can bring a tray. I think today the chores can wait so that we might do something together. What say you to investigating the hole in the wall Frank made, or finding the suites upstairs that belong to us?"

Mischief sparked in her eyes. "Once we have thoroughly investigated the ground floor of the tower, I would like the master of Mireworth to lead the expedition to our apartments. If you can remember the way?"

24

THREE DAYS LATER, the mage silver ring on Hannah's right hand tingled in a familiar fashion. She opened the conservatory doors, where she had been arranging the rediscovered and cleaned rattan furniture, and a sparrow flew into the room. The bird landed on the rim of the scrubbed pool and cocked its head at her.

"We are not far away, Hannah, and I so look forward to seeing you," her mother's voice chirped from the little bird's beak.

"I have much to tell you, Mother! I shall make sure the kettle is on." Hannah held out her hand and the bird hopped onto her finger. Then she took it over to the door, lest it become confused by the half-cleaned windows and batter itself trying to escape.

Wycliff, Frank, and Barnes worked to scrub the outside of the conservatory. Hannah shielded her eyes against the sun as she looked up at their progress.

"Wycliff, Mother and Father will be here soon. Probably in time for tea."

Wycliff slid down the ladder propped against the curve of the glass. On reaching the bottom, he wiped his hands on a cloth tucked into his waistband. "I shall go clean up before they arrive."

Hannah stared at the outside of Mireworth and worried her bottom lip. In the month of hard work they had put into the house, they had literally only scratched the surface in one small area.

Wycliff wrapped his arms around her waist and nibbled her ear. "You wouldn't happen to be worrying what your parents will think of the old pile, would you?"

She placed her arms around his neck and laced her fingers together against his skin. "I want them to fall under its charm as much as I have."

Humour twitched at his lips. "As I recollect, your mother said your father used to live in a hovel with potatoes growing in the corners. Mireworth's rooms are proudly potato free."

Hannah laughed and kissed him. Her mother had brought Wycliff into their lives when he bristled like a disturbed porcupine. If anyone could see beyond a concealing outer layer to the truth of what resided within, it was Seraphina Miles.

An hour later, the carriage pulled around by the stables and Hannah rushed to greet her parents. Sheba barked in excitement as the wheels rolled to a halt.

Timmy sat up front with Old Jim and called down to the spaniel.

Sir Hugh climbed down and held out his arms to Hannah. She flung herself into her father's warm embrace, while Frank untied her mother's bathchair from the back of the carriage.

"I have something for you. Cook mistakenly forwarded them to me, instead of to you." Sir Hugh pulled away to tug a fat parcel from his jacket pocket and hold it out to her.

Hannah took the plump stack of letters and recognised the writing instantly. "Why, they are from Lizzie!"

While she wanted to dive immediately into her friend's letters, they could wait until a quiet moment. Relief flooded her—Lizzie had not, after all, encountered pirates on the high seas or highwaymen along some remote Italian road. Or if she had, she'd survived to tell the tale but possibly lost her ensorcelled paper.

Hugh lifted Seraphina down and placed her in the bathchair.

Hannah hugged her mother and kissed her linen-clad cheek. "Welcome to Mireworth, Mother."

Seraphina held her daughter close. "I have missed you, my dear, but I rather think Dorset suits you. There is such a look of contentment about you." Then she turned her attention to the dirty stone exterior of the house. "Oh, Wycliff, your house is beautiful."

"I rather think you are overly generous, Lady Miles," he said with a glance at Hannah.

"I never said you didn't have a large amount of work before you. But Mireworth has an elegant bone structure and what is more, there is something about this location. Do you not feel it, Hannah? There is the gentlest whisper of magic against one's skin." She walked her fingers up one arm to demonstrate.

Hannah stared at the house with fresh eyes. Magic? "No, I've not felt that. But from the moment I crossed the threshold, I have had a sense of comfort and belonging, despite her outward appearance. As though I have found the place I am meant to be."

"Love will do that to you, Hannah." Sir Hugh winked and slapped Wycliff on the back.

Hannah took charge of the bathchair and wheeled her mother through the open doors into the conservatory.

"Ma'at! What an odd place to find you." Seraphina pulled herself closer to the pool and reached out to touch the statue in greeting.

"That is not the only mystery about Mireworth. But first you simply must tell me all about the Fae royal court before I burst from curiosity." Hannah dropped into a rattan chair and leaned forward, waiting for her mother's tale to begin.

Mrs Rossett took charge of sorting out accommodation for Timmy, Old Jim, and Helga—the formidable maid who assisted Seraphina. Then the young lad disappeared to run around with the spaniel, yelling he would be back at dinner time.

Hannah and her family sat in the sun in the conservatory while Seraphina described the royal court, accompanied by illustrations that danced over the brick floor. Then Hannah and Wycliff took turns to tell her parents of their encounter with the selkie and the engravings found in the tower fireplace. Only when they had dry throats and the sun had begun to fade outside did they consider moving through to the warmer kitchen. A bark heralded the return of dog and boy, probably drawn by the aromas of dinner wafting from the range.

"I rather think that before it gets too dark, we should see this tower," Seraphina said.

Hannah bounced on her toes, eager to hear what her mother would say about the hidden tower. Wycliff took Hannah's hand and they led the way as Hugh wheeled Seraphina. In the grand foyer, they paused at the bottom of the stairs.

"Griffins? An odd choice for this house," Seraphina murmured, stroking a wooden wing.

"I admit to being disappointed that Wycliff's ancestor chose a Greek creature for the newel posts, when Ma'at presides over the reflecting pool," Hannah said.

Seraphina muttered under her breath and brought her clasped hands together to breathe upon them. When she opened her hands, a golden orb appeared and drifted upward to hang above them, casting a yellow glow that lit up the room. "Perhaps Wycliff's great-grandfather was a cultured man who borrowed from many different tales. Or perhaps they are not griffins at all, but sphinx."

Hannah stared at the griffins with wide eyes. "Sphinx?" Surely not. How could she have made such an error?

"They are both winged creatures with the body of a lion, are they not?" Seraphina gestured to the light and it floated to hover above a griffin. Or a sphinx.

"That is a matter we can discuss later, Hannah. Let us take your parents up to the tower before we lose all the light." Wycliff tugged her up the stairs.

Sir Hugh swung Seraphina into his arms and followed them. Without complaint, he trod the halls and bent to navigate the narrow passage. The golden orb glided behind them. They paused in the little annex that surrounded the stone tower, so Seraphina could examine the construction.

"Oh, what a treasure this house conceals." Seraphina reached out and laid her hands flat against the stones. "What sin did you commit, my friend, that you were bricked away?"

Silence fell over the room as the mage communed with the spirit of the house. Then Hannah's mother turned to her. "Here is the source of the magical trace I feel, Hannah. Do you think this old lady will yield her secrets to us?"

Excitement built inside Hannah. Her mother confirmed that a magical mystery shrouded the tower. What would they uncover? Did the trace come from the engravings in the fireplace, or something hidden deeper still?

Once they reached the circular room, Hannah shook out a plaid wool blanket and laid it out in front of the fireplace.

Hugh set Seraphina down and she shuffled herself closer to peer into the fireplace. Wycliff and Hugh talked in hushed tones for several minutes, as the mage compared the engraved stones laid in either side of the surround.

At last, Seraphina sat back and gestured Hannah closer. "I say, Hannah, this is fascinating. Both sides are the same, are they not?"

"Yes, that is what I discovered from comparing the rubbings. But I don't know if the duplication means anything. It could simply be an eye-catching, but meaningless, decoration. Will you be able to discern what the writing means?" Hannah knelt on the blanket beside her mother. The fireplace was easily large enough to accommodate both women as they examined the drawings.

"It will take me a few minutes, but let us find out." Her mother murmured under her breath and passed her hand down the line of engravings. The hieroglyphics slowly began to transform in the stone and reform themselves, like dancers moving to unheard music.

Hannah stood and moved to stand by the window, to give her mother space to translate the pictures. The whispered magic brushed over her arms and she rubbed them gently.

"Are you cold?" Wycliff enquired. A frown marred his brow. Since her near drowning, he fussed over her like a broody hen.

"No, it's only Mother's magic tickling me." While they waited, Hannah gazed down at the overgrown lawn. In her mind, she imagined the years they would spend at the estate, and the ways in which they would improve it. Perhaps, one day, there might be children playing among the trees. Not necessarily their own, for there were plenty of children without families to whom they could offer shelter and a place to thrive. They could even establish a school within the grounds.

"Do you think it is possible to link this tower to the house in a way that is easier to access? I would like to be able to use this room, if possible," she said to Wycliff.

He blew out a sigh and looped one arm around her waist. "I have no idea. We will have to examine the plans and see what rooms are on either side of the passage to see if we can enlarge the corridor. You do seem rather taken with tearing down walls in Mireworth."

"That reminds me—I want to restore the library, too." She should make a copy of the house plans and pin them to a wall. That way, she could mark up areas to restore as finances allowed.

"I have it!" Seraphina called out at length. "This is a binding spell, but I cannot discern who, or what, it ensnares." She waved her hands and the letters she had been studying transformed back into hieroglyphics. "I think we are missing a third point to this triangle."

"What do you mean?" Hannah returned to her mother's side, pulled by the mystery contained within the fireplace. "There are only these two stones on either side. That is more rectangular than triangular."

Seraphina gestured to the stones on her left and right. "If these are two sides and we drew a triangle, where would it point?"

Hannah considered the proposition and in her mind, drew different variants of a triangle using the sides as two points. "That would depend on the direction of the triangle. It could point up, to something in the chimney or on the roof. Down to something in the room below. Across this room to the stairs or..."

"Or to the rear of the fireplace?" Seraphina suggested.

Hannah stared at the interior, coated with probably hundreds of years of soot until it formed an impenetrable mass. Had she missed something? "Hypothesise, then strategise," she whispered.

"Why don't I clean the firebricks first, before we decide to send Timmy up the chimney?" Seraphina patted Hannah's hand.

Her mother began to work a new spell, murmuring and waving her fingers as though she scratched an invisible itch. The rear of the fireplace vibrated, then a tiny chip of soot broke free and fell. Soon, baked-on charcoal shook itself from the rear stones and tumbled in chunks to the grate. Piece by piece it fell, revealing more layers behind. A fine black mist spread through the room as centuries of soot fell to the mage's magic.

Hannah gasped as time turned backward and the tower revealed another of her secrets. The rear of the fireplace held a single large stone, three feet square. Etched into its surface stood jackal-headed Anubis. On either side of the god of the underworld sat an enormous fiery hellhound.

"All a little too coincidental, don't you think?" Seraphina turned to gaze at Wycliff.

He knelt and peered over Hannah's shoulder at the creatures that had been living in the fireplace for centuries. "What are you suggesting? That these stones lugged back from the Crusades in Egypt had something to do with my men being slaughtered and my being turned into this creature?"

Seraphina gestured to the carving. "If you have another explanation, I am all ears. Until then, have you viewed this room as the hellhound?"

"No." He fell silent.

"Try?" Hannah asked. "For me?"

Wycliff nodded and walked to the other side of the room, away from them. He closed his eyes and his form shimmered around the edges as he commanded the beast to his side. When he opened his eyes, Hannah bit back her startled cry. His eyes glowed red with the hound's internal fire. His head swung back and forth as he studied the room. He closed his eyes and when he opened them once more, the hellfire had retreated.

"What did you see?" Hannah moved to his side and rested a hand on his arm as he shook off the last vestiges of the hellhound.

Wycliff stared at the fireplace. "The hieroglyphics and the images have a faint outline that glows purple. A pale lilac mist that feels the same rises up through the stone floor, like rain that falls upward instead of down."

"Now, isn't that fascinating," Seraphina said.

Hannah clasped her hands together. A purple glow? That was what she had seen in her odd dream, when her mother performed the renewal ceremony in her own tower in Westbourne Green. What could be in the ground floor of this tower that emitted a lilac mist? She turned to Wycliff with a thousand questions jockeying for attention in her head. "We simply must break through to the stone below, now."

"Tomorrow, Hannah. The tower has sat here for five hundred years. I think she can hold on to her mystery until tomorrow." Wycliff reached for her and in one fluid motion, swept her into his arms. "Just to ensure you don't sneak off and start immediately with the sledgehammer."

With that, he carried her down the stairs, her parents' laughter following them through the narrow corridor.

"Tomorrow, then, since you promise," she reluctantly agreed. She could wait another day.

Then one quiet idea swirled in a corner of her mind. The other ideas pulled back from it and left it isolated. Her mother had said the engravings were a binding spell. What if whatever made the purple other-worldly mist was bound by the spell to an eternity in the tower? Perhaps they should let it slumber undisturbed.

For now...

History. Magic. Family.

I do hope you enjoyed Hannah's latest adventure. If you would like to dive deeper into the world, or learn more about the odd assortment of characters that populate it, you can join the community by signing up at:

www.tillywallace.com/newsletter

Hᴀɴɴᴀʜ ᴀɴᴅ Wʏᴄʟɪꜰꜰ continue their journey in:

Hessians and Hellhounds

Fire erases all… even the undead….

One of London's most recognisable Afflicted is erased from the earth in a fiery way. Whispers spread that a hellhound prowls the streets, snatching the lost souls who have escaped the afterworld. Except, Wycliff is doing no such thing—could there possibly be another such creature in London?

While Hannah and Wycliff investigate the unnatural flames, unrest grows on the streets as someone seeks to unmask how the undead women stave off rot. Someone is agitating for all Afflicted to be eradicated, in a conspiracy that will set the common Englishman against the nobles.

To save the Afflicted and stop the uprising, Wycliff must face the void that whispers his name from an inky darkness. He plans to wrest Hannah free of the curse squeezing her heart, assuming they can get out alive…

Buy book 6: Hessians and Hellhounds
https://tillywallace.com/books/manners-and-monsters/hessians-and-hellhounds/

ALSO BY TILLY WALLACE

For the most complete and up to date list of books, please visit the website https://tillywallace.com/books/

Manner and Monsters

Manners and Monsters

Galvanism and Ghouls

Gossip and Gorgons

Vanity and Vampyres

Sixpence and Selkies

Hessians and Hellhounds

Highland Wolves

Secrets to Reveal

Kisses to Steal

Layers to Peel

Souls to Heal

ABOUT THE AUTHOR

Tilly writes whimsical historical fantasy books, set in a bygone time where magic is real. Her books combine vintage magic and gentle humour with an oddball cast. Through fierce friendships her characters discover that in an uncertain world, the most loyal family is the one you create.

To be the first to hear about new releases and special offers sign up at:
www.tillywallace.com/newsletter

Tilly would love to hear from you:
www.tillywallace.com
tilly@tillywallace.com

facebook.com/tillywallaceauthor
bookbub.com/authors/tilly-wallace